SOME MARLBOROUGH INVENTIONS

STORIES FROM A FOREIGN COUNTRY

John Maurice

The Book Guild Ltd
Sussex, England

First published in Great Britain in 2000 by
The Book Guild Ltd
25 High Street,
Lewes, East Sussex
BN7 2LU

Copyright © John Maurice 2000

The right of John Maurice to be identified as the author of
this work has been asserted by him in accordance with the
Copyright, Designs and Patents Act 1988.

All rights reserved. No part of this publication
may be reproduced, transmitted, or stored in a
retrieval system, in any form or by any means,
without permission in writing from the publisher,
nor be otherwise circulated in any form of binding
or cover other than that in which it is published
and without a similar condition being
imposed on the subsequent purchaser.

All characters in this publication are fictitious and
any resemblance to real people, alive or dead,
is purely coincidental.

Typesetting in Baskerville by
Keyboard Services, Luton, Bedfordshire

Printed in Great Britain by
Antony Rowe Ltd, Chippenham, Wiltshire

A catalogue record for this book is
available from the British Library

ISBN 1 85776 521 4

CONTENTS

PREFACE to
SOME MARLBOROUGH INVENTIONS   1

The Atheist   4
The Fall of the House of Robinson   22
Beginning at Home   36
Over the Hill   42
With Colours Idly Spread   48
In Xanadu   60
Visitors from Porlock   74
Ring of Fire   88
The Sound of the Sea   120

PREFACE to
STORIES FROM A FOREIGN COUNTRY   141

Anniversary Letter   142
'La Parolaccia'   154
At Porta Portese   158
The Human Heart of Dr Danakil   162

'Il Traforo'	170
Moonlight Sonata	180
The Flight from the Eagle's Nest	196
The Myth of Belamor	204
The Athenians	214

Some Marlborough Inventions

for my daughter Louise –
these stories which come as near as I dare
to the autobiography she wants me to write

A Preface to
Some Marlborough Inventions

These nine stories were written over a six-month period, around five years ago, when I returned to live in the place where I passed much of my childhood and youth. They grew swiftly – I could almost say obsessively – out of memories revived by that return. All the same, I must qualify the claim made in my dedication. Two of the stories are autobiographical only in the elusive way that all fiction is autobiography.

I present them in the order in which they were written, with the exception of 'The Atheist', whose proper place is sixth. I decided to pull this one out and put it first because it is Joel's story, not mine – except for the very large measure of imagination that went into it. He gave me the essential ingredients during a six-hour walk of seventeen miles from Putney to Richmond Park, some four and a half years ago. He was twelve, at the time. A year from now, I remind myself, he will be approaching his A-levels.

'Beginning at Home', the briefest of the stories, also owes almost nothing to memory. It was written for a story competition, where it sank without trace; an alert reader will calculate that its narrator is two decades younger than the narrator of the other eight stories.

For the rest, the autobiographical element grows progressively through the stories, but because they are all cast as fiction much was not quite as I now present it. Most of the characters are composites, drawn from life but each from several different models. Events are transposed in time and place, lines are deliberately smudged; and although I lurk everywhere, it is behind a variety of disguises.

But I still insist on the essential truth to be found in fiction – for in a sense, all memory is fiction, we are all self-created. As we grow older, the past becomes increasingly a book of well-thumbed pages.

These are some of mine.

Marlborough – February, 1999

The Atheist

Fifty or sixty years ago the long shadow of Victorian certainties still here and there clung on against the brash glare of the twentieth century. In our town, for instance, the churches flourished: Methodist, Presbyterian, the Wesleyan chapel, even a green tin shanty, housing recusant Romans, drew respectable congregations week by week; and the two parish churches, of St Stephen-Within and St Peter-Without, filled all their box pews and sometimes overflowed onto wood-and-wickerwork chairs in the aisles. The Church of England did not yet belie its name.

When the Reverend Jethro Jackson was appointed to the living of St Peter-Without, he was already a widower, and his son Joel some two or three years old. The advowson in the parish was held in hereditary right by Charles deWaigne, and it was commonly assumed that Jethro owed his preferment to the fact that as young men he and Charles were contemporaries at Balliol.

Be that as it may, it was also soon noted that there seemed to be little social or sympathetic commerce between squire and vicar. Jethro retreated behind the mellow stones and soft slate of the vicarage, assiduous always in his parish duties towards the poor and the sick, but otherwise eschewing the company and curiosity of his fellow men. He was recognized, and on the whole accepted without much resentment, as an austere recluse; not the sort of vicar one might expect to see at sherry parties.

In church he ruffled no-one. True, his sermons delivered from the high pulpit were stern, rather remote, a touch too intellectual for most of his congregation to follow with any confidence of understanding. But insofar as they could be followed, they were clearly pitched into safe and familiar territory, they steered a precise course between the rocks of High and Low, as did Jethro's liturgy and observances, exactly to the taste of his parishioners.

With a small son to look after, and his own material needs to be tended, although these no doubt were few, Jethro had brought with him a housekeeper: Mrs McGinty – a dour, indeed grim Scots lady, some sixty grey years old, who did not attend the church but worshipped instead, twice on every Sunday, with the Methodists. If this seemed to his parishioners a further oddity, it was at any rate consistent with Jethro's apparently sustained design to hold himself apart.

It was the child, Joel, who excited first the speculation and then the sympathy of those who felt, if not precisely disdained, at least in some thin and shadowy manner rebuffed, by such an absence of warmth in their new vicar. Spinster ladies of the parish clucked over the motherless infant, and slipped him small presents of sweets when they met him out walking with Mrs McGinty; these he accepted with grave yet mostly wordless good manners. He seemed as reserved as his father. But in one respect, he was gloriously different. The Reverend Jackson was a man of indeterminate middle age who looked, probably, much older than his years. Short of stature, his wiry frame still contained intimations of energy, but there was a stoop to his shoulders, an effect of myopia in his peering, tired grey eyes, and his hair had grizzled from a nondescript brown. Joel's hair, still allowed to grow long in a childish mop, was an astonishing tint of red, a blaze of autumn leaves, a riot of maple. Many a spinster hand, on those encounters, would reach out timidly, as though to touch; at the last moment to be plucked back, almost as if its owner feared to risk scorched fingers.

From a very early age Joel attended Mattins and Evensong on Sundays, sitting alone and dutiful in the vicarage pew below the pulpit. Until the age of five or six he was mostly an invisible presence, even when standing, but at about the time when that amazing beacon of hair began to emerge above the level of the pew, startlingly perspicuous all the way to the back of the church, it also became apparent that he sang with a notably sweet voice. So at seven, he moved from vicarage pew to choir stall.

It must have been about eighteen months before this, however, that the first of those two events occurred which were to crystallize a feeling in the parish: Jethro, it seemed, lacked any proper or indeed Christian sympathy for his son.

On a grey October day Mrs McGinty stumped, as was her custom every Friday afternoon, into Pickering's the butchers. But this was to be different from all the other Fridays.

'We shall want no more meat,' she said to Mr Pickering. 'You may cancel the weekly order.'

The butcher stared at her in some bewilderment, his face assuming a deeper shade of red.

'Was there something amiss with last week's order, then, Mrs McGinty? I've never had a complaint before.' If this was not strictly true, at least it held where the vicarage was concerned. Squire and vicar had always been given Mr Pickering's personal attention.

'No complaints,' said Mrs McGinty grimly. 'It is the vicar's word. We are all to be vegetarians now. A madcap notion he's taken into his head.' She sniffed, loudly.

'Yourself, too, Mrs McGinty? But surely, whatever he may decide for himself, the man can't require it of you – '

'He doesn't,' Mrs McGinty conceded, but her Scots eye flashed inwardly. 'Nevertheless. What's good enough for the bairn is good enough for me.'

It was Mr Pickering himself, probably, rather than Mrs McGinty (as reclusive and unsociable, almost, as Jethro) who spread the story. Not that it would have remained a secret. Joel had just started to attend the village school – another cause for mild censure, because he might reasonably have been expected to be entered at The Laurels, the private establishment of the Misses Kinsmith, who dispensed sound education from a Victorian villa in a leafy lane above the town. The county had recently instituted school meals, so that the village children no longer carried their sandwiches to school or went home at lunch time. Word came down from the vicarage about Joel's new regime.

The feeling in the parish about Joel was much the same as Mr Pickering's about Mrs McGinty: a sense of indignation, if not something stronger, that Jethro should impose upon a small and growing child the vagaries of his own eccentric conversion. The choice of school too, for his son, by a man of education and presumed breeding, seemed to proclaim an excessive Christian humility or, the less charitable supposed, an unchristian parsimony. Joel, as if to confound such suppositions, appeared to thrive, physically and intellectually, on private diet and public education.

By the time he moved, at the age of seven, from the pew to the choir, there was little enough for the censorious to get their tongues round. Under that burnished thatch his cool grey eyes, just flecked with blue, surveyed the world with extraordinary composure. His complexion, as might have been expected, was very white; his face faintly freckled; his frame skinny but by no means pinched – it had the wiriness of his father's.

His voice grew week by week into something of a marvel. The choir of that time was about fifteen strong, half a dozen of them children, both boys and girls; but for years the predominating sound had been Mr Pickering's strident tenor, blaring, intrusive, and always slightly and uncomfortably off-key. Now Joel soared above him, while old ladies dabbed eyes with surreptitious handkerchiefs and thought of Ernest Lough. Mr Pickering, abashed, muted his trumpet, as mesmerized by the boy's voice as anyone else.

The organist, Miss Merriman, who also coached the choir, was a better musician than generally graces a country parish, and drawing on her years as a Guildhall student, she gave Joel some rudimentary singing lessons. Then she began to let him loose on solos. St Peter-Without, which had languished a little under Jethro's austere and remote ministry, began to fill again. They drifted in from surrounding villages, they made clandestine forays from St Stephen-Within and even, it was suspected, from the Methodist and Presbyterian congregations. Only Mrs McGinty and the Romans seemed able to resist. Salisbury and Winchester cathedral choir schools sent out embassies, and much to Miss Merriman's relief were politely but firmly rebuffed by the Reverend Jackson. If her relief was secretly shared by most of the parish, there was also a feeling that once again Jethro was standing in his son's way, he was ordering Joel's life by principles too obscure to be understood or excused.

And then, some months past his tenth birthday, at Evensong one Sunday, Joel sang the solo part in Mozart's *Laudate Dominum* for soprano and choir, the one from the Vesperae de Domenica, K321. His voice was still two or three years from the treble's maturity, but it had grown astonishingly in power and control, so that it was hard to imagine where it might go from here. Miss Merriman had rehearsed the choir with assiduous tact and patience; inspired perhaps by Joel, they coped gamely (even Mr Pickering) with that glorious, arching sound while Joel's *cantabile* floated, effortless and serene, above them. For those of us privileged to be there it was an experience unlikely ever to be matched. I know, because I was there myself, younger even than Joel, and I can hear every note of it even now in my heart and memory, more than half a century on.

As the music echoed into silence, wreathed around stone pillars and wooden rafters, reflected from stained glass that blazed with evening sunlight, the Reverend Jethro Jackson climbed the spiral stair to the pulpit to deliver his sermon. I forget the text. I forget the sermon. What I shall never forget is the announcement that preceded it.

He clutched the rail in front of his reading desk a moment, as though for balance, and looked down at us for a long time in silence, his eyes behind half-lens glasses looking lost and thoughtful.

'That was very beautiful,' he said at last. There was another long silence. 'I have to tell you –' and surely there was a sadness in his voice – 'that it is the last time we shall hear my son sing. After today, he will no longer be a member of the choir.'

And indeed, although on the next Sunday the boy was back in his old place in the vicarage pew, and at appropriate moments his mouth opened and closed, even those in the nearest pews had to strain to hear anything they could with certainty ascribe to Joel. No explanation was ever offered, unless to the distressed Miss Merriman, and anything she heard was guarded secretly. It was left for people to speculate, which they did very freely. The consensus was that Jethro had acted out of jealousy, when he saw that it was his son who attracted all the attention and filled the pews and the overflowing aisles.

Within a month, St Peter-Without was emptier than it had been before Joel's singing had brought it sudden fame. Emptier, but by no means empty. In those days convention and social attitudes could still be relied upon to sustain a nucleus in any church, however unpopular the vicar; on the other hand it must have been a time of unusual prosperity for St Stephen-Within.

If it had not been for Jethro's final aberration, some sort of *modus vivendi* might have been achieved between priest and congregation. As it was, Jethro's last makeshift placed him finally, adamantly, beyond the pale.

Another year has passed. Joel is nearly eleven. One fine May morning a small group of early risers gathered in sunlight in the church porch for the first Communion service. This time the matter was lifted above drama, even above scandal, into the realms of outrage.

But before we can continue the story, we must return almost to its origins for a second look; because there is much in my account, so far, that has now to be corrected.

The vicarage study faced south across the valley, a spacious room lined with shelves, its two large casement windows allowing a flood of sunlight – a warm and friendly and smiling room. From his first days there, surrounded by all his books, Jethro loved it, and gave to it all the time his duties allowed.

We will follow him in.

His workmanlike desk is littered with papers in careful disarray; the only ornament under his eye is a standing black-and-white photograph in a silver frame, of a fair, misty girl with a faint smile on her lips and in her eyes – eyes which might be looking at him from as far away as Ireland, but which Jethro sees as both nearer and further than that.

On this first visit to his study we find him, as we often shall, at work on next Sunday's sermon. He writes this draft in pencil, in a small notebook: there is a tight stack of these in one of the desk drawers. Joel, who on this occasion is four years old, stands just behind Jethro's left shoulder. He has entered the room, as we have, not quite certain whether he has even been perceived.

'Father – '

This, his habitual form of address, is an old-fashioned decorum, of no ecclesiastical significance. Jethro, his eyes still on what he is writing with that busy pencil, reaches out with a straight left arm to the child standing half behind him, and his hand rests, softly and almost absently, as though unaware of its own persuasion, on Joel's shoulder. It seems a well practised gesture, familiar to them both. And here was the first of many ways in which his parishioners were mistaken about Jethro, for he loved his son with an extreme tenderness, and was loved by him in return.

'Yes?' he said presently, but still scribbling. 'What is it, then?'

'Father – what is St Peter without?'

The pencil stopped, and was laid beside the notebook. Jethro turned and looked straight into his son's grey eyes, his right hand coming to the boy's other shoulder.

'Without?'

'Yes. I have been wondering. Is it something we could give him?'

'St Peter-Without,' said Jethro. 'Well now, that's quite a thought. Perhaps we could.' Gently, he released the child.

'Actually, it's not quite what you supposed. But then again – perhaps it is. You see, there are two churches here, St Stephen-Within because it stands within the old charter boundary of the town, and St Peter-Without because it is outside, or without – in the old-fashioned sense.'

Joel nodded, satisfied.

'That's all right, then,' he said. 'You see, I thought it might be something he needed.' He wandered over to the window, and Jethro picked up his pencil. For a while, his heart so lifted, the words he wrote seemed winged, and perhaps they were, but he acknowledged sadly and silently to himself how often in their flight from the pulpit, over the ranked heads in the nave, those wings failed, folded, and the words crashed into the cold stone of the floor, to flutter, helpless wounded birds.

Was it on that or another occasion that Joel reached up, tiptoe, over the edge of the desk, to take the photograph into his small, safe hands? It was certainly at about this time.

Jethro watched him, calmly, yet with a distant pain in his eyes.

'She was my mother,' Joel said, without a trace of a question in his voice. But the question came.

'What happened to her?'

'She died,' said Jethro very steadily, 'as you were born.' He had answered this question before, but perhaps it was not that Joel had forgotten.

'What was her name?' The boy was looking with a sort of effortful intensity at the picture. 'Was it my fault she died?'

Jethro patiently followed the grasshopper leaps of the child's mind.

'Her name was Jasmine. No, it was not your fault.' He took the silver frame quietly from unresisting hands, and as quietly replaced it on the desk. 'A pretty name, don't you think? The name of a flower.'

'A *J* name,' said Joel, who was learning to read. 'What a lot of *J* names we have.'

Chance, at first, Jethro might have said; perhaps he did. But Joel's name was not chance; by then it had become design.

SOME MARLBOROUGH INVENTIONS

Mrs McGinty appeared in the open doorway.

'It's time for the bairn's tea, sir,' she said; stiff, remotely polite, with no hint either of deference or of Scottish truculence; yet surely we can catch a softening in her eye as it falls to encompass the child. Joel goes to her confidently, as to one in whom he has put his trust.

'Thank you, Mrs McGinty,' Jethro said. 'You remind us both.' His tone mild, comfortable, betraying no awkward edges. Another public misconception must be acknowledged. These two have no animosities. There may not be a real warmth between them, but there is respect, and tolerance, and recognition.

We must move on. A further fourteen months have passed. Another sermon is being prepared.

Joel sat in the worn leather of a large armchair, his feet projecting into the air. His head, somehow quiescent despite the red flame, was bent over an open book in his lap. He was by now a fluent and demanding reader, allowed to range the bottom shelves of the bookcases, which he could just reach. Perhaps it was the rustle of a turning page, after at least half an hour of apparently companionable reading and writing, that turned Jethro's thoughts from his sermon to his son. He laid down his pencil and very quietly shifted his chair, to improve the view. Reluctant to interrupt, he waited several minutes more until, with a small sigh of release, Joel came briefly up for air, a finger holding his place on the page. He saw Jethro looking at him, and smiled. To Jethro the smile seemed a sort of greeting, as if the boy was waking from a daze of sleep.

'I would like you to start school next term,' Jethro said, almost as though this was a continuing flow of conversation rather than an abrupt beginning. 'I have made enquiries at The Laurels. What do you think about it?' It may seem a small distinction, yet surely it reveals something of both Jethro and Joel, that the question (to a five-year-old) was not, as might be expected from a father who bothered at all to consult his son, 'Would you like that?' – but this invitation to discussion: 'What do you think about it?'

THE ATHEIST

The invitation was accepted.

'I thought I was to go to the village school, Father.'

Jethro, who had never himself considered this, was surprised.

'Some people might say it is not appropriate for you; they – the village children might not be thought suitable friends.' That Jethro could say something like this should not surprise us – it was a reflection of his time. But that he *did* say it was an indication, in fact, of how much Joel's observation had flustered him.

Joel's finger strayed from sentry duty on the page; all of his interest was now engaged.

'And is it ap- ap-propriate?'

Jethro seemed to know he was being asked this directly and personally – generalization would not serve either for question or answer.

'What people say is another matter, and a small matter here, I might add. But for my part I see nothing inappropriate, or unsuitable, in village children.'

'That's what I thought, Father. We ought to be the same, all of us.' But there was another consideration, clearly important to the child. 'Will I learn as much at the village school?'

'At whatever school you go to, you will learn as much as you wish to learn – ' and then, carefully correcting himself – 'as much as you determine to learn.'

'I think I should go to school where other people go.'

'Other people,' Jethro drily allowed himself to say, 'go to The Laurels.' – Perhaps he was curious to discover the boundaries of Joel's thought. The response was flat, and immediate.

'Yes, but *more* other people go to the village school. That is where I should go.'

Jethro understood by this, not a child's instinct to conform, or fear of the unconventional, but a more surprising determination not to seize an unfair advantage. For a moment he wondered how far Joel's reading had already ranged, in those lower shelves. But he decided that he agreed; and approved. And looking at his son he rejoiced secretly, too, in the knowledge that Joel was at the same time wholly different.

If we find ourselves thinking that Joel's part in all this was a touch questionable, if we are alarmed by such precocity, we must remember that Joel's two most constant companions were both adult, and that neither of them talked down to him, any more than the books he read.

So the Misses Kinsmith were deprived of a pupil they might reasonably have expected to see at The Laurels – no doubt he would have done them credit – and the village school, presently, was supplying a vegetarian lunch every day.

For this next domestic upheaval we must return, just a few weeks later, to that day of Mrs McGinty's last visit to Mr Pickering the butcher; the day that initiated the vicarage household into vegetarianism. (Yet another sermon interrupted in its composition.) I see Joel, on this occasion, as the one who takes the plunge, with a child's directness – a sort of transparency, without a trace of guile, although children are capable of this, too, and Joel no doubt at times was guileful. Not now.

'Father, there is something I want to say.'

The pencil laid carefully aside, Jethro looks up, expectantly. He is by now, we may suppose, accustomed to this; and welcoming.

'I've decided, but you mustn't mind – I don't want to eat meat.' Joel, unlike Oliver asking for more, seems quite serenely unaware of his own temerity in thus asking for less. There is a half-suppressed smile on Jethro's face, which is also tinged with weariness because there are other battles where he is conscious of losing ground in a grim retreat.

'Never?' he asked. 'You mean, you wish to become a vegetarian?' Jethro seemed to consider his own question from several angles. 'I think I would like to know why. Is it for sentimental reasons?'

'It's my tummy,' Joel said. 'It doesn't like meat.'

'I see,' Jethro said quietly. 'Then, in that case, we must alter our arrangements.'

'Not we,' said Joel in some alarm. 'I only meant me.'

And now Jethro did permit himself a smile. 'Just you and I, Joel. It will be a good discipline for me.' His hand reached out to ring a bell, and when Mrs McGinty appeared he gave her his measured reflections; and instructions. As we already know, that strange, surprising woman wrote herself voluntarily into the new charter too, and Mr Pickering lost some valued customers.

The time has come, I see, where I have to bring to this retelling of a story an element that up to now has all but escaped mention. There was a hint, perhaps, but hints will no longer serve. This has to be set down squarely, for it is essential to the pattern of events: Jethro had a secret, confided only to Joel, and only in part even to him. He suffered the terrors of vertigo.

'I remember, as a young man, I tried once to walk across Tower Bridge. I could not do it.'

As Joel grew older and their walks took them further afield, he was solicitous to avoid the steeper downland slopes, where he might have liked to play, knowing that for his father those airy spaces, familiar to the birds that Joel envied, were gulfs of dizzy treachery. But Jethro's most secret agony was the pulpit.

He might, I suppose, have chosen to preach his sermons from the chancel steps; or would he have seen that as the coward's way? I think in his tormented mind he had made a pact with God. He would endure the torment: God would keep him safe.

A half-spiral of stone steps led up, brass-railed, to the carved stone of the pulpit which stood, no ordinary Everest, just a modest eight feet above the level of the nave. There Jethro clung, in fear of what he saw: a clamorous swaying pitching swathe of faces, the wheeling vortex of the pit. No wonder then, that his words seemed to his listeners to come from such an austere and cerebral distance, or that to Jethro it seemed a recurring miracle that they came at all – albeit stumbling, in his haunted mind, and falling often before their destination, as we have seen. All this was inside him, and although it was no imagined chimera, but a clinically physical affliction of too solid flesh, it was an invisible as well as a silent battle Jethro fought each Sunday in the pulpit. Nobody knew; nobody noticed, or could interpret, such rare signs as slipped his obsessive leash.

Except Joel. Joel knew. But even Jethro could not be sure of this, for it was something – the one thing – they never discussed. Joel from love, and Jethro from fear, observed this privacy.

It must be borne in mind.

When Joel moved from the vicarage pew beneath the pulpit to a choir stall in the chancel behind, he was no longer witness of that agonized ascent, and this in a way made it easier for them both. Joel was now seven; then eight. Then nine. Report of his singing voice had spread, to the boundaries of the county and beyond.

One day: 'I have had letters,' Jethro said, 'and yesterday a visitor – he attended Mattins. The visitor was from Salisbury, the letters from Salisbury and Winchester. Both would like you in their choir and choir school.'

'A cathedral choir?' Joel seemed scarcely to reflect, and by now we need not feel too surprised by his response. 'I would rather stay here, at home. And sing in the church.'

If that was what Jethro would rather, too, it did not show. 'It would be a great opportunity. And the schools are good.' This had to be said, but he was careful of his emphasis. A fair man, Jethro, anxious to preserve neutrality. Yet he knew, I think, that the issue was already decided. Joel would stay. In this, surely, he was glad, as (each in their different ways) Miss Merriman too, and the ladies of the parish, were glad.

What did touch him, a year later, with a palpable grief, was Joel's next decision.

I have tried to take you a little way inside Jethro's heart and mind, that landscape of strange hopes, terrors, loves. What is far more difficult, a task before which I flinch, is a similar exploration of Joel. A child's mind, which may seem to us limpid, blessed by simplicity, untainted by adult perceptions, has its own mysterious opacities that guard against intrusion. When I listen to the conversation that I shall presently recount, I feel I can guess something of his thought; slipping between the lines, behind the words, I think I can understand what moved him to a gesture which on the face of it was a cruelty, to his father, to others, even to himself.

I may be wrong, but this is how I see it: Joel loved music, he loved to sing. When it began, his joy in his singing was as great as that of those who heard it. But as time passed he became aware, as others did, of a shift. It could not escape him that the church filled and overflowed each Sunday with people who had come, not to hear his father, not even to commune with God, but to hear *him*. Somewhere inside that mind which we cannot enter, ourselves, with any certainty, this offended; it seemed an impropriety. Could this be the truth of it? It would be of a piece with what we have already discovered of Joel. And there was something else as well in his mind, which bore on his decision; but this is still securely hidden from us, and from Jethro. It emerged only later, and must be left to await its proper place in this unravelling.

Joel, now past his tenth birthday, stood almost to Jethro's shoulder; and that familiar gesture, when Jethro was seated at his desk, Joel standing half behind him, had become a considerable stretch.

'I have something very difficult to say.'

Jethro turned to give him his full attention; he did not recall any previous such confession, and wondered what was to come.

'I don't feel *comfortable*, Father, any longer, in the choir.' Joel stopped there, the words delicately balanced. Jethro waited patiently, in silence, aware that there was more but uncertain what it might be. Perhaps a premonition plucked at him, making his silence more absolute.

Joel plunged, with a recklessness betrayed by his eyes which for once would not meet his father's. 'I think I must stop, Father. I must leave the choir.'

Torn from Jethro, with the passion that had ambushed him, two words:

'But *why?*'

Was there a flicker of fear in Joel's face? – he seemed to flinch. And Jethro, who had never seen fear in that face before, would have given anything to take back, if not the words, at least the passion.

Joel, as though deliberately resorting to a child's obstinate argument by repetition, his eyes still evasive, his muttering voice a stranger to his customary grace, replied: 'I told you. I don't feel comfortable.' He made a visible effort. 'I don't always like the feel of people listening. I used to. But sometimes, now, it feels wrong. As if they are listening for the wrong reasons.'

Jethro sensed their separate helplessness. '*I* listen,' he said. 'Is that wrong too?'

At last Joel's eyes could meet Jethro's. There was a warmth in them that belied the grey.

'I would still sing here. At home. For you.' There had been evenings when Jethro played on the old upright, rather stumblingly if I am to be honest, and Joel sang, and Mrs McGinty turned the pages of music or sat in a large chair listening, the clicking of her metal knitting-needles a discreet accompaniment.

Jethro was silent for a long time. He seemed now to be looking, not at Joel, but at that silver-framed photograph on his desk; with what was almost an appeal.

'Next Sunday,' he said at last, 'you were to have sung the Mozart. They have all worked at it very hard. It is music that I love.'

'I would like to sing the Mozart,' Joel said, with a surging eagerness. 'But not any more after that. Not in the choir.'

None of this was known, that Sunday, to any but the two of them. Joel sang, as I have described it. Jethro climbed, with more than his habitual fear, to the pulpit, to deliver that fateful message in which only now, not just in retrospect but with this new understanding, we can properly hear the cadence of its sadness. Never had the pulpit seemed so high, the gulfs beneath it so deep. And afterwards, the tongues began to wag.

If Jethro was at all aware of that canker dibbled in public opinion, imputing a shameful motive for a decision assumed to be his, this was a burden he could bear lightly enough; it could not touch him like that *Via Dolorosa* of spiral stairway to the pulpit.

I have come to the last of the conversations I must report. This one is different. We are no longer in the vicarage study; there is no sermon to prepare. Instead, on an afternoon of sunshine in early May, Jethro and Joel are walking in bluebell woods: three square miles where the ground is a shimmering carpet of blue, except for a few dark corners that have been planted with evergreens, where the bluebells won't grow. The new leaf is the palest green, and the sun heightens all the colours. Last autumn's leaves have dulled to a faded russet, dry underfoot, sprinkled among the flowers which mostly grow so thickly ranked that the leaves are hidden. Only Joel's head flashes a fire richer than autumn. Where the paths skirt the edges of the woods they catch glimpses through the trees of the North Wiltshire downs rolling away into hazy distances. This is the world, both natural and man-made, at its most luminantly beautiful.

All kinds of images tempt me – for instance, could Jethro have seen this as the first garden, a rolling woodland Eden blessedly free from precipitous edges? That is my fancy, but it is not so very far from reality. For both of them, Jethro and Joel, the image, shorn of its biblical significance, comes near to what they were feeling.

Joel's eleventh birthday beckons, but at this moment does not inhabit the surface of his mind. They have walked for an hour, zigzagging by woodland paths, often in busy conversation, but a silence has fallen recently between them.

Joel sat on a fallen log, and Jethro stood beside him, leaning on a slim strong stick, vee'd at its top, that he has picked up somewhere along the way. It occurs to me to wonder, for the first time, if there is a symbolic significance in this scene as I have described it, with its strange reversal of a pattern: the boy seated, his father now standing, as the silence stretches between them. Into that silence, which until now has seemed so easy, Joel flung his sudden, startling question.

'Do you believe in God?'

I am not sure how to interpret Jethro's stillness; his further silence. One might have supposed a more immediate reaction; maybe a gentle reminder that at least three times publicly every Sunday, and every day privately (we may presume) in his own room, he professed his faith. Evidently, he needed to shape his response, in his mind, before he made it.

At last: 'When I look around me, at the wonder and complexity of creation, I find it hard not to.' If he had chosen, he could not have found a better place for such a declaration. 'This world of ours – could not have been an accident. That simply doesn't seem possible to me.'

'It doesn't have to have been an accident,' Joel said. 'But there doesn't have to be a God, either.' It was clear in his mind, but he couldn't find the words to explain himself. 'People make up God to excuse themselves. And then they blame God for what they don't understand – or decide God blames them for what goes wrong. I don't want to do that.' He was clearly unhappy, but this was not for what he was saying, so much as for the effect he feared his words must have on his father. Declaration for declaration, his own had to be made.

'Father, I think I am an atheist.' And then honesty prevailed. 'I *am* an atheist. Do you mind very much?'

Jethro felt the oddest inclination (which he restrained) to laugh: not in derision, or alarm, but in something very close to joy. He had travelled a long journey with his strange and cherished son.

'No, I don't mind,' he said.

As they walked slowly the three miles home, Jethro was thinking about his pact with God. In his mind he saw the spiral stair climbing in front of him, as high now as Jacob's ladder. He knew, he could vividly imagine, that his vertigo was ever there; (Tower Bridge would always defeat him). But he had lost his fear of it.

One thread remains, still ravelled, in this Revised Version. We must return to a Sunday, on the face of it like any other Sunday, when Mrs McGinty took herself and her closed, unyielding demeanour, to the Methodist church. What silent prayers she may have spoken are quite properly hidden from us; nor can I say if she was in any way aware of what was happening half a mile away at the church of St Peter-Without. For there, where we left them a while ago, the people had gathered in the porch for the early service, and the late spring sunshine sang all around them, and they stumbled on a mystery.

The doors were closed against them, and pinned to those stout timbers on a sheet of white paper was Jethro's last sermon, pencilled in capital letters: GOD HAS GONE AWAY.

The Fall of the House of Robinson

I used to dream about the house falling down. Take *The Fall of the House of Usher* as an example: when I first stubbed a toe on that title – and this was long before those dreams – it was not the destruction of a family that I imagined, but the physical destruction of a building, crumbling downwards from the roof in terminal decay. (Another dream: all my teeth, like sub-standard cement, are suddenly a disintegrating rubble in my mouth.) The dreams about the house began years before we actually left it; but they symbolized a loss that I suppose my subconscious had already encompassed. The house has gone; nearly ten years ago now. Surprisingly, most of my teeth remain; stained by pipe tobacco, but still able to chew on a bone or two.

My mood, when I remember the house, is elegiac; and angry, when I allow it. Anger at such remorseless, ineluctable loss. And at myself, because it was not ineluctable. If I had chosen to thread a different path through life, I might have had the means to hold on to the house. But I despised material pursuits, and I think this was right; however successfully I had pursued them, I am fairly certain they would in the end have proved a rather inferior fiction.

So to those dreams.

My room was on the second floor, in the slope of the roof and under the attic. A low, uneven ceiling, bulging downwards in several places; the walls too, leaning at odd irregular angles. Did this plant the idea of imminent collapse? Yet there was a reassuring solidity about the room, even when the windows rattled in the wind or to passing traffic. (For years the traffic, behind the high retaining wall,

THE FALL OF THE HOUSE OF ROBINSON

was heavy and grew worse; until they opened the motorway.) A casement dormer window faced south across the valley. A sash window, set in the gable end, looked to the sunset, and to the river lost among willows across the watermeadows. It was a room that hummed with silence and sunlight, within the enfolding tranquillity of that lovely house. A servants' room once, perhaps, where maids huddled in frozen winters round bowls of frozen water. But I was not aware of a past, in that room or in that house. Two hundred and fifty years had left no ghosts, not even kindly ones; it was the house itself that brooded an enduring kindliness. And it was the house that split and teetered and slid to destruction in my dreams.

It always began in the roof, above me, while I slept. Silently the tiles would slip away, baring the timbers, which sagged and cracked, ugly distorted bones framed by the black stars. Sometimes those twisted beams would be fire-blackened, although in my dreams there was never fire. Often water would gush between them, eating the tops of the walls like sea water consuming a sandcastle; but in my dreams it never rained.

And we always got out. Nobody was ever caught in that destruction. From the dark hallway, I would look up skeleton stairs ascending to nowhere. Standing on the compacted gravel of the drive, I would see the wreck still reared above me, a vivid shadow of my inner despair; my desolation.

I have long held the positively vertiginous belief that reality is most certain of itself in fiction; for that is where it feels most at home. So what follows is fiction; I make no further excuses for this.

I must try to imagine Robinson.

He is, I think, in his middle forties, because that for most people is a comfortable age, and he is a comfortable person. He is a solicitor, something tells me, but that is unimportant – or at this stage in his story, it seems of little importance to me. I had always supposed solicitors to be a sedentary species, in the sense that once qualified and established in

SOME MARLBOROUGH INVENTIONS

a practice they tend to remain, all the way through to retirement, in the same place and probably even in the same house. But Robinson was different. He came from far away, in mid-career. Perhaps that gives an impression of adventure, of glamour: if so, it is an impression I must correct. Far away does not in this case mean exotic. Nor was there anything adventurous, that I am at present aware of, in his background. But North Yorkshire, let us say, or perhaps Cumbria, even in this age of instant and rapid communication, is still far away from the quieter corners of North Wiltshire.

Robinson is married. That is essential, but again at this stage I am not quite sure why. He has a round number of children, two or three probably, with no decimal points; but in most else he is, I suspect, pretty average. I am, I know, showing an annoyingly bare canvas – for the moment I cannot, even for myself, envisage features.

Which did he decide to move first, his job or his house? Reason demands that it was his job. Even in fiction, nobody is going to move two or three hundred miles simply because he fancies a house. So, work dictated the move. This too seems unlikely, but there is much that I don't know about solicitors, and Robinson has not confided in me. Given the move, and it will have to be given, it is easy for me to understand why he fancied the house. I have fancied it myself, to put it mildly, all my life.

Robinson is an orderly sort of fellow. Not for him haphazard tours round country lanes in the family Rover, pausing whimfully where FOR SALE boards lean from hedgerows or graft themselves on gateposts. He went straight to the Estate Agents (all three of them), so that his first view of the house would have been a photograph.

ROBINSON: I like the look of that one, by Jove. [Do people still say 'by Jove'? Well, Robinson does. I am helpless.] Georgian, I rather think.

ESTATE AGENT: Actually, the older parts are Queen Anne. (*Almost apologetic. Antiquity established, but the client's* amour propre *respected.*)

ROBINSON: (*to his wife, delighted*) Queen Anne, Ann!

We have established a name. Anne without an *e*. Robinson would be very particular about that. But Robinson himself has no name. Even 'Robinson' is a fiction, his real name remains a mystery to me. And Ann is no help; I cannot persuade her to tell me his name – I cannot persuade her to say anything at all as yet. She sits, demure and featureless. But she likes the house. Of that, at least, I am certain.

The children are at their boarding schools. (Robinson has old-fashioned ideas, it seems; and the means to pay for private education.) I am confident I shall soon be meeting them. They will be home for the holidays, which can't be far away – it almost always was the holidays in that house, as I remember it.

First, however, Robinson has to buy the house. He has prospered in the North, and I doubt if he has to concern himself with mortgages or bank loans. The boom in the property market has not yet begun, but it is only just below the horizon; as a solicitor he is perhaps aware of this. Perhaps he knows that in only four or five years, whatever house he buys is likely to double or triple in value. So they view the property.

It is love at first sight. I can get that out of the way with uncustomary confidence. The practised patter of the young man from the agency is superfluous.

ROBINSON: Of course, it needs quite a lot doing to it. [An innocent observation, I am sure, rather than a prelude to haggling over the price. All the same, it makes me wince. What horrors does he have in mind?]

They stroll in the garden, Robinson testing the delightful sense of prospective ownership that rises through soil and grass to his responsive feet.

ESTATE AGENT: (*they are gazing out over a small paddock towards a line of willows that defines the course of the river*) There are about twenty acres in all, mostly water-meadows. And fishing rights, although the present owners retain a small part of these.

ANN: Twenty acres, dearest. That seems rather a lot. [At last! She has spoken. On reflection, however, I have to say she has not told me much.]

Robinson bought the house, and about a month later they moved in. From a distance I see the furniture vans cluttering the drive. Soon I can hear the excited shouts of the two or three children – for the holidays have begun. There is so much for them to explore: the rambling three-storey house full of winding passages and strange recesses, the garden with its two lawns, the orchard, the many outbuildings, the water-meadows, the river.

I am reminded of my own childhood, and in spite of myself I warm in sympathy for these children, whose cries of delight I can distinctly hear, but whose faces I still cannot quite see. There are so many things I would like to suggest to them, things we used to do. But I can't. I must leave them to their own discoveries, which almost certainly will not be the same as mine.

Robinson has a mother, who lives in North Yorkshire let us say, or Cumbria perhaps. A dutiful son, he wrote to her every fortnight:

> Dearest Mother,
> So here we are, settling in if not yet firmly established, recruits to the ranks of the Landed Gentry! The house is a bit ramshackle – [ugh!] – but nevertheless a charming period piece. I feel sure you will love it when we have sorted ourselves out sufficiently to invite you down.
> There is much to be done. The fabric itself is sound – of course, we had a surveyor's report before buying – but Ann, quite rightly, wants to redecorate throughout. There is an immense ash tree in the garden, which must come down. I have been advised by the forestry people

that it is diseased, and threatens the house if a gale should topple it. I don't know what to do about the land. I have been told that the water-meadows are unsuitable for building development, but I shall seek further opinions on that because they *could* turn out a gold mine. I have sold the fishing rights – I feel at my time of life it is too late to cultivate new passions. The children love the place. Tom in particular [I have gleaned another name] is the complete water-rat, forever playing in and around the river. I am thinking of selling off the garage for conversion into a cottage – it stands well away from the house, so we would not be bothered by the propinquity of neighbours. It was originally a barn and stables, and is quite a pretty building in its own right, the same mellow brick as the house. If the planners give their permission, I feel it would sell like a hot cake. That's all for now. Ann and the children send their love.

Your loving son, Robinson.

I am worried by this letter. I do not like the mercenary side that is emerging in Robinson's character; nor did I intend this. I feel it is only half the picture, and hope that something will presently occur to redress the balance. The nice part is Tom; I see my distant self there; I am cheered by the reflection that a family that includes Tom has something going for it. It is a pity about the ash, but I suppose he is right; better to lose the tree than the house – but then, I remind myself, I *have* lost the house. As a child I used to lie in bed and see strange faces in the bare trellis of winter twigs etched against a white sky, framed by my bedroom window. In summer, its huge trunk rose out of a jungle of shrubs and elder behind the rockery.

At this point in my story, I feel the need to add to the *dramatis personae*, and so I introduce my cousin Jim. That is not his real name, because I have not thought to ask his permission, which I am not at all sure he would grant. Jim has little taste for fiction, except perhaps for some occasional Kipling, preferring, when he reads at all, biographies of military men, and fishing anecdotes. From this it follows, naturally enough, that he is a retired soldier and a keen fisherman, particularly with a dry fly. It was Jim who bought the fishing rights from Robinson, and on the strength of this transaction a mild friendship sprang up between them. He became a hero, moreover, to Tom, and taught him to cast a line. His bluff figure and soldierly bearing might have made him a hero to Ann as well, despite his sixty years, but for all his old-fashioned gallantry Jim remains an indomitable bachelor, so I need not pursue that line.

A summer afternoon. Ann is in the garden, a broad floppy sunhat on her head, a trug looped over her arm for the snapdragons she is cutting in the border beside the wall. Tom is across two fields climbing the hollow trunk of a willow that overhangs the river; the still vigorous branches of this rotting tree have trapped the fly with which he had hoped to trap a fish. His siblings – let me be decisive and say that they are two – are playing in the loft over the soon-to-be-sold-and-converted garage. And Robinson? It occurs to me that solicitors must sometimes go to work: Robinson is soliciting in his office in the town.

I regret that flippancy. It escaped. But I have set myself parameters that I am determined to observe, so I suppose it must stand. At any rate, it has cleared the scene for an encounter. Jim sweeps deftly in from the lane in his ancient Aston Martin, and brakes with a scrunch of gravel in precisely the spot where Robinson's Rover would have been parked if he had not driven it in to work. No symbolism is intended by this coincidence.

'Got some flies for Tom,' he said cheerfully. In the nick of time, if he had only known. 'Tied them myself. Not bad, for all that.'

'That's so kind of you,' said Ann, squinting a little because of the strength of the sun as she peered from under the brim of her hat. 'They look lovely.' She doesn't know an Olive Dun from a Little Marryat, as a matter of fact, but that is of small importance – neither do I.

'Would you like some tea? Robinson will be back soon, but we needn't wait.'

Fifty years ago a demure parlourmaid in white cap and apron would have emerged from the kitchen with a huge tray; a Crown Derby tea-set, china tea, cucumber sandwiches, *patum peperium* ('the Gentleman's relish'), a seed cake, all set on a garden table covered with Belfast linen. Ann would have poured from the Georgian silver teapot, and after such exertion have fanned the perspiration delicately from her face. But it is not fifty years ago, even if Jim would have preferred it so. Ann boiled the kettle on the Aga range which was earmarked for the scrap heap, put the tea bags in the pot, and a box of Mr Kipling's cakes on the tray, which Jim then gallantly and appropriately carried to the garden and placed, with careful decorum, in the middle of the wooden bench, so that they sat on each side of it.

'How are things going, then?' Jim asked. 'The family are curious, you know. Fond of the old place.'

'So are we,' said Ann quietly. 'We have been here scarcely a month. But it takes a hold.'

Jim nodded, fingering his grey military moustache, his silence comfortably confirming Ann's assertion. Presently the two children, both girls, I notice, and younger than Tom, appeared from the loft to eat Kipling cakes; made curiously shy by Jim's benign and jocular approval. They stared at each other silently, half inclined to giggle and not quite daring.

'And where's young Tom?'

'I think he must be down by the river. He nearly always is.' With sudden warmth, Ann turned full face to Jim. 'It really is so good of you to give him a free run at the fishing.'

'Not at all,' Jim muttered, in some embarrassment. 'Goes with the house. Or that's the way it always used to be.' It's not the way it is now, but Jim shies away from such complications.

A vignette of small significance, it seems to me, this impromptu tea-party. But thanks to Jim, I have learned a little more about Ann. I am not sure whether Jim left before Robinson returned, but either way this does not matter much because, as I have already indicated, any sort of romantic attachment between Ann and Jim (who is surely old enough to be her father) is out of the question – much to Jim's relief, I imagine.

A difficulty that faces me here is the apparent absence of tensions between and around my protagonists. Fiction thrives on tensions, they are as essential to the architecture of a story as precisely balanced stresses are to the architecture of a house. A story, like a house, is likely to collapse if that equilibrium of contrary forces is not maintained. Ann is too placid, Robinson is too anonymous. The house is too quiescent – but is perhaps a dormant volcano beneath which the magma, unsuspected, is building up. (I am haunted by those dreams, even if I do not dream them any more.) There *are* tensions, I realize. But they are between myself and my characters, which is an awkward admission to have to make, and even more difficult to convey.

Robinson became heavily involved in a case of municipal fraud among councillors in a neighbouring town. I don't know where his sympathies lay, or even which side he represented, but I do know that this proximity, not to corruption but to local government, sparked in him some mild political ambitions. Town councillor he decided, for a start, would sit well with his maturing image of himself as a settled and solid pillar of the community; it would suit the house, too. And he might get to know influential members of planning committees – for he still nursed hopes of building on his land.

Ann was less enthusiastic; but not to the point of tension. Theirs was a serene marriage.

THE FALL OF THE HOUSE OF ROBINSON

So Robinson began with some energy to promote himself. He made known his availability; he pushed, politely but firmly, at certain doors. Soon, although still unelected, he established his indispensability among local Conservatives. Guests were entertained to dinner; the old house began to stir, fitfully, unaccustomed to these manners. There is no saying where it might have ended, if Robinson's appetite had grown: town, district, county, region – perhaps all the way to Westminster. Was there a cabinet minister's baton hidden in his knapsack?

I have strayed from the domestic scene, but there is a reason. Robinson is a man of small imagination; which is why, perhaps, he is so hard to imagine. These details are at least something to hold on to, and presently they may even be seen to have a purpose, to fit the design I am moving, albeit crab-wise and capriciously, to accomplish.

Jim visits me occasionally, in the little house we have moved to.

'Odd chap,' he said to me one evening over a glass of port – 'Robinson.' The port was left over from Christmas, but still drinkable. 'Told me the other day he had dreamed the house fell down. I wouldn't have taken him for a fanciful sort of fellow. People speak well of him, as a matter of fact.'

If I gaped, Jim was too polite to notice. But this was inordinate. Not content, apparently, with my house, Robinson was appropriating my dreams. I hoped his teeth would fall out.

'He seemed quite worried. Wanted to get in another surveyor for a second opinion. I suppose your contract of sale is tied up tight? You never know with these lawyer chappies – tricky, some of them.' Cynicism, even so gentle, was rare enough in Jim to make me think twice about what he had said. But such hopes, false or at least tardy, were better squashed. I shook my head, and offered Jim the decanter.

When I began this story, I was sure that it must end badly

for Robinson. The title, for a start, makes this clear enough. So there is a sort of inevitability about the next bit.

I have done little to record the passing of the seasons, let alone the years. But a few years, by now, have passed. It is October.

Through my window I glimpsed a flight of starlings, tossed by the autumn rain between windswept trees: they seemed strangely happy. They flew, and pitched, and swirled, with an exuberance that defied the elements. That, at least, is how they struck me; but I got it wrong. In some important ways starlings are wiser than we, and now I know they were running for shelter, as fast as their frightened wings would carry them.

At about the time I saw the starlings, Robinson was walking his fields with his son. In October? Surely, Tom should be at school. Nevertheless, he and his two sisters are at home. I must contrive an epidemic of chicken-pox in their respective schools. So there they were, Tom and his father, under that wild sky; I see them clearly. Willows bent angrily to the rising wind. Robinson and Tom walked leaning into the gale, blown leaves hurled stingingly against their red, whipped faces. But they were both, in their different ways, happy as I had imagined the starlings to be happy. The wild weather lifted something inside each of them, the still rather inscrutable man and the much more visible boy.

Robinson had almost to shout to make himself heard to Tom beside him.

'All this will be yours one day, my lad.'

A familiar thought – yet new to Tom, who hugged it to himself. I would like to be able to warn him. But I can't.

Tom, in an excess of excitement, wants to walk as far as the top pool, but Robinson is pressed for time. He generally is, these days.

'Sorry, old boy. I must go back. I have a meeting in town this evening. I mustn't be late.'

There probably followed a good-natured lecture, man-to-man, on adult responsibilities and what awaited Tom when he grew up. Fortunately the wind, which by now was ferocious, renders this inaudible to us; and with a reasonable measure of luck, to Tom too.

So Robinson went off, presently, to his meeting, and Tom who often prefers his own company to that of others, retreated to his room at the top of the house. Yes, it used to be my room.

Afterwards, we learned to call it the Great October Gale, the one which nearly blew away Michael Fish; it acquired the comfortable flavour of a myth, source of endless bar-room anecdotes. At the time it was rather frightening.

It is a bit difficult to decide how to tackle this. I have been writing, cheerfully enough, for three days now; my good spirits should not surprise me – after all, from the start the story was intended to be a sort of catharsis. But I can't help feeling that any levity from here on would be inappropriate. It is an awesome task of destruction I have to accomplish; and I am aware, too, that I have already laid most if not all of my cards on the table. Face up.

By midnight the storm had declared its hand. This was no ordinary wind, but a bombardment, hurled round the roof-tops by primeval forces. It was not a moment to think of going to bed; nor was it a moment to consider venturing outside – so I was astonished when presently I realized, among all the other bangs and crashes around me, that someone was hammering insistently on my door.

It was Jim.

'Ann has phoned. Robinson has not come home. He's hours late. And the house is falling down.' There was a wildness in Jim's eyes that probably had not entered them since he faced the Germans in the forests of the Ardennes. 'Then we were cut off. The lines must be down. I'm going out there.'

It was an assumption more than an invitation. I was to go with him.

Wind and rain screamed round the Aston Martin. Jim steered recklessly past fallen trees. The house was only a mile and a half away, but on a night like this it was ten miles, it was a hundred miles. I have little memory of that desperate journey.

I stood on the compacted gravel of the drive, and surveyed my dream.

The lights of the Aston Martin, through the drift of storm, revealed it. The wind had ripped away the roof, but some of this, and the massive square chimney stacks, had fallen inwards, taking the upper parts of the walls with them. A few of the roof beams stood, jagged against the racing clouds. Through the open front door I saw that skeleton stairway, leading to nowhere.

Jim was bellowing beside me. Where was Ann? Where were the children? They were beside us, in the darkness, outside the pool of light cast by the car's headlamps.

Ann shouted, and somehow we heard her above the wind. 'We got out! We're all safe!'

We always got out. Nobody was ever caught in that destruction. Even Tom got out, from my room beneath the chimney stack.

And then Robinson arrived.

I never learned of his earlier adventures that night; I don't know what delayed him, or how he eventually made it through the storm. But I was there when he arrived. He climbed out of his car, and looked at the house – not at Ann, or the children. At the house.

'Oh my God,' said Robinson. 'The dream.'

Robinson's God had no seemly or sensible response to make, to this despairing cry.

Ann, and Jim, and the children, gathered round him; and I think by now he was able to see them, and to see that they were safe. Whether he saw me is another matter. Robinson did not know me; and on the whole I didn't feel it was a suitable moment to introduce myself.

No doubt he was prudently insured. But the house had gone, beyond repair, forever. I know the feeling. I knew what *he* was feeling. I knew, too, something that Robinson could not know: the house he thought he had bought, some few years ago now, had fallen down before we ever left it.

I must make amends.

Dear Robinson,

It was not your fault. In all honesty I can't think that it was my fault either, but still I feel a heavy responsibility. I have put you in my story, where you probably had no wish to be. I have done unforgivable things to you. Above all, I have not been fair in the portrait I have drawn of you. The trouble is, you were always so damnably elusive; I never really got the hang of you. Perhaps, if I tried putting you in a novel...

Yours, etc –

Beginning at Home

In 1964 I was eight years old, so my perspective on the events I propose to reveal here was, if you will forgive the contradiction, distinctly umbrageous. In that decade of light and flowers, of green hope (as it seems now), to be young must indeed have been very heaven; but to be very young was decidedly confusing. I make no special or romantic claim to innocence, but I must insist on our ignorance; in those days, and at our age, a great many books were closed to us that would have been opened today. We grappled with simplicities: foul language, a scorn for girls, an insouciant hedonism that was measured fairly precisely in summer by the sun's span, in winter trespassing only a little way into the hours of darkness – but artificial light, I remember, could sometimes make the blood race.

We were ten or a dozen – memory cannot be more precise – all boys, all in age within a year or eighteen months of each other, all living on the Meadowbank Estate, a red-brick development built in the 'fifties to replace the asbestos white of wartime prefabs.

What might have been no more than an aggressive and, to outsiders, obnoxious neighbourhood gang of small boys, was refined and precariously civilized by Mary Wollenplatz, founder and intrepid Akela of the 1st Meadowbank Troop of Cub Scouts (we called ourselves Wolf Cubs in those days). Her success, as unlikely as her name, owed little to Baden-Powell, almost all to the fact that every last one of us was hopelessly, irrevocably in love with her, although each would have died before admitting, or even hinting at, such secret disgrace. I cannot explain Mary's achievement in thus turning our values upside down, but I have a faded black-

and-white photograph, somewhat bent and crumpled by years of devotion, that might provide a pointer. Perhaps it would be relevant to add – I forget how this intimate knowledge came to me – that she was at the time just twenty-two. To be objective about this, I suppose it was not an entirely satisfactory situation for a conscientious Akela to find herself in, but Mary handled it, and us, with a cool and friendly sympathy that seemed effortlessly attuned to the demands and stresses of eight-year-old passions.

The Troop met twice a week, Tuesdays and Fridays, at five o'clock, in a shamefully dilapidated wooden hut, smelling strongly of creosote, that was sinking with slow patience into its water-meadow foundations beside the river. Try as I may, I could never conjure up in words, from such a distant past, the magic of those evenings spent with Mary Wollenplatz; but they glow in my memory, as I suspect they still glow in the memories of ten or eleven other middle-aged desperadoes.

The 1st Meadowbank Troop was divided into two patrols, which with a flair for the obvious we named the Bears and the Otters. Patrol leader of the Bears was a large and menacing boy, called Jake Stannard by his unsuspecting parents, but known immutably, to all of us, as Crusher. I was patrol leader of the Otters.

Crusher was the size of any two of the rest of us put together, and therefore to be respected. Although he took a pride in his place at the bottom of our class in school, he was illogically resentful of my place at the top of it. For a year I suffered bruises and the indignity of an all-consuming fear, but one day something (I still find this hard to believe) goaded me into retaliation, and in a moment of sheer improbablity I had a headlock on him – Crusher's own favourite tactic. His weight folded and collapsed, his rather slack white face gouged the earth, and he called enough. I had won my first schoolyard fight.

In spite of this, I remained impressed by Crusher's physical prestige which I could believe I had overcome only, as it were, by accident; and Crusher remained impressed by my intellectual pre-eminence, to which neither of us, however, conceded any public importance. On this odd basis we constructed an unsentimental if rather exclusive friendship.

It certainly excluded Lynn, Crusher's sixteen-year-old sister of whom he was bitterly and dangerously ashamed. Lynn worked in The Cinema (that was its unambiguous name) as an usherette, living in a daze of adolescent images of Cary Grant and Rock Hudson, but never failing to take particular care over the inspection of our tickets.

Early that autumn, two black clouds drifted metaphorically into our halcyon sky, as though to underline the passing of summer; of childhood, too, I am now inclined to believe. The first of these was financial: our Troop Headquarters, the shed by the river, was teetering towards collapse. Even to our uncritical eyes it was clear that the roof, at least, would never survive the rigours of another winter. But the other cloud was altogether more momentous, threatening to obscure the whole sky. Mary Wollenplatz had acquired a suitor. And to compound this betrayal she decided, with the uncalculating cruelty I have since learned that the kindest of women can contrive, to inflict him on us. When our two semicircles, sitting cross-legged on the splintery wooden floor, Tuesday and Friday evenings, responded to Mary's call of 'Dyb! Dyb! Dyb!' there was now an intrusive baritone mixed with the raucous treble of our reply: 'We'll Dob! Dob! Dob!' The intruder's name was Richard Bland, which was apt enough, for he seemed politely impervious to the eleven or twelve pairs of obsidian eyes unwaveringly wishing him dead. Mr Bland made it plain he was here to stay, and that we had better figure out a way to accommodate his unwelcome presence.

'Who cares,' said Crusher once, out of adult earshot, and with a mortally wounded scorn, 'who cares what she does? Old Woollen-Plaits.' But this single instance of wit in Crusher fell flat; nobody had the heart to laugh, or the nerve to disagree. It was, after all, true that there was a Teutonic cast to Mary's style and colouring of hair, as well as to her name.

There was also a Teutonic directness in her response to our financial straits. She organized, in the course of one Tuesday evening, what would nowadays be called a sponsored walk. Perhaps she could claim to have invented the concept.

'We must collect money for ourselves. Charity begins at home,' Mary reminded us. She was not one to blink at a cliché if it could advance her cause; a quality I see now as not merely endearing, but actually as a sign of strength, of blithe self-confidence.

The walk, Mary declared, was to be of eight miles, four out, into the neighbouring forest, and four back. Her eyes challenged, as backsides shifted uneasily on the floor. But we knew we could deny her nothing. And the forest, if not the eight miles, was familiar to us.

'I will walk with the slowest of you,' Mary said, and that immediately meant all of us, even those who had begun to wonder about the distinction, and perhaps the rewards, of finishing first.

'And Mr Bland,' she added, making this up as she went along, to judge by his startled expression, 'will be waiting in the charcoal-burners' hut at the furthest point, to check your names.' Mary took a realistic view of Cub Scouts.

I shall always remember that walk; for the way it ended of course, but also for the magic that preceded disaster. The trees blazed with autumn colours under a cool, thin sun; someone, somewhere, was burning fallen leaves, and even now that smell can haunt me. We jockeyed, viciously, for a place next to Mary. Our laughter set squirrels to flight. We knew we were in the morning of the world.

And then Jimmy Pardoe decided to jump a fallen tree-trunk, and slipped, and broke an ankle. His screams, before Mary managed to quieten him, had cracked the day, irretrievably. They were more an expression of fear than of pain, and somehow that fear was communicated to us. But our trust in Mary was not misplaced. She encircled us all, briefly, within invisible arms.

'We cannot go on,' she said. 'We must carry Jimmy to the hospital. One of you – ' and she looked at her two patrol leaders; first at Crusher, then at me – 'one of you must run on and tell Mr Bland.' Her eyes lingered. 'Peter, you will be faster.'

I knew then, as I was never to know again in the same measure, the heady pride of the elect. My feet were winged. I sped down grassy rides, soldier of Miltiades running the first Marathon, and reached the charcoal-burners' hut at least thirty minutes before Mr Bland could have expected the fastest of the walkers.

It seemed deserted.

A cobwebbed window.

I peered through it, tiptoe, puzzled by silence; and saw what I palely knew I was not meant to see. If the glass had shattered, in my face, I would not have known or heard it. Mr Bland and Lynn Stannard, in attitudes mysterious to me, decorated the dark interior.

Presently they emerged, Lynn looking frightened, Mr Bland with extravagant unconcern.

'Don't tell Mary,' he said, with extraordinary lack of emphasis.

Looking back, I think I recognize a kind of contempt in my feelings, for them both; but also a tearing, unforgiving alarm. They were pulling me in so many ways – not just Mr Bland and Lynn, but Mary as well, and Crusher – even, obscurely, something in myself, distorting myself: so that among all those clutching, dragging hands I sensed, terrifyingly, my own. But I remember, too, my ignorance. If I had really understood what I had seen, I suspect I would have gone straight to Mary, and told her. Perhaps Richard Bland read this in me.

'Don't tell Mary,' he said again, with a note of desperation now. 'Pete, please. Remember what she said. Charity begins at home.'

At the time, I hadn't the faintest idea what he meant by this.

Now, when it is so far too late to matter much, because a

great weight of water has flowed past the site of that abandoned Scout hut, long since disappeared – now, I think, I begin to understand.

Over the Hill

I had better start by giving myself a name – a prescription that can be missed in the heat of developing a narrative, but an oversight, if allowed, that leaves both author and reader, from their different perspectives, awkwardly stranded on the shoals of anonymity. Roderick Slim, I think, would fit the *persona* I want to assume. If, from here on, I tend to drift in and out of the first person, take it as a symptom of the identity crisis that is liable, occasionally, to beset any writer of fiction.

As Roderick, then, rather than as my uncertain self, I returned recently, after an absence of thirty-five years, to my native town. This is an experience that tests the imagination as much as the memory. On the whole, I wanted things to be as they once were, so I wandered the town and its surroundings with selective vision. Windy chalk paths over the downs would distance change and soften the jagged edges of the intervening years. Up there, Roderick could almost reconcile himself with his past – the art of nostalgia, which I was determined to master, depends as much on forgetting as on remembering. I walked an easy pace, three and a half miles to the hour, comfortably dressed, sensibly shod, my only companion a well-used thumbstick. While my feet reeled off the solitary miles, time closed up behind me, a secretive lacuna; hill-fort and burial chamber, Wansdyke and Ridge Way, each assumed the lineaments of its origin, closer than yesterday to that eternal landscape.

But one day a chance encounter was to shatter such gentle fancies; I came face to face, for once, with my authentic past.

Roderick's own face, I suppose, needs some definition

here. The morning mirror provides a suitable opportunity: looking, less casually than usual, Remington in hand, at that reflection, what do I see? The eyes first, a much-washed and tumble-dried blue, accustomed to foreign and exotic horizons. A thin and military moustache. Cheeks tanned, and sculpted into wistful hollows. Salt-and-pepper hair, cut with tidy precision. It is a face I think I would recognize in a crowd.

And so to that moment of intense and disconcerting drama.

Two days of snow had taken me to the highest escarpments, but a rapid thaw set in on the second afternoon, and the next day was one of warm and gentle sunlight, a trailer for the spring feature that was still more than a month away. Impulse rather than decision, I am inclined to believe, took me that morning along paths I had never walked before; perhaps it had something to do with the change in the weather. I forsook the heights and set out for the valley to the east of the town.

Many years ago a branch railway line crossed the valley, skirting an area of ramshackle and peripheral light industry. The line was closed down even before Dr Beeching had the chance to declare it redundant; but Roderick, as a child, had collected a few coal smuts in his eyes, hanging his head hopefully through carriage windows as the little train chuntered up and down tree-lined gradients and out onto arable and open downland. This haunted relic was where I walked. I had seen from my Ordnance Survey map that like many another abandoned railroad this one remained a public amenity, a right of way.

It was, somehow, an unnerving experience. The ghosts were too vivid for comfort. The rumble of lorries on the trunk road across the valley was ambiguously threatening – I looked uneasily ahead, or over my shoulder, expecting at any moment to see a 2-6-2 Hall class locomotive spitting smoke and steam as it bore down on me.

This was galling. I had after all, on my walks, looked

eagerly enough for such sweet and melancholy reminders of vanished times, illusions of immortality. But there was, too, a perversely exhilarating aura about the place: the dizzy height of a bridge over the river that crawled below, the wild-grown banks of steep-sided cuttings, the vault of interlacing trees interrupted by a mouldering brick arch where a lane crossed above. So it was in an appropriately schizophrenic frame of mind that I first saw, two or three hundred yards ahead of me where, if they had not been torn out half a century ago, the railway lines would have all but converged on infinity, two figures: a small woman, I decided, and a large dog, walking purposefully towards me. I was relieved to see the dog. On my walks I had met remarkably few people, but a woman alone always made me uncomfortable – I felt guilty, by association, of all the horrors retailed by the tabloid press; I was bound to be suspected of the wish, if not the intention, to rape and murder. So the dog was in a way as much my protection as hers.

We drew steadily, inevitably, towards each other, and I was able to discern detail. A dumpy figure, with more than a touch of eccentricity about it. A brown tweed jacket, almost shabby but evidently cherished, a rimpled deerstalker from which grey curls escaped, dark blue woollen trousers encased to the knee in scarlet stockings, and boots as serviceable as mine. She was smoking a pipe, held at a natural and practised angle in her generous mouth. The dog, a wild black creature with a glint of mischief in its eye, bounded in front of her, its jaws clamped precisely at the point of balance on an immense piece of timber that protruded a good yard each side of its wicked face.

I prepared a civil greeting, to mumble as we passed each other; it was never to be spoken.

She stopped, grey eyes widened in an expression I could not begin to fathom, and removed the pipe from her mouth.

'Good God!' she said. 'Roddy Slim!'

At the same moment the dog thumped my legs, numbingly, with its baulk of hardwood, thrashing its tail in an ecstasy of pride.

'Leave!' she bellowed – 'Leave, Saracen! You vile, unmannerly mongrel.' But this was spoken more in love than recrimination. 'You haven't the faintest idea who I am, have you?' She looked at me in lenient silence, now puffing thoughtful curls of smoke from that unlikely pipe.

'Amabel,' I said, making the miraculous connection; and then, mistrusting inspiration: 'It is Amabel, isn't it?'

Saracen, who had dropped the log, was sniffing my boots with fastidious interest.

'How very impersonal, after all these years. But yes, it is. I am.'

Amabel Leigh-Palmerston, a dashing girl to hounds, I remembered. That was the least of all I was remembering. For reasons (of State, I am tempted to add) that will presently become clear, I cannot use Amabel's real name here, but it is a thin disguise that I have chosen.

In the meantime Roderick was slowly reassuming command of himself. Observing covertly, but more closely, this extraordinary woman, it was just possible to fit Before and After together. I was swept by invigorating memories.

'You are looking wonderfully well,' I said, cautiously.

'I am very fit, I don't deny. But – oh Roddy, the years are so unkind.'

She was thinking, I knew, of Before: in her day, cover girl for *Vogue* and *Country Life*, deb of the year, living a whirligig of excitement. For one breathless spring and summer, Roddy had been granted a brief share; just a toe in the door.

'You haven't changed *at all*, Roddy.' She seized my two hands, and I nearly lost my thumbstick to Saracen. 'Tell me the secret.' But her wide grey eyes were laughing. I saw that, after all, she had not lost a stitch of her ravelled beauty.

'What an amazing chance, Roddy; meeting you here. I was just thinking about you. Well, not exactly about *you*; about *then*.'

I, too, I realized.

'What idiots we were,' she said. '*You* were. You should have slept with me.' I stared foolishly at the pipe.

'But you wouldn't let me,' I said indignantly. It was not for want of trying, I might have added.

She sighed impatiently. 'Papa was rather strict. The dear, silly man.'

This seemed an odd description of Edward Leigh-Palmerston, who in his way was also a Before and After man. Wealthy barrister and Member of Parliament when I knew him, he had already the intimidating air of a future Prime Minister. Roderick Slim, callow youth, found himself frequently tongue-tied in the great man's presence, and suspected that he was viewed with little favour.

Only once did I summon up any kind of courage.

'Don't keep my daughter dangling,' he said to me over brandy, in the small hours after a party.

'It's Amabel who does the dangling.' I dared the contradiction, but in the mildest of tones. He grunted, I supposed in disbelief. It was, I remember, always a reprieve – to part from Edward Leigh-Palmerston.

Saracen chased a rabbit into a burrow somewhere above us, and stood guard, noisily. I spread two empty supermarket plastic bags on the damp turf, and we sat down. Amabel seemed in a mood to reminisce.

'We were married on the same day; within five miles of each other. Did you know?' (I did. We had sent each other invitations.) 'It didn't do either of us any good.'

'How was America?' I asked. 'He *was* an American, wasn't he?'

'Awful.'

'So was South Africa.'

Amabel rested a hand on my shoulder.

'Poor Roddy. We both messed up our lives. Oh yes, I have followed yours; from afar.' She stuffed the pipe into a jacket pocket, and stood up. 'We should have messed them up together. Too late now. Over the hill.'

'What happened – in America?'

She looked at me, in some surprise.

'Papa, of course. Too goddamned much for them, you

see.' She smiled. 'Goodbye, Roddy.' A piercing whistle through two fingers brought Saracen scrambling down the bank. 'We go that way.' She pointed down the valley, but it wasn't necessary. Five miles along a footpath through the water-meadows, to the village I used to visit. To the same house perhaps.

'Will I see you again?'

'If you want to. If there's any point.'

Roderick Slim resumed his solitary walk, haunted now by other ghosts, and a distant scandal. The Right Honourable Sir Edward Leigh-Palmerston, Home Secretary, had reached camp six on his political Everest, when his foot slipped. Two days before that year's party conference, he was obliged to duck hastily out of sight; he turned up a week or two later in Moscow to keep a more pressing engagement with his old friends Philby, Burgess and Maclean. Roderick, reading the story in the South African press, found it hard to believe; Sir Edward, he reflected, had shown himself to be a master dangler.

The next day I walked, alone again, a piece of the Ridge Way, feeling nearer to the sky than I have ever felt atop the Drakenbergs, or on Welsh or Cumbrian or Scottish mountain. In that clear air, I have noticed, it is difficult to sustain the enigmatic shifts of fantasy. I was ready, I realized with some relief, to discard Roddy Slim, moustache, thumbstick, bruised blue far-seeing eyes and all. He had served a purpose, but I never felt at ease within his alien frame.

Nor have I yet walked the five miles down the valley to Amabel's village.

With Colours Idly Spread

This all happened such a long time ago that I have to furbish it with some care, not trusting too blithely to the impulsive and deceiving flow of memory. Much of what I want to relate will have to be shown through Timmy's eyes, so first I must show you Timmy himself – I am aware that I am an interloper here, and aim to slide as near invisibly as possible between the lines.

Timmy, then, was a slight fair child, ten or perhaps eleven years old. With no brothers or sisters, and no handy neighbourhood children for friends, he was accustomed to his own company but at ease, too, with adults. He didn't confuse solitude with loneliness. For Timmy the world was a bright and beckoning place, and he its geographical centre, for this is how children generally view their environment, outwards, in all directions, from themselves. He lived in a large house in the country, with a father and a mother and several more elderly relatives who clung to a real, but rather faded and wistful, gentility.

I must trespass briefly at this point, because while externals are easily carried on a story line, it is important to know something of Timmy's inner character, of his unique and private psyche; of what he felt about things. An essential element in this was his reluctance to impart, to confide his feelings in anyone else; which is my excuse for this intrusion. He wasn't one to start at shadows, but he was nervous in the sense that he was often acutely aware of ideas, sensations, phenomena, that were incompletely understood. This never troubled him in any urgent way – he perceived it, I suppose, as a part of that outward exploration from the centre of himself that I have already mentioned, the experience of growing through childhood. But this larger sensitivity at once reinforced his isolation and heightened his response to the excitements of the physical world around him.

That world was full of satisfactions for Timmy. As he roamed the fields and tracked the banks of the little river that wound through a gentle valley, his heart was often lifted in recognition of immediate and overwhelming happiness, an emotion that he treasured and perhaps already could distinguish from the sere and treacherous attractions of nostalgia. To know that you are happy, he conceived, was a gift; one that was properly rare but for him, then, miraculously prodigal.

The river constantly drew him in his play: ice-cold and fordable almost everywhere, but still deep enough to sustain a quantity of shy brown trout that lurked in streaming weed or flickered over the chalky stones. Willows were plentiful – phoenixes of the river bank, some of them, in a second or third incarnation; for as, trunks hollowed in old age, they fell and rotted, new shoots would spring from the dead wood, a new tree emerge. Timmy climbed among their branches and through their hollows. Stretched on a branch over the water, he could observe the life of the river: trout, grayling, mallard and moorhen, hovering dragonflies, water-rats plying their trade like busy little tug-boats. Walking the fields, his feet would sometimes come near to crushing plovers' eggs.

Empty cartridge cases, collected when he went with his father and great-uncles over their rough shoot, after pigeons and rabbits, or the occasional partridge or pheasant, made wonderful craft to race down the river. The oiled cardboard shells were resistant to waterlogging, the brass caps a perfect ballast to float them upright. A series of dams created waterfalls where in their scarlet or blue or green racing colours the cartridges leaped and gyrated, bobbed, vanished, emerged. Best of all, if they had survived all the other hazards, was the Mill race. Here the river broadened, and deepened, and slowed, in deceptive calm. It seemed to end against a stone wall, a grassy bank, and the mellow brick of the Mill itself. Twenty yards above this apparent cul-de-sac, the water was released sideways in a roaring torrent, through hatches let into the river bank, over a stone sluice set between ivy-grown walls, to tumble in a froth of turbulence into a wide quiet pool. Some of those cartridges would prevail even here, buried in white water but popping up again – gasping, surely, for breath – to float peacefully round and round on the currents of the pool until caught up in the tailwater and at last swept on.

But we have arrived; at the centre of the centre of Timmy's world.

A lawn sloped to one edge of the pool and dropped to the water in a wall formed by two courses of massive roughcut stone. Willows cast cool shadows over the far bank. A small island of mud and reed emerged in summer when the level of the river fell.

The Mill stood above the lawn, set obliquely to the race, turned three-quarters to look the other way. The half-gabled end wall had no windows, although there had evidently been one, bricked over now, high up near the roof, from which perhaps the sacks of flour had been winched to the ground. But there was a low green-painted door, which Timmy could open, and stoop to peer through. Inside was a strange space where once the water had passed to turn the mill-wheel. The wheel was still there, vast and rusted, lying at a slant because it had been lifted off its axis at one end. A dim light filtered through the entrance passage from the upper river, overgrown with reeds. There was a heady smell of mud, and damp brickwork, and spiders. It was possible to scramble down there and climb over the wreck of the wheel, stepping in ooze to dark cobwebbed corners. It was cool, like a cellar, even on the hottest days in summer.

If I have seemed to linger too lovingly over these memories, I have to acknowledge that this is because they belong to me, as much as they ever belonged to Timmy. On the other hand the story I have to tell is his, almost exclusively. There may be little bits of it here and there that I can recognize; but these are secrets I feel I must reserve to myself.

A few years before the war, the Mill had been converted by a fashionable London physician into a weekend cottage. During the war, the military requisitioned it; a rough and insensitive soldiery then left it in a state that had little appeal for its tenant, so Timmy's family took it back, in the year after the war, set it right, and looked for new tenants.

By chance, Timmy was crossing the Mill drive when they arrived. This was an event he could not conceivably have failed to notice; he stared in near disbelief at the behemoth that had turned in from the lane. The shining dark green monster, open-topped and perched on enormous steel-spoked wheels, glaring at him through immense brass headlamps, growled and throbbed slowly up the drive. Huge leather straps secured the quivering bonnet, as though to restrain the engine inside from bursting out. Black smoke belched negligently from its chromium-plated exhaust tubes. As the car came alongside, it eased gently to a halt, its thunderous engine cut to an ominous muttering; but the young man at the wheel, who had perhaps been bellowing conversation on the open road to the woman beside him, did not immediately adjust his voice; so his first words to Timmy were almost a shout.

'Have we found it? Is that the Mill?' He nodded ahead. A superfluous question, really, for the Dutch doors and the small irregular windows and the wooden wheel mounted decoratively on the wall, were all a dead give-away.

Nevertheless: 'Yes,' said Timmy, aware that his mouth had been hanging open. He shut it firmly.

'I'd switch off, for a talk,' said the young man, 'but I'm afraid I'd never get the brute started again. Hop in. You can be our guide.'

There were only fifty straight yards to go, but this was an offer Timmy couldn't refuse. He climbed on the wide running-board, struggled briefly with a door handle, gave up the struggle, and pitched himself head-first over the side of the car into the commodious leather of the back seats. He sat up and craned between the couple in front of him.

'Straight ahead,' he said, enjoying this. After all, he had been elected guide. 'You can't miss it.'

'Away we go then.'

The engine roared. The young man waved a gloved hand in the air, and then put it nonchalantly back on the outsize steering-wheel.

'Come along, Nathalie old girl, don't keep us waiting.'

The woman put two hands to the gear lever and pushed it forward.

'I'm Simon,' the driver shouted cheerfully over a shoulder, as the car began to move. 'She's Nathalie. Who are you?'

But Timmy didn't reply. He was staring at Simon's jacket. The left sleeve was empty.

The car stopped in front of the Dutch doors. Nathalie put on the hand brake. Simon swung round, with an easy smile, and said, 'Let's try again. Who are you?'

'I'm Timmy.' And then, still looking at the empty sleeve, and in a voice that surprisingly didn't change in tone, 'Was it the war?'

Simon glanced down where Timmy stared.

'Oh, that. Yes. Battle of Britain.' His pale face seemed serenely untroubled. 'We'd better get that out of the way.'

Timmy chose to take this as an invitation.

'Spitfires?' he asked.

'Hurricanes. Not quite the same degree of glamour, I'm afraid; but the ones that did the job.' Simon put his remaining hand to the door beside him and flung it open. 'Come on, all ashore! Stir yourselves!'

Timmy, transformed from guide to native porter, helped them unload the mountain of suitcases and packages strapped to the back of the car.

In the days that followed, Timmy stepped gladly, eagerly within the compass of the spell that Simon and Nathalie seemed to cast around him. He had never met anyone like them.

Nathalie was Belgian. In slightly fractured English she wove her magic.

'Darling, you must show us *ev-rrything* in this *merveilleux* place,' the *r*'s bubbling in her throat. Timmy, who squirmed at the 'darlings' of enthusiastic aunts, found this one exciting.

In the car, as if in the cockpit of his Hurricane, Simon had seemed impetuous, swept by strange energies, but in the climate of the Mill house and its garden, established 'ashore' as he had put it, Nathalie became the driving force. Perhaps it was because, for all that she was so small, she was ten years older than Simon. For Timmy, it was simply that she was beautiful – more beautiful than he had imagined a woman could be, and with a beauty different in kind to any he had ever experienced. For this was not the domestic and affective beauty of his mother. Nathalie was volcanic fire, she was dancing light on rippled water. And her continental presence was also new to Timmy: *svelte* and *chic* were words he probably didn't know, but were what, in her black trousers and scarlet sweaters, smelling of strange French scents, he knew insensibly she was.

In contrast Simon now, towards Timmy, was cool, amused, unruffled. He seemed at moments almost to apologize for Nathalie's excesses. But at the same time he excused them, he condoned, for his every gesture, every inflection of his voice, made it clear that she could do no wrong. And this was at the heart of their attraction for Timmy, even though it was something he could not fathom: they had married just a week before they arrived at the Mill. Life stretched before them, enhanced in a peculiar fashion by that reversed disparity in their ages, a continuing honeymoon to which they could envisage no end. They were cathode and anode; erotic sparks leaped between them. For Timmy, who could sense but not understand this, it was bewildering. All he knew for certain was that he liked them, enormously.

Fortunately, his family liked them too. Even the aunts and great-uncles surrendered swiftly to the spell.

'What an exotic pair of lovebirds!' said Aunt May, with the pensive, veiled enthusiasm of the spinster.

And Simon's mutilation inspired silent sympathy and approval in the great-uncles.

'The very best sort of young fellow. We owe that lot everything, Timmy. Just you remember.'

Timmy remembered. And nobody thought it out of place that he contrived, as that summer holiday slowly unwound, to spend more and more time with Simon and Nathalie. For their part, it seemed to amuse them – but avoiding condescension – to have him around. It was as though, so totally were they wrapped up in each other, they needed the unthreatening company of a child as a sort of safety-valve, so that they could keep this lightest of touches on the other, outside world.

One evening Timmy slipped out after supper and crossed the small water-meadow to the Mill. He crouched on the lawn near the water, watching the endlessly fascinating patterns of drift near the edges of the race. And the sun cruised gently, silently down the sky behind the willows, streaked with thin high clouds. He had a capacity – his mother sometimes ruefully called it a flair – for losing touch with time. Perhaps half an hour passed; all in the blink of a dabchick's eye.

'*Darling* Timmy! What do you do here? So still. So late?'

'Look!' he said urgently, almost at the same moment. A shimmer of turquoise and emerald and darker blue, and a flash of red: a kingfisher arrowed low across the water, angled itself steeply upwards over the sluice wall, and disappeared. Like a Hurricane in a dogfight, he thought. He turned and saw Simon and Nathalie standing silently behind him. Simon's one hand was holding one of Nathalie's; they seemed always to need to touch, to hold on in this way as though each were seeking some singularity in the other. It was a soft, warm evening and Simon wore a short-sleeved shirt that only just concealed his stump. Timmy had lost his curiosity about this, but it was something he could never entirely forget.

'I came out for a walk,' he explained – as if, belatedly, to answer Nathalie's question.

'Then we shall walk together,' said Simon. 'What about it, old girl?'

They crossed the bridge over the weir, and followed the fisherman's path up the river bank. Nettles and thistles grew thick in places, so that they had to walk carefully. They came to a stile.

'Darling,' said Nathalie, but this time it was Simon darling, not Timmy, 'are you sure you can manage?' And then, with sweet and loving malice, 'Must Timmy and I lift you o-vairr?'

'I have two legs, woman. And one hand is enough to beat you with.' They stood before the stile, and kissed. Lingering. While Timmy waited, patiently.

Beyond the stile they walked beside a post-and-wire fence, which marked off a rough and tufted water-meadow to their left. Here the willows had been thinned, so the fishermen could cast their delicate lines. The sun had sunk below the distant slope of the downs, and the sky from which it had gone was on fire. They came presently to a place where the river widened into a small, mysterious pool; fringed by reeds, the water ran slow and deep, darkly still except that the sunset sky had spilled its colours over the dazed surface. The fence, on both banks, stepped out into the river, to make drinking places for grazing cattle. They stopped, as though powerless now to move, clenched in their separate apprehensions of the evening, of its imperative beauty.

'Whistler's Pool. I love it here,' said Timmy simply.

'Darling, I am so happy.' Nathalie held each of them by a hand: impossible to tell who was darling now. Both, perhaps.

'Where's Whistler?' said Simon, looking round. 'He should be here to paint this. One of his *Nocturnes*.'

'He didn't *paint* it,' said Timmy doubtfully. 'But he – somebody called Whistler drowned here. Years ago.' This was often the way, he might have added, that the river acquired its names.

Beside him Nathalie seemed to shiver; he could feel it through her hand. There was, indeed, a damp chill in the air as the last of the day faded. But Timmy's cup brimmed. Did it overflow?

The evening had seemed to confirm, in Timmy, all that he

felt about his friendship for Simon and Nathalie. He hugged it to himself as he fell asleep that night, and he leaped with it from his bed when he woke in the morning. Therefore it was as much with disbelief as shock that he heard them, as he approached the Mill after breakfast, loudly quarrelling. The top half of the Dutch door was open, and they were somewhere in the room behind it. Most of the noise came from Nathalie, for Simon never raised his voice except, from necessity, in his car. But there was unmistakable anger in his tone, and a shrill bitterness in Nathalie's. It was this emotion that Timmy heard, rather than the words, which perhaps he couldn't distinguish, or if he had heard them, have understood.

He stopped, yards away, wondering what to do. At that moment the lower door was flung open and Nathalie burst out, blindly, into the dazzle of morning sunlight. She stood a moment, blinking, so small and woeful that Timmy wanted to go towards her, to comfort her somehow. And then she saw him.

'You!' she screamed, as though furnished with a new focus for her rage. 'What are you doing, always hanging a-rround us?' An unimaginable fury seemed to well within her, shaking her small frame, bursting through dark fissures. 'Always hanging a-rround *Simon*! Go away! Go away!'

In his horror Timmy was rooted, the earth had seized his feet and would not let him go.

'Nathalie!' Simon had appeared behind her, his pale face now white with anger and despair. 'Leave him alone. Leave him out of this. How could you?'

But Timmy's feet, miraculously, had been released; he could escape. He ran, stumbled, swerved round the corner of the Mill, seeing nothing, his mind desperately seeking a distance, a haven. He was flying blind, through impenetrable cloud, the sunshine all around him a lie. For a long time he neither knew nor cared where he was, where he went; all that mattered was to run, to keep going.

At last he stopped, breathless, gasping with dry and unremedial sobs. He could not bear to think.

Gradually he became aware of his surroundings. His unnavigated flight had apparently brought him in a wide semicircle round to a point across two fields from the Mill; here the long back gardens of a row of cottages in the village sloped to the edge of the field where he stood. He could see the Mill, flashes of old red brick through leafy willows. But he could not run any more. He moved slowly along the fence beside the allotment gardens, pausing irresolutely from time to time. What could he possibly do now?

'Shelley!'

A strangely raucous voice, somewhere near him, behind him. He turned round, but there was no-one there.

'Shelley!' Strident. Demanding attention. 'Good morning!' A chuckle. 'Good morning!'

Timmy looked, wildly, around him.

'Good morning,' he said, doubt and hope and bewilderment all informing his voice. 'Where are you? Are you hiding?'

And then he saw it. Hanging on the fence a few yards behind him, a large wire cage. Inside the cage a gnarled and mouldy-looking parrot, its green and red and blue plumage conspicuously stained and ruffled. It muttered grumpily to itself, and preened, and squawked again:

'Shelley! Good morning! What's your name?'

The parrot began to climb ponderously up the side of its cage, gripping with claw and beak. When it was near the top and half upside-down, it cocked its head and fixed Timmy with a very beady eye. Evidently it expected answers to its questions.

'Timmy,' said Timmy, taking a fascinated step nearer the cage. 'Who are you?' As Simon had asked him once.

'Shelley!'

Timmy studied the parrot politely; its conversation seemed to excuse its shabbiness.

'Do you live near here?' he ventured, in an experimental spirit.

'It's a small world!' screeched Shelley. This oblique reply delighted Timmy.

'I live over there,' he explained, pointing over the Mill and across the valley. 'Do you come here every day? I've never seen you before.'

'Monday, Tuesday, Wednesday, Friday, Thursday...' Shelley's words ended in an indignant squawk. Not being able to speak with its mouth full, it had released the hold its beak had taken on the wire, and in this precarious position a claw had slipped. It lowered itself with careful dignity to the floor of the cage.

'*That's* better!' said Shelley. Timmy was not sure he could trust his ears.

'Do you really understand me?' he asked.

Shelley blinked, or winked, a single eye; scornfully.

'A friend indeed...' But the parrot stopped, as though to look over its words, aware that something had gone slightly wrong. 'A friend in need...' it tried again.

'I do need a friend,' said Timmy, and was surprised that he could say this with so little fuss.

'You have one,' said Simon behind him. 'As a matter of fact, you have two. As I came to explain.'

Timmy turned sharply, too startled to consider running again.

'Talking to yourself?' Simon asked kindly. 'First sign of madness, I've always heard. But don't be mad with us. Please.'

'I wasn't talking to myself. I was talking to a parrot.' This seemed easier, safer for the moment, as a topic of conversation. 'It's called Shelley. It talks. I mean, it talks *sense*, Simon. It really does.'

But Simon was not to be deflected from his purpose.

'That was rather a prang, back there, I'm afraid. She's sorry, you know. So am I. She didn't mean it, old chap.'

Timmy's eyes were fixed on Simon's stump.

'It wasn't fair,' he said. 'You have a bit missing.' He wanted to explain, but this was as much as he could say. Simon seemed to consider it.

'Everybody has bits missing. It's just that some are more visible than others.' He, too, was finding this difficult.

'Before – earlier – Nathalie had a sort of a bit missing. But I think she's found it again now. At any rate, she wants to see you – if you wouldn't mind.'

'Will she be angry with me again?'

'No, Timmy. Our friend here – ' he pointed at Shelley – 'said it once, a long time ago.' Simon was looking over Timmy's head, not into his eyes. 'She lifted the painted veil, you see. That was the trouble.'

'I know parrots can be very old,' said Timmy, who was struggling to understand.

'I was thinking of another Shelley, actually. *Lift not the painted veil which those who live/ Call life...*'

Simon walked to the cage, and stood looking at the parrot.

'Love and jealousy are hard things to understand,' he said. 'Impossible, at your age, if you don't mind me saying so, old chap... *Though unreal shapes be pictured there,/ And it but mimic all we would believe...* Come on, Timmy. I think we should go and find Nathalie. She can be hurt too, you know.'

They began to walk slowly away together.

'Good morning!' shrieked Shelley after them.

'Goodbye!' called Timmy, turning round. 'I'll come and see you again. Tomorrow.' But Shelley's cage was never hung out on that fence again, for all that Timmy passed there hopefully on many days.

Nathalie was waiting for them at the Dutch doors. In silence, she drew Timmy to her, and gave him a very thorough kiss.

'Darling,' she said.

Timmy buried his face in her scarlet jersey.

In a way, he realized afterwards, his affection for her had been deepened. But it contained something new – a wariness, a knowledge. Nathalie was the same; only the eyes that viewed her were now changed. He was, of course, too young for the lesson in love she had given him; but she had left him with an inkling of its force.

In Xanadu

A few days ago I realized I would have to revive Roderick Slim. Fiction is a perilous balancing act, for both writer and reader, and Roddy's mature and seasoned outlook, as I see it, may help both of us to a surer footing on those vertiginous slopes. If I borrow a small dog too (let's call him Henry), I shall have another of the ingredients necessary to my purpose.

This story starts with a downland walk. I think I had dispensed with the thumbstick, considering Henry sufficient company under that windy sky. Picture us then, as I do, the man at ease with himself and with the wide and empty spaces that contain a history and a heritage at once more mysterious and more manageable than the distant landscapes of Southern Africa, which still lurk, perhaps, behind the spangled blue of his eidetic eyes; and the dog, an elderly Cavalier of limited intelligence and boundless energy, zigzagging the rabbit runs, white plume streaming behind him.

There are three river valleys within easy walking range of the town, small chalk streams winding between hills that are clumped here and there with trees, sometimes growing straight out of old burial mounds; but mostly these uplands are great bare arcs of arable or sheep-mown turf where one's thoughts can move with the freedom of the wind. Which of the three valleys with its surrounding hills forms the arena of this story is something I must reserve: the privacy of the imagined, too, should fitly be respected.

We walked a track that followed the line of the hill, near its crest, and overlooking a long, lazy curve of the river – I shall call it the Rush. In the distance I could see a cluster of cottages and the square stones of a church tower, all half hidden by willow and poplar – the village of Rushbourne St John. The hill here was grassy, and rippled where it fell away more steeply below us, like the sand of a low-tide beach; and scarred with deserted rabbit warrens. I saw the dogs when we were still perhaps a hundred and fifty yards short of them. Two or three little brown heads, ears pricked, just showing above the edge of what appeared to be a natural hollow, or earthwork, almost exactly on the skyline.

Then they leaped from cover and ran, as a pack, straight towards us. They were five; black-and-sandy-brown Border terriers.

When, still in silence except for a few half-stifled and involuntary snarls, they sprang upon Henry and turned him over, I knew that all five were of a single dedicated mind: they intended to kill him.

I seized one, tore it off, and hurled it away into a clump of gorse. It ran straight back, contemptuous of me, seeking Henry's throat with its terrier teeth. I pulled more of them off, but they kept coming back, all of their silent and unswerving fury locked upon Henry. So sudden and unsolicited an attack had scattered my wits; I did not even have the time to regret my absent thumbstick. In that heaving mass of little dogs my hands found Henry, and lifted him into the air. Shock or terror had rendered him as silent as his attackers, but I think he squealed once, because two of the terriers still had their teeth into him and hung there a moment before dropping to the ground. A third leaped snapping still at Henry as I held him shoulder high.

Something snapped in me, too. Henry, as I have said, was borrowed, but I know him well and that afternoon he was *my* dog. As the third terrier fell back to the ground I kicked it, with my heavy walking boot, full in the head, with all the power and deliberation of a place-kick on Twickenham turf. I heard the crack of leather on bone, and the little dog flew, a bundle of stunned brown, yards into a fold of grass, where it lay twitching. Sickened by what I had done, and what they had done, but ready to kick again, I carried Henry away from them.

Their mute frenzy had died, as mysteriously as it had arisen. I held Henry shivering in my arms, the white and brown of his coat streaked with blood; the pack had begun to move back, almost furtively now, towards the point on the skyline where I had first seen them. It was inexplicable. I had never encountered such motiveless aggression in animals before; nor had I ever imagined myself responding so ruthlessly.

My first concern, of course, was Henry. Back in the town, I took him straight to the vet, who cleaned his wounds and patched him up. Once he was home, lying still dazed and mistrustful in his basket, I set about my second concern.

I live now, conveniently I have sometimes supposed, no more than two hundred yards from the police station, a red-brick Victorian building earmarked for demolition and reconstruction. So, but a few minutes after Henry was settled, I was already at the desk reporting what had happened, to the duty sergeant.

'A pack of wild dogs. Border terriers – harmless enough you might think, but completely out of control. Up there on the downs, and not a sign of anybody with them. A public menace – a danger.' With some precision, I described the place where we had met them. The sergeant, who knows me slightly and likes to use my discarded military title, was calmly impressed.

'We'll look into it, sir. Sounds very nasty, 'specially for your poor little dog. It could be they'll turn on people next – a kid, maybe.' He made some notes, and I went back to Henry, who had fallen into an uneasy sleep.

He still had not stirred from his basket when, past nine-thirty that evening, I was roused from the recuperative cadences of Pergolesi's *Stabat Mater* by the pert vulgarity of my front-door chime, which I am too lazy to replace. Through frosted glass and dusk shadows I saw the loom of a blue uniform; when I opened the door, however, it was not to my friend the sergeant but to a young black-bearded constable who was a stranger to me.

'Colonel Slim?'

'Roderick Slim,' I said, with that compulsive affability that police uniforms seem to inspire in me. 'I have retired.'

'Not for the night, sir, I hope,' he said, with intelligent and inoffensive humour. His voice had a pleasant trace of Wiltshire burr.

'Certainly not. Come in, come in.'

'Just for a moment, sir. If I may. It's about those dogs.'

'I thought it might be.'

I switched off Pergolesi, and offered him a drink, which he accepted without fuss. His name, he told me, was Ernest Culley.

'It was an odd thing,' he said. 'We found the place. Easily enough, with the directions you gave us. And the dogs were still there.'

'Did you have any trouble with them?'

'No sir. You see, it was a sort of vigil they were keeping. If you'd got any closer, you would have seen it for yourself. If they'd let you. I suppose it was because you had your own dog with you that they didn't. There was an old lady up there. Lying in the hollow. She was dead – heart attack, we think, but we'll know for certain tomorrow. Most likely she was out exercising her dogs and simply keeled over, right there in the hollow, where she couldn't be seen unless you went right up to it as we did.'

I put my own drink carefully on the table beside me. 'So they were – looking after her? Hapless creatures.' (Roddy has an old-fashioned turn of phrase.) 'I couldn't have known. And even if I had, there was still Henry to protect; but I hate to think of it, all the same – the way I treated them.'

'It wasn't to be helped, sir,' said Culley. 'They were very unusual circumstances. The dogs are being looked after, by the way; but I don't know what can be done for them long-term.'

'You can be certain they won't want to see me again.' And then, in some embarrassment, 'I didn't mean – '

'And nor did I, sir.' Culley seemed almost upset, but swiftly recovered his good humour, to go on cheerfully: 'As a matter of fact, hers is the second dead body I've seen inside a week. Fished a young fellow out of the canal only last Wednesday. But this old lady was a bit of a sad case. Lived up on the hill above Rushbourne, in a house full of dogs. Always scrapping with the village kids – they thought she was a witch. Now if it had been cats, you could understand that. A real recluse, and a bit batty, people reckoned.'

Something stirred in my unwilling mind.

'What was her name?'

'Lucy Venables. She was a widow.' My question could not have seemed as casual as I had tried to make it. Constable Culley looked at me sharply. 'Do you know her?'

I nodded. 'I did. Years ago. I have been away thirty-five years, you see. But I did.' And then I decided I owed him a further confidence. 'As a matter of fact, she was a fairly distant sort of cousin.'

A second cousin, to be exact, but our large Victorian families had spread the generations so that in age Lucy was halfway to being an aunt. In my very earliest memories of her, with that slight displacement brought by the perspective of childhood, she seemed already a young adult. The sheen of straight black hair falling below her shoulders, the wide dark thoughtful eyes set in a face of white and candid purity, even the long assertive Norman nose, gave her for me the vivid quality of a picture, perhaps of a mistily primitive Italian madonna. This was appropriate in its way, because at eighteen or nineteen she went to study painting at the Slade.

I remember her diffidence about her art. She favoured landscapes, in oils sometimes but more often gouache; the drawing was accurate and naturalistic but she had a private and slightly disturbing concept of colour. Praise embarrassed her, and I think if she could she would have kept her art entirely from her family.

She must have been nearly thirty when she married

Ranald Venables, and he two or three years younger. I think it was probably Lucy who drew Ranald to our part of the world – had they once, perhaps, been fellow students? At any rate he appeared, I don't know from where, and lived for a year or so in a small cottage in the forest. When they married, they removed to the extraordinary house on the downs above Rushbourne St John that I shall call Xanadu – not its real name, but equally inappropriate. The move seemed to confirm a local suspicion that Ranald was a man of independent means, for in one respect the house lived up to its name – it was a notoriously expensive property. Ranald, emphatically, was an artist, as his dress and manner extravagantly proclaimed. I remember how his Byronic sweep of hair in those mean pre-'sixties years, falling well below his collar, somewhat illogically scandalized a few of my more elderly and Victorian relatives.

There was nothing Victorian about his painting, which was uncompromisingly abstract and, at least to our small and unsophisticated community, pretty well incomprehensible. Once a year, the local Artists' Association held an exhibition, to which Ranald conceded half a dozen canvases. More bewildering even than the pictures was the price he put on them: four or five hundred pounds, in those days and in that context, was an assertion that most could only interpret as a joke. He never, so far as I know, sold a single painting. And although there were rumours, when he disappeared from time to time to London or Paris, I am unaware that in those years he was any more successful away from home.

As for Lucy, we saw no more of her work, at the annual exhibition or even more privately at Xanadu. The demands of being married to a genius, she gave us to understand, had brought her own artistic dabbling to an end; she had hung up palette and paint-brushes.

Although this is not in any way my story, I have reached a point where I have to pitch myself back into it, briefly, in a walk-on part, and a word or two of explanation is necessary. At the time, scratching on the door of adult life, I was approaching, unaware of it, a watershed. Only a few years after the events that concern us now, I was over the slope and pursuing a rackety military career around our diminishing and then vanished colonies in Southern Africa. But this was still to come. In those days I imagined, with youthful and misplaced enthusiasm, that I had it in me to make myself a writer – a folly that the years have enabled me to view at last with more indulgence than embarrassment.

So, while I could contemplate Ranald's pretensions, I hope, with some detachment, I sympathized to an extent with the artistic statement that his style of life proclaimed. I allowed myself, not at all unwillingly, to be drawn into the small circle of disparate misfits who regarded Ranald, for a variety of mostly undisclosed motives (frivolous in many cases, I am sure – as essentially were my own, I now suspect) as some sort of minor prophet.

In Xanadu, from time to time, the circle was entertained: to cheese straws and straw-covered bottles of Chianti – the wine in those lean post-war years an eloquently Bohemian touch, but a well-heeled Bohemia, it was (not too discreetly) made plain to us.

The house was one of those strange expressions of the 'twenties – a white flat-roofed structure with porthole windows and brass-railed balconies that made it look for all the world like some brash and glittering cruise ship sailing the green seas of the downs. It was easy to see how its ugly vulgarity appealed to Ranald, to his urgent instinct for the outrageous.

Conversation, on these occasions, was hazardous, for Ranald could be by turns surly, ebullient, arcane, quizzical, and more often than not downright rude. For us, I suppose, there was some sort of perverse attraction in riding this psychosocial roller-coaster; at any rate, the same people always seemed to be coming back for more.

Given the chance, I would have guarded the secret of my novel from that company, and more particularly from Ranald – not because I had any doubts about its quality, but because it was as yet unpublished (it never would be published). Lucy, however, by grace of her family connection, already knew.

'How clever of you,' she said to me, in a moment when Ranald had paused for breath, 'actually to have *finished* a novel. So often one has a brilliant idea and dashes down the first page, but it never seems to come to anything.'

Not to be admitted, I had often had, if not the same outcome, at least the same fear. Perhaps it was simply the fact of having stuck to it through to the end that gave me such misplaced confidence in my novel.

'It's a matter of planning,' I explained kindly, with all my weight of experience; 'of knowing where you're going.'

Ranald put a hand on my shoulder, as if in benediction.

'Anybody can write a novel,' he said reassuringly. 'All it takes is a little application. Now, the short story is something else. The short story requires a real talent, a real writer.'

Some hero, whose name I have forgotten, wickedly risked all. 'Have you written any stories, Ranald?'

'A few,' said Ranald, dismissively. 'Not for publication. For myself. My search for self-knowledge.'

Was all our conversation this banal, and this self-centred? Certainly, at the time I did not think so. I felt an exhilaration, a sense that here I could at least snatch at the hem of the real world (the artistic world, be it understood) as it trailed across my excited vision, or as I stood callow and tongue-tied in front of Ranald's latest masterpiece – the inevitable cynosure and axis of each Xanadu party. I think that even if I suspected, buried within me at depths I did not care to excavate, that Ranald's work was worthless, that Ranald's bullying words were a bluff concealing a void, he still represented for me a stance, a belief, an alternative, that I prized and wanted to make my own.

So Ranald's death was as much a shock to me as to anyone else. He drowned himself, one sunny afternoon, in two feet of water, in the Rush.

In those days suicide was a legal as well as a social solecism, so I think, if memory serves me, that it was passed off as an unfortunate accident. Nobody on the inside of the story, however, was in any doubt. Whatever the outward appearance of that benign afternoon, Ranald had come suddenly and terribly face to face with a dark reflection of himself; he had seen into the abyss, into the utter emptiness of his own artistic bankruptcy, and it had overwhelmed him.

The irony of this was exemplary: it was all unnecessary. For Lucy, as soon as she had overcome her immediate grief, released to the world Ranald's secret shame. Stored in an outhouse studio at Xanadu were fifty or sixty canvases, oil-paintings of quite extraordinary power and originality, yet of a representational immediacy of the kind that, living, Ranald had mercilessly flayed in others. An exhibition was mounted in London at the Portman Galleries. Ranald Venables, in death, took the art world by storm. These pictures commanded thousands of pounds, where his abstracts had failed to sell for hundreds; a few of those abstracts even, I believe, now swung through on the coat-tails of his posthumous success – there are always people who will pay for a signature.

Lucy tended the flame. On the few occasions that I saw her before I went away, I was struck by her devotion to Ranald's memory. She remained at Xanadu, and intimate friends could always drop in; but party time was over. What had been a serenity in her, lightened by gentle good humour, became somehow detached, dedicated. There was indeed something nun-like in her withdrawal, as though she were at once founder and single postulant of a new religious order. The house became a shrine to Ranald Venables; yet oddly it contained not one exemplar of his great paintings – instead the walls were serried with those stubbornly uncommunicative abstracts. I did not care to ask her why.

All this, perhaps in less detail, I told young bearded P.C. Ernest Culley. He was an appreciative audience, with an intelligent sympathy, I fancied, for a world that had existed and passed before he was even born. But it was getting late, and he was tactful too; presently he took himself off into the night. I returned to Pergolesi, and to a few memories; but my sleep that night, and unlike Henry's I suspect, was dreamless.

Next morning, my breakfast was interrupted by a telephone call. It was Timothy Fiennes, junior partner in a firm of local solicitors; I had met him once or twice since my return, and found myself rather swiftly on quite familiar terms with him.

'Roddy,' he said. 'Sorry about the hour, but I wanted to be sure of catching you. It's about Lucy Venables. I was going through the file last night.'

'Already?'

'The police were onto us as soon as she was identified. It's her will. She named us, you and me, her executors.'

'Good heavens! But we'd completely lost touch. I haven't seen or heard of her for thirty-five years.'

'All the same. It's down in black and white. And Roddy, there's something else. Something rather odd. I think we'd better go up there as soon as possible. To the house. Could you come round this morning?'

By ten o'clock I was in his office. Timothy looked at me with veiled curiosity.

'Didn't you try to see her?' he asked. 'According to the will you were some sort of cousin.'

I had been thinking about this, a touch uncomfortably, myself.

'I've only been back a few months. And it was all so long ago. I didn't even know if she was still alive.' But this was lame. 'I did think about it a bit. I suppose I planned to scout around first – no, planned is putting it a bit strong. But yesterday, if it hadn't turned out the way it did – I was only a mile from Xanadu. Perhaps I was headed that way – I honestly don't know.'

Timothy gave me a friendly smile.

'Well, we're headed that way now. Look at this.'

He handed over a bulky brown envelope. Written large across it in Lucy's spidery, artistic script was this emphatic instruction: *To be taken by Roderick Slim and Timothy Fiennes, in the event of my death, to Xanadu; and only to be opened there, nobody else being present.*

'I have the house keys,' Timothy said. 'The police found them on Lucy. Shall we go?'

I have always loved the drive up that valley. The road used to meander almost as much as the Rush beside it; now it is broadened and straightened and burdened by unremitting traffic, a trunk road. But the valley, once the town with its sprawl of new estates has been left behind, is as it ever was. The line of the hill, over the little river on our right, where I had walked the day before, was unchanging. On the near side the downs climbed in lazy ventilated sweeps to the sky. Ahead, the unspoiled roof-tops, thatch and weathered tiles, of Rushbourne St John, and the square church tower, lingered through the pale green of water-rooted trees.

Timothy's silent car made short work of those two or three miles. In Rushbourne we turned off the main road and headed up a narrower valley along a lane that climbed to the skyline, past a golf course. Another right turn, into a byway now, took us back a few hundred yards along the top of the hill. There, almost on its edge, overlooking the Rush valley, stood Xanadu.

The chalk of the byway turned to weed-grown gravel as the car scrunched softly up the drive. Xanadu, after all these years, seemed a ship adrift, an abandoned relic of the ocean. The walls were streaked with grey where the white paint had flaked from concrete, the brass rails were gone, the iron rims of those round windows rusted to a bilious green. The garden was overgrown, frozen in windswept shapes. A stone bird-bath had slipped on its pedestal, its mossy surface now angled to the ground. Timothy switched off the engine and we sat in silence for a moment, oddly reluctant to move.

A pigeon crooned gently behind the dark curtain of a matted, canting cypress tree.

'We must go in,' he said. Clutching keys and brown envelope he led the way, uneasily, to the door. For a moment, as I stepped behind him, I could imagine I saw the earth a-tilt, the angles somehow wrong – house and garden, even the downs and the sky above, seemed to have assumed the shapes, the blind enigmas, of one of Ranald's abstracts.

'He left his mark,' I said. 'In a peculiar way.' Timothy was too young to have known Ranald, but he knew something of him, I suspected. His silence bore a kind of complicity.

'Let me,' I said, taking the keys. 'I know the house.'

The drawing-room had always been Lucy's. Sun streamed through French windows and the wide portholes, making the whole room bright and cheerful. The furniture was mostly handed on from Lucy's family, but she had chosen with taste, the smaller pieces, favouring the elegance of the eighteenth century. On all the surfaces stood silver-framed faded black-and-white photographs, family pictures running back a hundred years or more – shrubby moustaches, military uniforms, pompadours, crinolines, little boys in sailor-suits – I recognized many of them; some of them I possess for myself, duplicates, tucked away in drawers or at the backs of cupboards.

A half-size Steinway stood in one corner. Timothy put the envelope on its shiny surface (there was not a speck of dust in this sparkling room) and opened up the keyboard. He played, competently enough, a snatch of Chopin.

'Come on,' I said, restlessly aware of the blank scrutiny of Ranald's abstracts on the walls, 'let's see what it says.'

'And what it contains, besides a letter,' said Timothy, closing down the piano. 'But I think I know, by the feel of it.'

We stood rather solemnly by a small walnut table, from which Timothy had taken a conveniently placed silver paper-knife. He slit the envelope and drew out a single sheet of paper. Then he up-ended the envelope and slid into his hand a largish ornate brass key.

The same black-ink script – that careful and conscientious spider – covered the sheet; but not much of it. The message was brief.

The key is to the studio shed. The pictures are mine. You will know what to do.

'I'm damned if I do,' said Timothy. 'Where's the studio?'

I led him through the house and out across a small yard at the back. Ranald had built the studio (not, of course with his own hands, but to his own design) to match as far as possible the eccentricities of the house; but instead of the flat of Xanadu's upper deck, it had a shallow pitched roof, set with yards of skylight window. The brass key seemed out of place, but it turned the tumblers of the lock. We stepped into a dazzle of breathless colour.

Aladdin in his cave, Carter at Tutankhamen's tomb – the images are worn, but no less imperative to describe our feelings here. Down two long walls, the canvases were stacked four or five deep; more hung above them, covering every space. Their colours, and their authority, were overwhelming.

Timothy stood, hands deep in his pockets as though to hold himself together, a thin whistle – an echo of Chopin perhaps – all that his lips could dare. I walked slowly, the length of that spacious airy room, in a dream. These pictures, I had seen at a glance, were second-period Ranald, a continuation of those marvellous canvases Lucy had discovered and revealed to the world after Ranald's death.

And yet they were not.

I still held that declaration in my hand. '*The pictures are mine*,' I read aloud to Timothy. 'Lucy painted these pictures. And it means – '

'It means she painted them all,' said Timothy quietly. 'Yes, I have heard the story. We even have one of the pictures at home. My father bought it, from the Portman Gallery exhibition.'

We stood in further silence, for a while the only possible tribute to what surrounded us. Timothy began to tilt through some of the stacks, revealing treasures.

'Ranald knew,' I said with sudden certainty. 'It explains his death, properly, at last. I always found it strange, and so hard to believe, that he allowed anything so trivial as failure to pierce his conceit. But this was different.'

He could cope with failure – after all, in his eyes it was the world's failure, not his own. What had defeated him was something else – his recognition that Lucy's art, of a kind he affected to despise, was infinitely greater than anything within himself. In a way, and to his credit, there was a sort of honesty in his suicide.

There remained Lucy's final, farewell sentence. *You will know what to do.* I marvelled at her confidence.

'She doesn't want anyone but us to know,' I said, as if to test the idea.

'So what do we do?'

'I don't know. We'll have to think. I suppose another exhibition and sale at the Portman is a possibility. In Ranald's name, of course; bequeathed by his widow.'

'It would make millions,' said Timothy. 'But ethically – in my position – I would be lending myself to a fraud.' He looked at me anxiously. I felt I could reassure him on one point at least.

'The money is no problem. We could see it went to an appropriate charity.'

But I was thinking of a different kind of fraud: the one Lucy, if I was right, wished to practise on herself. In this, if I was to abet her, I was as uncertain of my own ethical position as Timothy, the careful solicitor, had seemed of his. My eyes swept again those hundreds of canvases, lingering on one here and another there: and each a perfect short story, I thought. Lucy had never been able to finish a novel, she claimed – yet even in that, Ranald had been right in his way: it didn't matter. What surrounded me now was the life's work that Lucy had accomplished.

She was asking us to give it all to Ranald.

About a month later I borrowed Henry again, just for the day this time. Physically, he was completely recovered; but I couldn't be certain that the experience had not touched his psyche – as it had touched mine. So although we walked at least nine joyful and contemplative miles over the downs that day, I was careful, with the route I chose, never to bring him within sight or scent of Xanadu.

Visitors from Porlock

David tells me we quarrelled, ceaselessly, for all of the three days and two nights our expedition lasted. This surprises me, for it is not at all how I remember it, except perhaps towards the end and after the events that concern me now. On the other hand, I would be equally surprised if David remembers anything of those events – he would more probably deny that they ever occurred. Writers of fiction, I remind myself, have certain esoteric privileges.

It was all, anyway, a very long time ago, and I can't help finding David's embarrassment now, when he looks back on his behaviour then, a touch excessive. After all he was, by his own account, only twelve; which would have made me sixteen. On this, I am inclined to trust his memory.

David and I are first cousins, and up to that time we had seen quite a lot of each other. We overlapped a year or two at the same school; but more than this, in those austere wartime and post-war years, long before families had learned to take nuclear and exclusive holidays abroad, we were often sent in a complicated game of general post to stay with an inexhaustible supply of uncles, aunts and cousins, and on reciprocal occasions entertained the cousins at home. As a system to maintain an extended family, it had much to recommend it.

At that time I must have been nudging six feet, and gangling with it, but David was a veritable beanstalk, and broad-framed too, which may explain my initial difficulty in accepting his recent assertion that he was only twelve in that summer of our adventure. It also explains the more considerable difficulty the two of us had in cramming ourselves, and all our gear, into a canoe.

I don't think the canoe was actually home-made, but compared to today's moulded fibreglass it was archaic: a sort of black tarpaulin canvas, as I remember it, nailed over a wooden frame, and quite incredibly heavy. Bow and stern were covered, and here we stowed enough equipment for a month's expedition up the remoter reaches of the Congo or Limpopo: tent, camp beds, blankets, cooking utensils, tinned food, changes of clothing, a pile of books no doubt – in those days I never went anywhere without books. The middle section was an open cockpit, where David and I sat with our double paddles, seeking an at first elusive unison. All this was not for the Congo but for an unqualified few days, four at the most, on the Kennet and Avon canal.

For many years now, annually at Easter, the élite of the canoeing world have gathered at Devizes and set off on a non-stop race by canal and river to Westminster. I have, occasionally, seen some of them pass at different points along the canal, and whenever this has happened I've been unable to escape the smug reflection that these bronzed and singleted youths don't realize how easy they have it. David and I were among the pioneers, back around the time of the first race although certainly not in it, decades before the canal was at last cleaned out, restored, and opened to holiday traffic. Not a lock or a swing bridge functioned then; even now of course, with his feather-light craft, a canoeist will carry his boat, one-handed probably, round the locks, unencumbered. But for us each lock meant a back-breaking twenty minutes of unloading, porterage, launching and reloading. Perhaps this was the source of most of those quarrels David remembers.

Even more of an obstacle was the neglected state of much of the canal. Overhanging trees trailed in places to the water; long stretches were carpeted with solid weed, trapping blades and clinging to the sides of the canoe, which advanced reluctantly, like some black and shiny slug.

Our goal, by present standards, was modest: not Westminster but Reading, where the Kennet joins the Thames; or perhaps a few miles short of this, at a point due south of David's home – we would see how it went. And we started, I remember, just east of Devizes, to avoid that incredible stairway of twenty-nine locks that climbs over a mile of Caen Hill, through the town.

Already, I see, I seem to have prepared the ground for a detailed account of our expedition; but this was not my intention. If that is the story David wants, he will have to wait for it – or write it himself. There was a particular encounter along the way, that in the strangest manner was only very recently illumined for me, and that is the part I propose to write about now.

Two or three weeks ago I began reading the published correspondence of a literary mandarin, dead now some twenty years, a man who could be described as having loomed a long time on the remoter fringes of Bloomsbury. It is a fascinating collection, casting unexpected swathes of light on all sorts of odd overlooked corners of British literary life over the first half of the century. But none, for me, so curious or revealing as a brief exchange between the great man and Perivale Wolcott-King, which I did not come across (I am a slow reader of books I enjoy) until two days ago. I should explain that the mandarin, as well as being man of letters was master of a small, discreetly famous publishing house. I must leave a fuller account of that correspondence to its more proper place in my story, but I can't resist one brief quotation here:

'Damn your visitors from Porlock,' he wrote. 'We have a contract, I would remind you. Don't buccaneer with me – I want your MS not later than November.'

We started in sunshine, near the beginning of the summer holidays. A little of that first day needs to be described, I think, if just to set the scene. From Devizes to Pewsey the canal follows the contours of the Vale with such cunning that for twelve miles or so there isn't a single lock. Setting forth from Coate Bridge, behind the Le Marchant barracks, we might therefore have expected to make good progress over this first part of our passage. But several circumstances combined to slow us down. An initial lack of skill and practice in handling that obstinate and clumsy craft might easily have brought the expedition to an abrupt, sodden conclusion in the first half mile. But while we wobbled and zigzagged on a crab-like course, somehow we avoided disaster, and stayed the right way up. Then there were those long stretches of blanket weed, bringing us at times to a frustrated standstill.

To begin with, David sat in front of me – until I thought of the advantages, for cramped legs, of the forward position, and we began to take turns; for David's legs were at least as long as mine. No doubt this was another source of friction.

So was steering. We had independent ideas about this, and at times the canoe seemed to have a third, of its own. The canal was a fourth factor, frequently twisting and turning to hug the line of a hillside. There were straight reaches too, and here the canal behaved like a railway line, plunging through cuttings or striding high above the surrounding country, on embankments less ancient but as impressive in their way as the Wansdyke up there on our left, over the skyline of Tan Hill.

I still remember the beauty of that morning, heavy with summer, so a part of my mind at least must have been able to free itself from anxious exertion. Down at water level as we were, the canal banks obscured the view immediately surrounding us, but the hills on each side of the Vale were often in view, touched by a cool haze that seemed to refresh the eye as the day grew steadily, stickily hotter. There wasn't a cloud in the sky, but in mid-morning we heard a distant rumbling like thunder; it could have been a storm somewhere over the horizon – but a kind of regularity about it betrayed its true source. We were listening to artillery practice, far away to the south on Salisbury plain.

The landscape was a disheartening guide to progress; a hill that we thought we had passed twenty minutes earlier would suddenly swing into view again, ahead of us, as the canal took another sharp turn towards it. We stopped for lunch (sandwiches) at Honey Street, by the wharf, and stretched our legs. I think we were both a little dismayed, by now, at the dimensions of an enterprise so lightly undertaken.

In the late afternoon we paddled, a mite more skilfully now, under the road bridge by The French Horn, outside Pewsey, and started to look for a likely campsite. We had had enough, for a first day.

Moored to the wharf was the only other craft we had seen all day – and surely, those years ago, the only craft of its size on the whole of the Kennet and Avon canal. It was a narrow-boat; at that time, to me, a type totally unfamiliar on any waters. Painted like a Romany caravan above its black steel hull, it shone and gleamed and danced with colour, a floating country cottage – there was even an incipient cottage garden tumbling over the long cabin roof; so the name, wreathed in painted flowers on bow and stern, seemed strangely inappropriate: *Marie Celeste*. A curl of smoke from a cowled chimney suggested that this one was at least inhabited.

The wharf and its environs seemed to offer no corner to pitch a tent, but on the other side was a broad meadow, and beyond it the outskirts of an overgrown village, so we paddled across to the high grassy bank, looking for a landing.

I forget what it was we wanted from the shops; there was certainly something – milk, perhaps. Also, across the meadow, we noticed a small farmhouse, where we thought it good policy to seek permission for our tent. This was amicably granted, and we pressed on towards the village, which was further than we had imagined, a good half mile from the canal. The weather must have held, for I remember the evening as green and gold, while the blue of the sky gradually softened: buttercups, I suppose, sprinkled over the meadows. We returned to the canal side, and pitched our tent a few yards back from the water, in long lank grass. Our thoughts turned towards supper.

Eggs, scrambled over a primus stove, marked the height of our culinary ambition; but the year before in Cornwall, in a fit of *cordon bleu*, David had carefully collected large snails from the crannies of a dry-stone wall, and thrown them in with the eggs. I had cooked my own separate supper that night; and now mistrusted the look in David's eye as it roved the vicinity. No stone walls, I was relieved to see. I think we hadn't got far in our preparations, when two people approached us along the canal bank.

Looking back to that moment over so many years, I realize that my first sight of Perry and Mabel needs some rather careful description. Out of curiosity I looked him up yesterday, under his real name, in the *Dictionary of National Biography*. Born 1874 – which would have made him around three-quarters of a century old that August evening. In some repects he looked much younger: in his agile, hopping walk, for example, taking at least two electric steps for each tweed-skirted stride of the woman beside him. He was a pocket-handkerchief size man, quite improbably tiny, but his neat and wiry frame effused an urgent energy, all barely contained by immaculate navy-blue blazer, brass buttons flashing an anchor insignia, and spotless white duck trousers. Only his face, beneath the peak of a white-covered yachting cap, was old – older than his years in a way, hatched deeply with a maze of criss-crossed lines, weathered like old leather, but still animated by a pair of the most sparkling blue eyes I had ever seen, under an immense bush of eyebrow.

His consort, equally remarkable in her different way, towered above him. Despite the heat of the day, which the evening had not noticeably diminished, she wore a thick brown country tweed suit, the wide skirt swinging amply over formidable hips and bottom, to a line halfway between knee and ankle. Her feet were cased in heavy brogues, the grey curls of her head jammed under broad-brimmed brown felt hat. Her face, if I may permit myself this economy of description, was extraordinarily reminiscent of Margaret Rutherford in the Ealing comedies of the time. She carried a heavy walking-stick, which had the air more of companion than necessary support.

With what I recognize now as a certain inevitability, this strange pair stopped as they reached us, their eyes taking us in where we crouched by the primus, the eggs still unbroken in a china bowl. The walking-stick swung thoughtfully over our canoe which lay at the top of the steep bank.

'Would you trust yourself to that, Perry?' the woman asked. 'Shall we engage them to ferry us across?'

'*I* might,' he said. 'But you, my dear, would be foolish to try it.' With a casual rudeness that rather took my breath away, he explained. 'It would undoubtedly sink under your weight.'

She nodded agreeably. 'I do believe you're right. We had better walk round by the bridge.'

I think at this point an uncertain sense of etiquette brought me a bit awkwardly to my feet, but David who was staring at them both with open curiosity seemed quite at ease where he sat in the long grass.

'It takes quite a load,' he said, a touch defensively, for it was his canoe.

'So I see,' said Perry, surveying the tent and all our gear spread around it. 'But on the whole, I think we won't risk it. Have you come far?'

'From Devizes, today,' David said. 'We've been rather slow. It was more difficult than we expected.'

'Expeditions often are.' I didn't then know what wealth of experience lay behind his words.

He peered, with apparent interest, at our preparations for supper.

'What's it to be?' he asked.

'Scrambled eggs.' Perhaps it was foredestiny that made me add: 'Luckily, David hasn't found any snails.'

I explained.

'David sounds a true gourmet,' Perry said. 'But snails need garlic. Have you any garlic?'

'We haven't any snails,' I reminded him. He considered this, with evident care. It was, I soon discovered, characteristic of this singular man to throw himself, whole-hearted, into every situation, however trivial. He held nothing back.

'Mabel,' he said, 'am I right in remembering a tin in your store-cupboard? A tin of French snails?'

Mabel folded her double chins in contemplation, and then nodded vigorously. 'You are,' she said. 'There is. A splendid idea.'

'Then,' said Perry to me, 'you must come across and have supper with us.' He nodded, somewhat superfluously by now, to the *Marie Celeste*.

'But I don't like snails,' I said, alarm overcoming good manners.

'David does.' Perry was undisturbed; indeed, distinctly high-handed, I thought. 'You can bring your eggs, if you like.'

We left everything as it was, even the eggs if I remember, spread around the bank and the edge of the meadow; in those days one could still expect, with a certain confidence, a communal respect for other people's property – ours, anyway, was in full view of the *Marie Celeste*; and walked the hundred and fifty yards to the road, and over the bridge, and back along the far bank to the mooring.

A narrow plank to the after-well served as gangway. It wobbled a bit, and there was nothing to hold on to, but Perry who led the way and Mabel who presently followed after us, crossed it with practised ease. I concealed my qualms, but David looked at it with deep suspicion. Perry was already disappearing into the cabin.

'It takes my weight,' Mabel said cheerfully behind us. 'It should take yours.'

David, halfway across, looked carefully over his shoulder. 'It's not its *breaking* that bothers me,' he explained, 'but it might *slip*.'

'Probably will, one day. The last one did, and that was a proper gangway. Sank without trace in the mud.'

'That's what I'm afraid of,' David said feelingly. 'I mean me, not the gangway.' Perry's laughter echoed within the cabin, but David seemed unoffended. We were across, and into the well, most of which was filled by an iron tiller, thin, curved and immensely long. Squeezing round this, we ducked through a low doorway into the main cabin.

Mabel disappeared through a far, curtained opening, into the galley, leaving us to Perry's not very tender mercy.

'Have some wine,' he said, and then, no doubt taking in our startled faces, 'well, cider then, if you must. Filthy stuff.' He settled us side by side on a long bunk-bench and sat himself on the other side, facing us across a table. Small though he was he seemed able, still sitting, to conjure bottles and glasses out of handy cupboards; and arrayed these on the table. David and I were both looking around us, with more than a little curiosity. Mabel, or Perry himself, was evidently an enthusiastic housekeeper, for everything was spotlessly clean and almost obsessively tidy. It was the nature of that everything which drew our eyes, as to hungry magnets, for we were surrounded by an amazing collection of exotica. Hanging on all the available wall space, placed on every available surface, were objects surely gleaned from all the corners of the globe. We might have been sitting in a somewhat bewilderingly pandemic department of a museum of anthropology – or perhaps its annexe, a storehouse for rejects and duplicates and pieces of doubtful provenance. Perry, who had certainly expected and was clearly enjoying our astonishment, reached for a wicked-looking spear which had caught David's eye.

'A Somali of the Ogaden stuck that one in my shoulder,' he explained. 'I took it from him, as a souvenir.'

'What happened to the Somali?' David asked, with morbid interest.

'Well. We exchanged souvenirs,' Perry said with a bright smile. 'But I doubt if he still has mine.' He reached for another object on a shelf behind him. 'A Tibetan prayer-wheel. Do you say your prayers?' This, I think, was to David, who nodded silently. 'If you had this, you wouldn't have to. Just write them on a piece of paper, stick it up outside, and the wind does it for you. It certainly seemed to work for me, once.'

He began a Himalayan tale, of extraordinary ferocity and no little humour. As the smell of garlic drifted in from behind the curtain, and prompted by more of those eloquent relics of his travels, Perry followed one story with another, Ancient Mariner to a pair of wedding guests.

If I am to be truthful, I must qualify that last observation. David, I could see, was fascinated by all he heard. But with what I hoped was a more adult scepticism, I discounted much of the fanfaronade, while freely enjoying the entertainment of those stories. Perry, I decided, was a most engaging liar.

A few years later, when I came across some of his books, I had to adjust that verdict. But I still feel, even in his books, and certainly in his conversation of that evening years ago, that he was inclined (to put it as kindly as I can) to improve on the truth in the interests of a good story. And this, as I have since discovered for myself, is something that all tellers of tales must do. At the time, and knowing nothing at all about him, he seemed to me a mountebank; this was my mistake, and quite unfair. I don't need that entry in the *Dictionary of National Biography* to remind me of the details of his astonishing life – or that some even of the wilder passages were shared with Mabel, then still invisibly busy in the galley. Perivale Wolcott-King's was a name to conjure with – traveller, explorer, sailor, pirate. Half a generation older than Wilfred Thesiger and near contemporary of Henry de Monfreid, he was known to both and somewhat in their mould. He had roamed East Africa, the Sudan, the Arabian sands, the Hindu Kush. For three or four years as a young man he had sailed his dhow in the Red Sea and the Indian Ocean, pearling, smuggling hashish, even perhaps running slaves – in his book *Cargo of Innocents* he examines in some detail the ethics of the Red Sea slave trade in the early years of the century, making the point (it may well be self-serving) that most of the African slaves were eager volunteers for the good life on the Arabian shore. But to be fair to him he did not, in his writings or over the table to two stray boys plucked off the bank of a Wiltshire canal, pretend to any particular morality. Life, as he saw it, was simply something to be seized, and enjoyed. Its rewards went to the daring, and the strong. For all his diminutive size, Perry was both.

At some point, this spinning of yarns had to come to an end. Mabel appeared from the galley, bearing snails and a more pedestrian dish for me.

'Has my old pirate kept you amused?' she asked. 'Tread on his toes if he begins to bore you. It's the only way I know to stop the flow.'

'Very sensitive, my toes,' Perry said, with unruffled good humour. 'I'll tell you how that came about, if you like.' And as we ate, he did.

While the others relished their snails, I toyed with my own food, feeling uncomfortably outside the gastronomic circle that David had entered with such enviable ease. I felt gauche, foolishly young; stepping carefully, as though to avoid the cracks between invisible paving-stones. I think Perry noticed this, and took pity. He insisted that I should drink some wine, which I did, not knowing how good it was. Outside, unobserved, the night had drawn round the boat and the canal and our camp on the far bank. My eyes, from the wine or the day's exercise, both unaccustomed, were suddenly heavy.

'Perry, we must send these boys back to their tent. They are both cracking with sleep.'

David, I think, would have liked to deny this, but his gaping yawn would have belied the words. I remembered, with remote trepidation, the precarious gangplank, and the thick summer darkness.

'Yes,' I said. 'We really ought to go.'

'But first,' said Perry, 'after such an evening, we must introduce ourselves properly.' He was reaching into the breast pocket of that impeccable blue blazer, and took out a slim wallet of gaudily tooled leather, a trophy perhaps of some Egyptian bazaar. From this he extracted a white card, which he handed to me with old-fashioned courtesy.

'My visiting card.'

I took it, in some confusion, and read there for the first time his full name: Perivale Wolcott-King; with an Ebury Street address.

'I'm sorry,' I said. 'I don't have one to give you.'

And David made his fateful intervention.

'But that's all wrong,' he said. 'It's the wrong way round. *We* are visiting *you*.'

I suppose it is only with hindsight, now, that I see Perry – at that blinding moment – as another Saul on the road to Damascus. Yet it must have been then, immediately, that the special significance of David's words, for him, struck home. It is there, in his own next words:

'Where did you say you had come from?'

David looked surprised at the unexpected question, and its intensity.

'From just this side of Devizes,' he said.

'Oh.' Perry seemed for a moment far away. 'I thought it might have been Porlock.' He stood up, suddenly in a hurry, and reached for the prayer-wheel.

'I have several of these,' he said. 'David, this one is for you. Write a prayer on it for me, if you wish.'

Neither David nor I was sure what had happened; but we both knew something was changed. So, I suspect, did Mabel; but I doubt that even she had worked it all out yet. We gave our thanks and said our goodbyes in such a daze that I have no recollection now of crossing that rickety gangway, or even of our stumbling return in darkness to the other side of the canal. When we woke up next morning, the *Marie Celeste* was gone. Not far, I knew, because on that unnavigable canal she was as circumscribed as a goldfish in a glass bowl; but somehow I knew she had gone the other way, where we had come from. We would not, and did not, see her again.

That was not, of course, the end of our expedition. It lasted the best part of two more days until, somewhere around Aldermaston and exhausted by an unremitting succession of locks, we admitted defeat to each other, and telephoned to be rescued. I suppose we were both a little ashamed of that surrender, but we never went back to try it again, and it's certainly too late now.

Perry's neatly engraved visiting card has survived the years – it lies with a few others in a small wooden box on

SOME MARLBOROUGH INVENTIONS

my desk, within reach as I write these words. (Mine is a very small treasury compared with the collection Norman Douglas made – but in his day visiting cards were common currency.)

I must remember to ask David, when next we meet, if he still has the prayer-wheel.

So what was it all about?

I was puzzled at the time, but not to the point of pursuing the matter. I might have forgotten it entirely if I had not, some ten years later, come across Perry's books and read them with a rare insider's relish. Nevertheless, I was not a true insider until I stumbled, so recently, upon that revealing correspondence. At last, I know.

Some further extracts, this time from Perry's letter to the mandarin, quoted in one of those footnotes so extensive that one wonders why they can't be incorporated in the text:

> I'm sorry. *The Last Adventure* has foundered. Sunk without trace like a gangplank in the mud. Torpedoed by the chance remark of a twelve-year-old (so he *claims*; he stands taller than Mabel). He and a cousin, gallivanting on the canal, my visitors from Porlock...
>
> The older boy was an amiable nonentity. It was the younger one, David, who did the damage. Just one careless remark – 'It's the wrong way round,' the innocent said, and I saw the awful abyss at my feet. The whole structure of my masterpiece, my finest book, erected on a misconception, topsy-turvy, the wrong way round. Revealed to me by a child. You must see it. You know my mind. You must see that the book can never now be written...

So that's what David did. I should have seen something of it sooner – not the whole, but at least a little, even right back there at the time it all happened. There are no excuses: I had been studying Coleridge only the term before at school.

When I showed David this story that I had spun out of our expedition along the canal in that now distant summer of our youth and childhood, he had two things to say – or rather, one to say, and a question to ask.

The first was to deny, flatly, that it ever happened like that. He had no recollection of the *Marie Celeste*, or of Perry, or of Mabel. He even denied the snails. I expected this.

The question was significant.

'Why visitors from Porlock?'

It was the opportunity I had hoped for. I ribbed him gently for inattention in his English classes all those years ago. At the time, the story of the interrupted genesis of *Kubla Khan* was one that every schoolboy knew.

The curious, now (those few who have forgotten), must excavate it for themselves. It would be tedious to tell it again here.

Ring of Fire

There are two stories here and the two never touched – except in my mind, because I was witness in a sense to both.

I do not need to be reminded of either; they are too securely lodged in my perception of the past. And if the past is a foreign country to which, as L.P. Hartley instructs us, entry visas are not easily acquired, our minds at least are littered with faded travellers' snapshots of those distant landscapes, pressed between the imagined pages of old albums, sere and haunted reminders of scenes and people and places we may not revisit in the flesh.

No, I didn't have to be reminded; I had simply, when a few days ago an occasion asserted, to remember. With peculiar resonance, present and past came together; in the shape of two elderly women. The peculiarity lay in their shared age, because fifty years separated them: one stood before me in the present and the other belonged to that time I am remembering, when the woman of today was a child. Nor did they ever meet, or know anything of what they shared, except here and now, where I bring them together in my mind.

Tasha, if I am to be literal, stood behind me, but I could see her face reflected in the wide wall mirror as she wielded deft scissors round my vanishing hair. For it was such an innocent pursuit, a visit to the barber, that entangled me in these coils of memory.

I did not know her. How could I have connected that sombre face with the child – smiling, impetuous, farouche, in memory – encountered so briefly half a century ago? I can see it now, vividly, that time. I can hear its echoes, channelled down the sonic kaleidoscope of the years. It must have been in late summer, for the blackberries had started. In age we were no more than ten – both born in that calamitous year when Hitler's rule began. And it was only the inside of a week she spent, that year, in our town.

No, there would have been no recognition, on either side, nor any ground probably for this story now, if it hadn't been for the idle chatter that sometimes stirs around the barber's chair, and which for once struck such an urgent, unexpected spark.

It was my third visit, since my return to the town, to the little shop below the walls of St Stephen's churchyard. *Men's Hairdressers*, the sign proclaimed: a faded, run-down establishment it seemed, but rather surprisingly the single-handed enterprise of a brisk and cheerful young woman – or so I had concluded from my first two visits. (It has since moved to brightly refurbished premises next door.) But on that day the face reflected in the glass before me was very different: deeply lined, scored with a remote and secretive sadness, an embattled face; and yet undefeated. Could I really read so much into it, so soon? There are faces that tug at the memory, not because they have been seen before but because they remind of other faces. I think it was then, even before we began to speak, that the teasing vision floated into my mind, of a person I hadn't seen for fifty years and who must have been dead for half that time at least: of Mrs Wilhelmsbach, sitting patiently beside me at the piano; or leaning over the keyboard as she played, herself – lost in a dream of Schumann; or cranking the handle of that old gramophone with its improbably enormous papier-mâché horn. These eyes now in the mirror, intent upon their work but sometimes raised to meet mine, had that quality I remembered: not of suffering in itself, but of suffering surmounted, encompassed, understood; and perhaps forgiven.

She smiled briefly, her expression drawn closer – to me, to the ordinary amenities of our commerce. Mrs Wilhelmsbach receded, a quietly fading intruder.

'It has been a good summer,' she said. The scissors snicked emptily around my head, as if to humour me. My hair grows reluctantly; there is so little of it left I like to hang on to it as long as possible.

'Warm and dry,' I agreed.

'But we must not talk about the weather.' She picked up a comb. 'You seemed so silent, you see.'

'I was thinking,' I was startled enough to confess.

She laughed, her face transformed; handsome, I am mysteriously guided to assert.

'I know. I could see you were thinking. But I couldn't see your thoughts. Not even their nature. Were they pleasant thoughts?'

'I'm not sure. Not entirely, I suppose.'

'Thoughts are sometimes uncertain of their own character, I know.' She snipped, and paused; the scissors now stilled, half-opened, hesitant. 'I have not seen you here before.'

'I have been. Twice. It was a young lady, then.'

'Ah. My daughter. She took it on when I retired last year. It is her shop now. But she has a holiday, so I am here to keep the business ticking over; I do not want her to lose customers, I think.' There was no trace in this of Mrs Wilhelmsbach's thick Austrian accent, but there was something in her phrasing, in the words she chose, that reminded me again.

'I've been away,' I was obscurely moved to explain. 'For a very long time.'

'And now you have returned. To stay.' This spoken with odd conviction.

'It was where I was brought up, you see. Where I spent my childhood, and a few years after that.'

'Yes. The places we live in as children are always important.' The scissors went to work again, but circumspectly, with frequent pauses, feather-light against my drowsing hair. 'Were you here, then, during the war?' It seemed an idle question, yet I felt it somehow concealed a design. It mattered.

'For some of it. Not for the first two or three years.'

At the age of nine I was sent back from India, a year ahead of the rest of my family, to go to school. I lived in the holidays with my grandmother, whom rather oddly, a childish nickname, I called Da; in the house that I loved, in the one place that through a nomadic childhood I could with certainty and comfort call home.

I looked up into the mirror, and found my eyes seized by hers, by their strange, dark intensity. I can see, now, that she had begun to understand, to know; at the time I was only aware of a silence, a compelling stillness, and of my own unease. Her face seemed to retreat into an impenetrable past and once again, this time with a clarity that shook me, I saw overlaid the anguished, desperate features of the old Austrian Jewess, the refugee teacher of piano and singing. In my confusion, I was for a moment adrift in time.

'You remind me of someone,' I said, dazed by the impossibility. 'From that time. The war years. Did you live here then?'

'I came here twice,' she said slowly. 'We did not live anywhere. I never had.' Very carefully, as though she no longer trusted or believed in them, she placed the scissors on the table, between a pair of clippers and a leather strop. I felt her hands, gently on my shoulders, and then she had turned the swivel chair so that there was no longer a mirror between us, and she was suddenly very close.

'John,' she said.

And then: 'Do you remember a little girl, who rode through a ring of fire? Who escaped with you afterwards to the forest, and picked blackberries?'

And so I remembered.

'But it was someone else I was thinking of,' I said. 'It was this time of the year. Early September.' A swirl of images, clamorous, imperious. 'Yes, Tasha. I remember.'

The house was an early eighteenth-century farmhouse, of mellow brick, three storeys high, the attic dormer windows set into the mossy clay tiles of the roof which age had settled into gentle undulations. Twenty acres, mostly of water-meadows, remained of the farm. A quiet chalk trout-stream, flanked by ancient willows. A converted Mill and miller's cottage. Paradise, as I remember it. No doubt it rained, sometimes; but in my mind that landscape is blessed with perpetual sunshine. For two years, in India, it had haunted my dreams.

For a while Da had filled the house with evacuees from London, and there would still have been room for a few, but my great-uncle was back from the war, I was there in the holidays, and rooms were kept for a succession of other relatives who appeared briefly, from time to time, on leave. So for a year, I do not remember that I had the company of other children. This didn't seem to matter.

Da, whom the First War had widowed, was ever busy; most often in her green WVS uniform, but her activities were multifarious, and Da herself apparently inexhaustible. I think she felt rather heavily responsible for me, but mostly disguised this weight because her instinct for kindliness was as strong as her formidable conscience. I remember very little tension between us at that time, and I believe I was given a measure of independence that today might seem quite perilous. For hours in the day, I was accountable only to myself.

There was what I think of as a Victorian simplicity in many of Da's attitudes and actions – I mean those simplicities that flow from the ability to dismiss Darwin and to remain wholly, innocently, unaware of Freud. She saw the possibility that Christmas might be a difficult time for me, deprived of my immediate family, and devised a distraction – a treat. We went to stay for a few days, half a mile towards the town and in the shadow of the parish church, with Uncle Will and Aunt Connie. Uncle Will was a courtesy great-uncle, married to one of Da's many sisters; crippled now by lumbago, in earlier years he had been a rugby international, which in itself in those days might have been enough to recommend him for his position as housemaster at the College – a nineteenth-century foundation, intimately connected with our town and family. But Uncle Will had other qualities too, beneath that florid, bullish exterior and his walrus moustache; of sensitivity and intelligence, and an educated love of music.

On Christmas Day, at Mattins, I sang the hymns and carols with a fervour and fortuitous accuracy that charmed Aunt Con.

'There's nothing more beautiful,' she sighed, 'than a boy's voice. What a pity we don't have a choir.'

Uncle Will's was what they called an Out-House; a barrack of a building about a quarter of a mile from the College centre. I remember how strange it felt, when I pushed through swinging green baize doors and stepped from the housemaster's residence into hollow, deserted, silent rooms and corridors where in term-time fifty boys roared and battled and struggled to survive. I had read *Stalky*, with fear and fascination – it informed all my ideas of what I supposed a public school to be. One afternoon in his study, Uncle Will had pulled open a drawer of his desk to show me, with jocular ferocity, a bundle of canes.

So in those spaces smelling of dusty wood and cast-iron pipes, other imaginary smells seemed to linger: sweaty, joyful, apprehensive refractions of those fifty anonymous spirits, playing on the fringes of an airy perception. It was a world of peril I felt no impatience to be a part of.

Somewhere in that beehive labyrinth there was a larger space, I suppose some sort of assembly hall; with a small stage, I remember. And just below the stage, a battered and jangling upright piano. When I discovered this, it gave a focus to my explorations. Cautiously at first, but with growing abandon, I sat and strummed it. With extraordinary patience I picked out single-finger melodies – all of one morning, it took me, to master and remember the tune of *God Save the King*. I had no knowledge of harmony, but I found when I became frustrated by my stumbling search for melody that the black notes, played in haphazard sheaves, yielded a strange and sympathetic consonance.

I was overheard, and rather to my surprise, approved. Aunt Connie was most impressed by my one-finger rendering of the national anthem.

'He is musical,' she said. 'Something should be done.'

Da and Con had been brought up in an age when well-educated girls were drilled, by governesses, in French and Music.

'I hated it,' Da said, of the piano. 'Not music. I loved music. I hated not being able to play; and I tried so hard.'

This was after Christmas, after we had returned home.

'Would you like to learn,' she asked me; 'properly?' And then, because she never forgot to emphasize the importance, and scarcity, of money: 'Lessons are expensive. But music is such an important gift. I thought I might make you an extra Christmas present. But only if you are sure, and prepared to work hard at it, darling.'

In the next village, Da had discovered, there was a teacher of music who gave private lessons.

'Mrs Wilhelmsbach,' Da said. 'She teaches singing as well as the piano. Aunt Connie thought she might train your voice a little, too. You sang so nicely in church.'

It was arranged. Once a week I was to bicycle by the back lane, narrow and twisting and hilly, a mile and a half to that village where years ago Da's family had lived, in a house much bigger and grander than the one we lived in now.

'She is a refugee from Austria,' Da explained. She had made enquiries; had even, I discovered later, made a call. 'A Jew.' She paused. 'In these times we have to be par*ticrally* good to them.' It was a word that always gave her difficulty.

'Why?' I asked. 'Why particularly good?'

'Because they have been treated very badly,' Da said. Her face closed a little, as though she doubted the propriety of what was in her mind to say, but honesty forced her on. 'I don't believe they are to be blamed, now, for what happened two thousand years ago.'

I didn't understand, but I think I could sense her discomfort, which I believe I carried with me, in a way, on my first visit to Mrs Wilhelmsbach. I remember feeling acutely nervous as I cycled over. I would have welcomed a puncture, as an excuse to postpone the visit, but didn't quite dare to contrive one.

She had settled in a small thatched cottage of whitewashed stone, on the steep hill that leads to the lower part of the village. My wheels cracked ice on the puddles as I swerved to the side of the lane and stopped at her gate. I leaned the bicycle against a fence, and walked reluctantly to the porch, where an iron bell-pull silently challenged. But before I could persuade my hand to grasp it, the door creaked suddenly open, and Mrs Wilhelmsbach stood, scarcely defined in the shadowy interior, before me. I sensed, more than saw, that I was the object of a brief, intense scrutiny. Then a hand emerged from the folds of a black silk sleeve and somehow my own hand, poised for the bell, had found its way into hers, and I was drawn towards her.

'It is John,' she said. 'Welcome. I have been expecting you.'

I could smell violets, and lavender, as I followed her down the short dark passage into a small room which that winter afternoon was a bright pool of artificial light. It was a room made to seem even smaller by the bulk of all it contained. Two or three armchairs, a gleaming table of dark polished wood, a half-size grand piano, the keyboard open but its lid closed to accommodate a few silver-framed photographs, and on a smaller table against the inner wall, the gramophone. A log fire blazed cheerfully, in a hearth out of all proportion to the room.

She turned, and smiled at me with an extraordinary tenderness, and I do not have to recreate that moment in my mind to remember how instantaneously I was conquered.

'Now you must sit down,' she said, 'and we shall have some pastries, and discover what we can of each other. That is important. Next time, we shall have music first and then tea. Do you like tea? But this time we are getting to know each other. Tell your grandmother that I do not charge for this afternoon.'

Yet there was, unless memory fails me, music on that first occasion too. Some awkward moments, while I sat at the piano and demonstrated my total ignorance of musical notation. Patiently, Mrs Wilhelmsbach explained staves and clefs, crotchets and quavers, and wrote out a C major scale on score paper for me to take home and study.

'Practise on a table,' she said.

'But we have a piano.' Da had found an old upright somewhere; another extra Christmas present.

'But practise first on a table. To exercise the fingers.'

And then for five minutes she sat at the piano and played to me. I didn't know the music – I didn't know any music then – but she caught my mood.

She turned to look at me.

'Schumann,' she said. 'What did it make you feel, *Liebling*? You don't mind that I call you *Liebling*?'

'Sad, and happy,' I said, with no hesitation. She seemed pleased by my response. 'What is *Liebling*?' I asked.

'Just a little word, that I used to call my grandson, my Sascha.' Her eyes sought one of the photographs in front of her, of a solemn little boy of three or four, with dark, wistful eyes. 'In English, you would say *darling*.' I was aware of shadows in her own eyes. 'How old are you, John?'

I told her I was nine and a half.

'That is Sascha's age,' she said quietly. 'I have not seen him for a long time.'

She struck a chord, fiercely, on the piano.

'Let me hear your voice.' She opened the chord, playing the notes of the triad separately, up to the octave, and down again to the tonic. 'Sing la – la – la – la – la – la – la.'

I sang, nervously. She repeated it, with a different chord.

'You have an ear,' she said. 'Perhaps we can do something with the voice.' But of this she seemed less certain, and I shared her doubts. Singing solo was somehow like undressing in public.

So there was music, that first day. And I am certain that it ended, like all the days, with a record on her cherished gramophone.

There were rituals, in listening to recorded music of that time, which would puzzle a generation born to remote-controlled and digitally mastered CDs. The turntable had to be cranked by hand. There were metal needles, but for those who cared for their records and sought a better sound there were slim, hardened thorns or, as favoured by Mrs Wilhelmsbach, a triangular wedge of wood, cut with a special pair of clippers to a clean point after each playing. Uncle Will had a machine with a horn much like that on the HMV trademark. Our own merely incorporated a sound box. Mrs Wilhelmsbach's was like nothing I had seen before, although I have come across one or two since. The horn was so large that, the size I was, I believe I could have crawled into it. The effect was not so much to increase as to mellow the sound.

'Let us listen to some Haydn, *Liebling*. So that I may remember my old Vienna. The trumpet concerto.'

I think that was the first time I ever listened to orchestral music. I had heard it, of course, from time to time, on the wireless, but as a background noise – pleasant enough, no doubt, yet without any particular shape or meaning or purpose. With a few spare words here and there, softly murmured, Mrs Wilhelmsbach began my education. There was a moment, in the slow movement, of peculiar intensity – in her even more than in the music – when she grasped my hand.

'There,' she breathed, 'do you hear the violas? That is my Sigi.'

When it was finished, she crossed in a rustle of silk to the piano and took another of those photographs into her hand. She didn't show it to me at once, but pressed it to herself.

'My Sigi was first-desk viola player in the Vienna Philharmonic. My husband. That was before the world went mad.'

She stroked the photograph against the silk of her dress. Her face, even to my innocence, seemed slashed with grief, and I felt suddenly, ignorantly afraid. Almost as though aware of this, she looked up at me and her face softened into the shadow of a smile; she held out the photograph.

'There are things you do not know,' she said. 'Things you *should* not know.' With brittle, aching cheerfulness, she insisted. 'Look, at my Sigi. Is he not a handsome man?'

I saw, sepia-tinted, a domed forehead, wise and gentle eyes, and a small moustache and triangular beard, neatly trimmed.

'He looks nice,' I said. 'And young.' I meant younger than her. She smiled again, this time more easily.

'It was perhaps a long time ago, the picture. And now, *Liebling*,' she was suddenly a bustle of energy, taking back the photograph, steering me with a hand on my shoulder across the crowded room, 'now I must send you home. How late it is. How dark it has become. What will your poor grandmother be thinking?' We came to the front door. 'You have the music I gave you to practise? You will come again next Tuesday? Oh, *mein Liebling*, I do not like to send you into this dark. Will you mind?'

'I have lights,' I said, with more confidence than I felt. The blackout ensured that they were minimal.

The air crackled with frost. I knew that Da would be worried, and cross; I had overstayed by at least an hour. Yet as I cycled cautiously home, I floated, buoyed on a warmth of melody and promise; and of mystery, too. Mrs Wilhelmsbach seemed to be beckoning me into an unknown territory; one with its darknesses as well as its light, but where, in that bright cosy room and in her benignly gnostic presence, I felt I would always be safe.

I forget what Da said, or how cross she was, but it couldn't have been too bad, because on the next Tuesday I went back. Then I had to return to school, and I didn't see Mrs Wilhelmsbach again until the Easter holidays. Da had arranged for more piano lessons at school, and to begin with, as often happens in a learning process, I seemed to make rapid progress. On my first visit of the holidays to Mrs Wilhelmsbach I plodded proudly through a little minuet from Bach's *Notebook for Anna Magdalena*.

'John! *Liebling*, I am so proud of you. But there is much that you have not understood. We must work hard. The left hand – '

We worked. That left hand, obstinately refusing to follow its separate but correlated course, continued to trouble me. I listened, enraptured, as Mrs Wilhelmsbach's own magic fingers showed me how – effortlessly measuring and shaping the notes, releasing sounds that sang and flowed, lifted altogether out of the percussive dimension that my ear expected of the keyboard. Sometimes, not often, I could coax her into a display of rare virtuosity, and she would lose herself in dreams of her favourite Schumann. They were dreams which the music seemed to invite me into, to share; so that I could follow a little way – not understanding much – to glimpse that secret landscape of light and shadows her mind inhabited.

Through April the evenings were drawing out, and I could linger without fear of arousing Da's anxiety. We would sit in rapt silence by the gramophone, while those old 78s crackled round and the huge papier-mâché bell cast its soft acoustic spell. Looking back now, I can see a design, a plan, in what she chose to give me. It was a strange one. There was little of the dramatics of Beethoven, not much even of Mozart or Haydn. She offered instead, as though this was where music should begin for a child, choral and orchestral pieces by Bach and Handel – Purcell – and, ranging further back, Monteverdi, and English church music from the Elizabethan era. At the time I was little aware of styles, of period; it was simply music, a new world for me, that even then I knew, transmuted by the imagination, to be an intimate and essential part – more than a mere reflection – of reality. I did not, could not know, that for Mrs Wilhelmsbach music was more even than reality: it was the saving quality that, if anything could, made the world bearable.

Easter came and went; for Da, the most important moment in the year, a spiritual fulcrum, the point of balance for her certain faith; a perpetual promise kept. I don't remember it at all precisely, that year – or whether it fell early or late in its mysteriously movable fashion. It has retreated, in my mind, into the collective Easters of my childhood. But I do remember the return to school at the end of the holidays, and the sharp sense that this time I was losing more than the securities of home, and Da, and my unusual measure of independence. My homesickness embraced, also, Mrs Wilhelmsbach.

She wrote to me, for my birthday, which always fell ten days or a fortnight before the end of the summer term. It was a letter which, for its eccentricities, I hid carefully away – aware that, once revealed to my schoolfellows, it would expose me to endless indignities.

> *Liebling,*
> I think of you with love on your tenth birthday. I would send you a present, but I am fearful of it breaking in the postage. It is a record of a most beautiful Handel aria sung by a boy, that I will give you, so soon now, when you come for your next lesson. *Where'ere You Walk,* it is called, and on the other side is a piece from *Messiah*. I think of you when I listen to it. Also I think of my Sascha. Oh, *Liebling,* I am so afraid. It is a so cruel world. But God will preserve you from its cruelties, of that I am sure.

Did I read this somehow as a cry for help, from me? I remember how her letter disturbed me; but I knew so little. All I can be certain of now is that I felt that inexorable tug of love, and knew that her unhappiness made me unhappy.

The start of the summer holidays, as it always would, dispelled such clouds. Eight glorious weeks stretched ahead of me – almost an eternity. On the first Tuesday, I was back with Mrs Wilhelmsbach, listening to Master Derek Middleton's singing. It was the first record I ever personally owned.

My piano playing had stuck, just as records sometimes did in those days, in a groove. I think we were both beginning to recognize, and accept, my limitations. One afternoon, after a particularly trying session, Mrs Wilhelmsbach rose from her chair beside the piano stool, and walked quietly to the window that overlooked her small garden. For a long time she stood in silence, her back to me. I took a handkerchief from my pocket and wiped the nervous sweat, first from my fingers and then from the white and black keys I had touched. I wondered where her thoughts had gone, knowing how they could stray, and fearful that they might have deserted me completely. Suddenly she turned.

'*Liebling*,' she said, 'I must tell you a thing. It is known to clever people who study these matters that the human brain is capable of thinking only three thoughts together, all at the same time. It is also known to these same clever people that a concert pianist, on occasions, has to be thinking of nineteen different things in just a single moment.'

She looked at me with the gentlest of smiles.

'How shall we resolve this riddle, *Liebling*? – I don't think that we can.' She moved back beside me, and placed a thoughtful hand on my shoulder. 'We will go on, because it is good for you, for your musical education. But I do not think, my John, that you will ever be a concert pianist.'

Nor did I, nor ever had I. And strangely, her words seemed to lift a weight from me, so that I found myself smiling back at her, without resentment.

'Have you thought,' she asked, 'of another instrument? Something that is perhaps less demanding, although nothing in music is easy?'

'My uncle plays the flute,' I said. 'Perhaps he would let me try.'

'The flute! That is perfect, *Liebling*. And a lovely instrument. I do not know, but I believe those clever people might decide a flautist has only to think five or six thoughts at the same time.' She laughed, and holding my face in both hands she bent to place a gentle kiss on my now untroubled forehead.

The piano lessons continued and, freed at last from some of my anxieties, they went a little better. Tuesday afternoons were islands of memorable delight, dotted over that drowsing summer sea of sunlit happiness.

It was a Saturday, however, that leads me back to the other of these two stories: and to Tasha.

On the far side of our town, just off the London road, in the valley below the forest and bordering the river, lies the Town Football Club. It is still there today, but housing estates and a sewage farm have crept around it over the years, so that now the open space is much straitened and confined. In those days there was a long meadow beside and beyond the football pitch, visited from time to time by itinerant fairs and circuses as an alternative site to the Common above the town, which in wartime was liable to be conscripted for military purposes. On this occasion it was neither fair nor circus, briefly camped on that convenient stretch of land, but something else; something that to me, at least, was even more exotic and enticing.

I have said that I was without companions of my own age during the holidays. But there was one boy, who went away to the same boarding school; so our families thought it appropriate for us to meet occasionally at home. His father was sports master at the College, which gave us convenient privileges at the huge open-air College swimming pool, fed from the icy waters of the river. Apart from that, we made little effort to meet; I don't think he liked me any more than I liked him. I will call him Robin Geeley.

One day Mr Geeley telephoned Da. The Cossacks, he said, were coming to the town. Would John like to join Robin for a family visit to the show on Saturday evening? Da felt certain enough to accept on my behalf, without even consulting me. But I didn't resent this; the thought of seeing the Cossacks again far outweighed, for me, the disadvantages of sharing them with Robin. For I had seen them once before, a year or two before the war, and although my memories were muddled because I had been only four or five years old at the time, they were also, however inaccurately, vivid. They had that quality of mythology which attaches sometimes to memories from early childhood. In particular, etched into my mind's eye, was the ring of fire. I saw it as a huge blazing arch, towering into darkness, and through flames and billowing smoke the blackened shapes of galloping horses and men – apocalyptic, leaping, vanishing, appearing, dancing in the sky.

The show began in early evening, timed to reach its climax just as dusk deepened into night. It always ended with the ring of fire.

I am not sure where my knowledge came from, but I knew something of this nomadic band of Cossacks. They were what we called White Russians – a political not ethnic description – refugees from the civil wars that had followed the Bolshevik revolution, exiles now for twenty years from their homeland, who had learned to make a living out of their extraordinary horsemanship. They roamed, no longer the steppes but all the counties of England, displaying feats of skill and daring on horseback that dazzled belief. Some of their routines were familiar to us – they were the same as those presented by circus trick-riders: leaping on and off a galloping horse, singly, in twos, in threes – sometimes as many as six of these small lithe men riding one horse. But mostly, their exploits seemed geared to their military past, adaptations of mounted warfare. They lanced hoops, they picked up wounded comrades from the ground, at full gallop, and held them, shielded from enemy fire, along the horse's flank; they swung themselves completely beneath the horse and hung there under its belly, their heads just inches from the thundering turf, as they discharged their rifles.

It was all a blur of excitement, of reckless courage, of an exalted disdain for danger.

In such an atmosphere of time suspended, the day had passed, unperceived; it was dusk, it was almost dark. Mr Geeley peered at the luminous dial of his large wrist-watch.

'Nine-thirty,' he said. 'It must finish soon.'

Neither Robin nor I, in a state of unexpected truce, wanted this.

'Not yet,' said Robin. 'Let it go on.' As if this somehow depended on his father.

'There's still the ring of fire,' I said. 'It can't end before that. And then it does.'

'What ring of fire?' Mr Geeley wanted to know. Evidently he hadn't seen the Cossacks before.

'They make a great blazing circle of flames. And then they all jump through it.'

'Sounds very dangerous to me,' Mr Geeley said; but not as though he meant it. More, I felt, to humour us. I didn't mind. He would see.

It was at this moment that half a dozen little men dashed out across the field and began to hoist into the air the arch which until then had lain unnoticed on the ground. A metal framework, packed with straw. The warm evening air wafted a strong smell of petrol towards us.

'How do they get round the rationing?' Mr Geeley muttered. In the darkness Robin flashed me what seemed strangely like a look of apology.

The men were spreading straw over the ground between the uprights of the arch. One of them drenched this from an upturned can. A match was struck and thrown, and the six men fled into what was only briefly darkness. For as they ran, the flames roared round that circle, and seemed to scorch our faces even at the distance where we stood, behind a rope barrier.

From the thicker darkness beyond the blazing ring we could hear a crescendo of hoofbeats, and suddenly there they were, the whole troop one after another leaping out of darkness through the fiery light and searing heat of the ring; ten, fifteen, twenty horses and their demented riders, rending the night air with ancestral battle-cries. They were through, and charging towards us, some brandishing their long lances, some discharging a fusillade of rifle blanks, as they rode us down. For it was clear that nothing could stop them, and the crowd swayed involuntarily back from the rope barrier, in confusion. Only a yard, it seemed, from the front rank of spectators – from a visibly startled and incipiently angry Mr Geeley, and from a pair of hypnotized boys – within a single stride, from a full gallop they had come to a quivering, steaming halt. There was a sudden, unnerving silence. It was like that moment which sometimes overtakes a concert hall, when the full sound of a symphony orchestra achieves its thunderous conclusion but the audience, so dazed by sound and waking from such dreams, cannot persuade itself that the end has come, or begin the applause.

And into that deliberately contrived lacuna was inserted something stranger still, an improvised and unofficial coda that startled the performers as much as a moment earlier they had startled us. I could see this, stamped on the features of the rider nearest to me; red-bearded, his blue eyes reflecting points of fire from the ring which still blazed against the night sky.

A shrill cry had split the darkness behind the fire, and suddenly, flying through smoke and swirling ashes and the flaring straw, came one more horse. Small and black and streaked with lines of sweat, it seemed little more than a pony. And this was appropriate, because as they burst through the ring there was enough light left from the dying flames to reveal its rider: a little girl, her hair as black as the horse she rode, her eyes wild with triumph.

She pulled up a few yards short of the others and sat there a moment, very still and poised, her eyes daring the group of riders. Then with a small, tight smile, directed I could have sworn at the man with the red beard, she flicked her hair from her face with a sharp twist of her head, wheeled the little horse with the reins against its neck, and cantered off into darkness. Red-beard shouted something after her that I couldn't understand – I supposed it was in Russian. I thought his voice sounded angry, but then his head went back and the shout turned into a roar of laughter; one by one the other riders took this up, until they were all laughing together while the crowd, puzzled perhaps but polite, gave them their postponed applause and then began to disperse. As we walked away I felt I must be the only one there so caught, so entangled, in the romantic and inexplicable mystery of the black-haired child who had ridden the ring of fire.

On Sunday morning I went to church with Da. We had a fight about this, I remember, because I was moved by a desire obscure even to myself: there was something else I wanted to do. Da could not, would not understand that there was anything more important than going to church on Sunday – particularly if it was for something I couldn't explain. It was only when my obstinacy had reduced her to tears – the one time I ever remember seeing her cry – that, appalled by what I seemed to have done, I surrendered. It was a very quiet walk that morning down the lane to church, both of us I think, for different reasons, ashamed of our behaviour.

As soon as lunch was over, I slipped out; ostensibly to the fields and river, my habitual domain. In fact, to walk the mile and a half, back past the church, and through the town, and out the other side to the Football Ground.

They were still there, with their caravans and horse-trailers, camped between the pitch and the river.

I don't know, now, what I hoped to achieve by this return to a scene that haunted me. I was too young to have learned the impossibility of turning the pages back, too firmly anchored in childhood's perception of time as a single dimension that spreads imperceptibly from the central present, whether backwards or forwards. So I must think I was luckier than I deserved. As I wandered over that field, eyeing the blackened scorch marks in turf that was scored with hoofprints, I came upon her without any fuss or preamble, sitting quietly among clover and buttercups.

'It was you,' I said, 'last night. You rode through the fire.'

I don't suppose I have ever, before or since, made such a direct and simple approach, or with less apprehension, to a total stranger. I had not stopped to think, and even when the words were spoken they didn't need thinking about. She looked up quickly, her dark eyes brimming with excited pleasure.

'You saw me, then? You saw me do it? Uncle Grigor pretended to be so angry, but I had told him. I *swore* that I would do it, even if he did not let me.'

I believe I sat down then, and that presently we exchanged names; but there is much I have forgotten. Much I remember, too – particularly of that first day; and there were only a few more, three or four perhaps, before they moved on to their next town. But it is not easy to arrange these memories in my mind, to say with any certainty *this* she told me on this occasion, *that* we did on that day. What I do remember, though, is the strange mixture – of ordinary childhood chatter that filled most of our conversations, and then of those moments when she seemed to lead me briefly into a different, shadowed world, where I was aware of mysteries but had no inkling of their nature. It has taken me fifty years to make the connection, to understand that what puzzled me in Tasha, what stirred in me such a formless and anonymous disquiet, was exactly what puzzled and stirred me in dark moments with Mrs Wilhelmsbach. So that I can believe it was only chance, or lack of chance, that I never stumbled into betraying Tasha as I betrayed Mrs Wilhelmsbach – although Tasha, too, was to be betrayed, as I now know.

Tasha's moods were bewildering: so still and quiet, as I had found her sitting among the wild flowers; such flashing energy at another moment, as when she suddenly leaped to her feet, dragging me after her.

'Come! You must meet Uncle Grigor!'

We ran across the football pitch towards the line of caravans. Uncle Grigor, I was not surprised to see, had a red beard and piercing blue eyes; and a ferocity of expression that did not for a moment deceive. He was sitting on the outside step of his caravan, whittling a piece of willow with an enormous clasp-knife.

'What has Tasha found?' He glared at me, but there was bright laughter in his eyes. 'A boy? The Saints preserve us – it is a boy!'

'He is John, Uncle Grigor. He saw me ride the ring.'

'Did he, now? Then he saw a great foolishness, my little girl. As I cannot tell you often enough.'

Tasha's own eyes flashed, wickedly, and she muttered something I couldn't understand.

'We will speak English, Tasha.' There was a real but gentle authority in his voice now. 'We must not be impolite.' Tasha's mouth was stubbornly compressed, saying nothing in either language, but her eyes were eloquent, and Grigor seemed to be answering them, although it was to me he spoke.

'You see her eyes? They are like naughty blackberries. Yes?'

Tasha giggled.

'How can blackberries be naughty?' I asked him, doubtful and yet intrigued.

'For that, you must ask Tasha.' Grigor calmly whittled his stick. 'She knows all about being naughty. If I was her father, I should beat her with this.' He sighed. 'But I am only her poor foolish uncle.'

Now, when I remember, I can see the force in that description of her eyes, although I search for it in vain in the Tasha of today. At the time, it merely flickered through my mind, an image that briefly aroused curiosity and then was forgotten in another that it suggested.

'There are blackberries on the edge of the forest,' I said. 'Millions of them. They might be getting ripe by now.'

Tasha jumped up.

'Then we shall pick them! Take baskets. Uncle Grigor – '

But Grigor shook his head. 'I am happy here in the sun. You children go.' He stood, and I was surprised to see how small he was. Sitting, he had somehow loomed large, but that was for his vivid eyes, his force, his presence; when he stood he revealed himself slim and slight – I stood higher than his shoulder. He looked at me, momentarily thoughtful.

'Where do you come from, John? Will your parents perhaps wait anxiously, wondering where you are?'

'They are in India.' I stilled my conscience. 'My grandmother won't worry. If I am back for supper.'

Grigor nodded, but made no comment beyond an indeterminate grunt. He turned, to fetch two wicker baskets from the caravan.

'We have learned,' he said, handing these to us, 'to live off the land. Mushrooms, nuts, sorrel, wild raspberries sometimes. So now, blackberries. Good picking, children!'

We crossed the road just above the railway bridge, and struck right-handed, diagonally up the steep turf slope towards the edge of the forest which stood less than half a mile from the town, upon its hill. Halfway up seemed a good place to pause, and catch our breath. We sat, looking down on the tiled roof-tops of the town, the silver streak of the river threading here and there between trees and houses. I am almost certain it was here she spoke of her father. Mine, I had told her, was in India, to fight the Japanese.

'Where's yours?' I asked. 'Is he in the war, fighting Germans?'

'Everyone is fighting,' she said, 'everywhere.'

And then, with what I think I recognized – although something else escaped me – as an extraordinary care: 'He is fighting against the communists. The Bolsheviks. Uncle Grigor is his brother.' She seemed to let her words float, oddly inviolate, so that my curiosity stumbled, was checked, retreated cautiously; here was a world beyond the comprehension of children, which she had seen into, briefly, but could not enter. I could not even see it.

We took up our baskets, and climbed on towards the line of trees. Presently we found blackberries, and began to pick.

I had been wrong, it seemed, to number them in millions. Our mouths were soon streaked with purple juices, but the baskets filled slowly. Tasha wore faded brown dungarees –as a child I never saw her in a dress – her pockets filled with things appropriate to a boy: a smaller version of Uncle Grigor's clasp-knife, ends of string, a polished year-old conker. There was a knot tied in her grubby handkerchief.

'To remind me,' she said. But I forget what it was she had to remember.

'Shall we go further in?' I asked. 'I'm sure there were more blackberries last year. And bigger.'

The trees were bigger, too, as we pushed deeper into the forest; oak and beech and elm, growing tall, filtering out the September sun. We came to a high and formidable barrier.

'It must be the Army fence,' I said. 'They store ammunition in the forest.' But we had found the real blackberries, glistening on thick brambles beyond the wire.

On my own, or even with Robin Geeley, I would not have dared. But Tasha could ride through fire, and did not hesitate.

'We must climb over,' she said. 'We must find a way.'

Beyond the tangle of brambles I could see the curved corrugated roof of a Nissen hut.

'It might be dangerous. We could be blown up. A sentry could shoot us.'

'Look! There is a tree. Its branches go right over the top.'

It was an easy climb, and there was indeed a branch that took us over the top of the fence, but it was a long drop on the other side; even as I dropped, I wondered how on earth we were going to get back. I rolled over, hitting the ground, spilling all the blackberries from my basket. Tasha helped me recover them, and then we began to pick again – and this time there really were millions. The baskets were soon full.

We looked at our tree. There was no way we could reach that branch.

'We'll find another tree,' Tasha said, with a fine careless confidence. 'It will be easy.' She led, squeezing between fence and brambles, and turned a corner.

Square in front of us, legs planted wide astride, rifle slung on shoulder, stood – towered, I should say – an enormous GI. I knew he was an American from the pale colour of his uniform, but also because he was black, and negroes (in those days we had not been taught to shun the term) were not to be found in the British army. I felt the terror, clear through me; I was frozen like a rabbit in the mesmeric eye of a weasel. Tasha was very still beside me, but somehow I knew she did not share my panic. And very slowly, revealing a flash of white teeth, the soldier smiled.

'Well – well – well.' The words spaced, and easy. 'What do we have here? – I declare – ' I can still hear that voice, mocking its own Southern drawl – 'Hänsel and Gretel, I do believe.' He took a giant, gentle step towards us, peering into our baskets.

'Blackberries!'

His eyes scanned the bushes on the far side of the fence, and then those beside us, and his smile became broader still.

'The grass is always greener, so they say – '

'We were looking for a way out,' said Tasha firmly. I could not fault the misleading truth of this; nor did it escape our soldier.

'So how did you get in? Fell down a rabbit hole, I guess – or stepped through a looking-glass.'

Hank – he told us his name was Hank – seemed to see everything in terms of stories, and evidently he knew a good many. Already I was feeling comfortable with him.

'Listen, kids. Everything gets easier over a Coke. How about we all go back to my place, and discuss this? I'll feel a heap happier when I've snuck you out of here.'

Hank's place was the Nissen hut on the other side of the brambles. He sat us down, and flipped the lids off three bottles of Coke. It was the first I had ever tasted. A muddier colour than blackberries, but it settled well on the top of our earlier feast.

It seemed to be party time. Tasha offered him blackberries, which he ate with noisy pleasure; and then he reached lazily behind him to take down a guitar that was hanging from a nail on the wall. He strummed a chord or two, and began a slow sad cowboy song, all about the lonely starlit prairie and the girl he had left behind him in some distant log-cabin home.

He broke off suddenly, in the middle of a line, as though the song had somehow become too urgently real for him, and no longer a story.

'Say, kids. Can you sing? How about some carols?'

I stared at him. 'But it's not Christmas. Not for ages yet.'

Hank rippled the strings of his guitar. 'That doesn't matter. Christmas is when you feel like it. I guess I want any day of the week to be Christmas right now.'

A shadow darkened the door. Hank looked up, and then without any sign either of haste or truculence, came easily to his feet.

'Some strays I found in the forest, sir. I've been trying to figure out a way to get them home. Without using the gate.' He paused, pointedly.

An extraordinarily young face looked thoughtfully at each of us in turn. This was an officer, a British one; a Lieutenant. The war made experts of all small boys: in uniforms, in aircraft, in tanks and guns and ships. But it is only now that I wonder what sort of military detachment it could have been, detailed to guard the ammunition, that so oddly mixed British officers and American GIs. Clearly, these two were familiar with each other, and at ease.

'Hank will think of something,' Tasha said.

There was a flicker of amusement on that pale and handsome face.

'Oh, so it's Hank, is it? In that case I am Stuart. And who are you?'

With a demure yet prideful formality that surprised me, she replied: 'I am Natasha Alexeiev. And this is John.'

'Well, Natasha Alexeiev, and John – I suppose I must conspire with Hank to smuggle you out of here. I could pull rank at the gate, but I think it might be better if we are more discreet. How did you get in?'

'We climbed a tree,' I said. 'But it was too high to climb back.'

'Let's go and look at this tree of yours. And see if we can help you into it. And then,' he looked with the briefest of smiles at Hank, 'arrange to cut it down.'

With Hank's great height, it was easy enough to lift us to our branch, first Tasha, then me, then our brimming baskets carefully handed to us. We climbed along the branch, over the fence, and slid down our tree into the civilian world. Stuart and Hank stood looking at us.

'Don't come back,' said Stuart, but in tones stripped of all unfriendliness.

And as we walked away, Hank shouted after us: 'Sing a carol for me! When the real Christmas comes round.'

Tasha turned, and waved. 'Any day of the week!' she called, and I saw Hank's face split in that shining smile.

On the hill above the town, without a word spoken we stopped in the same place as before, and sat down.

'They were nice,' I said. 'But I was a bit scared when I first saw Hank.'

Tasha hugged her knees. 'I like Hank, and I like Stuart,' she said slowly. 'But I don't like soldiers.'

'I told you there were soldiers there.'

'I know.' And then her smile was as broad as Hank's. 'But I like blackberries.'

The sun slanted across the town. I didn't know the time, but Da lay rather uneasily on my conscience. I had not forgotten our quarrel.

'I think I must go home soon. Will I see you again?'

'We are here for a few days, resting.' She seemed uncertain. 'Perhaps until Wednesday or Thursday.'

It was not much, to have lodged so firmly in my mind and memory, the title of friendship; but I did see her again, two or three times. And Uncle Grigor. And Tasha's black pony, Scimitar. And on one of those afternoons she came to our house, and Da in her modest way was very kind to her.

Then it was Wednesday, or Thursday, and the caravans

departed. That was half a century ago – a long time to hang on to a memory.

I had sacrificed a Tuesday to Tasha. There was only one left of the summer holiday.

As I dismounted and wheeled my bicycle to the cottage gate, I was rehearsing apologies in my mind. But they were to remain unspoken, for when I saw Mrs Wilhelmsbach all my own preoccupations were suddenly swept from me; she was so stricken. There was something in her of the quality I had come to think of as her 'moods', but infinitely magnified. It was only with an effort that she recognized me.

'John!' She swayed in the doorway, blocking my entrance. 'I had forgotten. I should have telephoned, to tell you another day. This one is so terrible.'

I stood, shaken and embarrassed by her emotion, which I could not understand but which defined itself as something so far beyond and behind my experience that I feared its truth.

'Mrs Wilhelmsbach. I'm sorry. I'll go away.' I stammered, searching for solid ground. 'I – I'll come back tomorrow.' My hand was on my bicycle.

'No! No, *Liebling*, you are here. And perhaps that is better.' She stood aside, and as on that very first occasion, it was her hand that drew me in, holding mine. 'Just for a little while. But I do not know if there can be any more music – never any more music.' Her face seemed to me as alien, as alarming, as her words. We came to what I thought of as the music room, and she stood beside the piano, clutching a crumpled piece of paper.

'Oh, John, you do not know what they have done. I have feared it all this long time, but I could not believe. And now I have heard.' She dropped the paper, and swept those silver-framed photographs from the piano top into her two hands, clasping them to her.

'All, *Liebling*, all! Because we are Jews! Even my Sascha – but Sascha is not a Jewish name! His mother was not Jewish, and they took her also. They took them all – and my poor Sigi too.'

'Who took them?' I asked, bewildered. 'What have they done?'

'What have they done?' Her hair streamed wildly. 'Nothing! All they have done is to be Jewish, or marry a Jew, or have a Jewish father like Sascha.'

The photographs slipped from her hands. The carpet saved some, but as they crashed together the glass shattered in others, into starred splinters, and a frame broke across one corner. She stared, unseeing, at that wreckage.

'Sascha. Sigi.' And she wept.

I would like to be indulgent, to my memory of myself; to remind myself that I was only ten years old, and innocent of what the world can contrive. But Sascha, too, was only ten; and innocence had not spared him an adult understanding, nor an adult consummation. All I knew was that this gentle woman I had thought I loved, for herself and for the music she had given me, I feared instead; as we must always fear what we do not understand. Her feet cracked glass, as she moved closer to me, and she took my head to bury my face in her black silk dress. It was her own comfort she sought, but this too I didn't understand, and was something else to fear. I struggled. I remember the burning, icy touch of that silk, and the desperate body beneath it. I choked for breath.

'What has *happened*?' I cried, shaken by tears that were all for my own predicament and blind to hers.

'They are all dead,' she whispered. 'Killed because they were Jews.'

At last I broke free; or she released me. My tears were hot, and frightened; hers were cool, despairing, and remote.

'*Liebling*, I did not mean to hurt you. Can you see, no-one who has been hurt as I have been would ever wish to hurt another?'

And in my fright and my own despair, those terrible words escaped me, that I have never forgotten or forgiven. No, not escaped. I must be truthful. I hurled them at her.

'The Jews killed Jesus!'

It was not what I believed, or Da had taught me. Only St Peter, with memories of a garden in Gethsemane, could know what I feel now.

I looked at her in horror, and saw only a remote sadness in her own face, where the tears had dried.

'*Liebling*,' she sighed. Oh, *mein Leibling*.'

They were the last words she ever spoke to me. For I turned and fled, running from myself as much as from her, because I could not face either.

It didn't take me long to discover that we can never escape ourselves; but years passed before I understood that I had not escaped her, either. The love she had spared for me, in her anguish, and that I had so cruelly rejected, remained a buried secret in my mind, nourished I would like to believe by music, until at last a time came when I had grown enough to look at it squarely and welcome it back, as it had been offered, without guilt or reproach. I was sixteen or seventeen when I cycled out to her cottage, finally resolved to make amends. There was a stranger in the garden, a bald middle-aged man smoking a pipe and wielding clippers on a hedge.

'I was looking for Mrs Wilhelmsbach,' I said. 'Does she still live here?'

'Mrs Wilhelmsbach?' He looked puzzled for a moment, and then his face cleared. 'Oh, you mean Mrs Williamson. The old Austrian lady.' He put a match to his stubborn pipe. 'She moved away, a long time ago. Around the end of the war, it would have been. Now let me see, she went – I believe she went to – ' he scratched his shiny head, and named one of the villages on the Plain, fifteen miles to the south. 'Or it might have been another. I don't remember now.'

I took the lane home, very slowly, thinking about that change of name and residence. Evidently she had wanted to forget, as much as such things can ever be forgotten. Why rake over the ashes of that past? My presence could only remind her.

It was another twenty years before chance took me through that village on the Plain, and I was no longer looking for her. By then, she must certainly have moved on again – to some other village, I would like to believe, where Sigi and Sascha were quietly waiting for her.

Tasha closed the shop, and we walked up through the town to a little café which in the summer spreads continental tables and umbrellas over the pavement. It was still warm enough to sit outside, but there was no need to seek shade and most of the umbrellas were furled.

Somehow she had contrived to make me talk about myself – easily done in other circumstances but not what I wanted now.

'And you, Tasha,' I said at last – 'what brought you back?'

'Memories,' she said, with a little smile. 'But mostly, a husband. It was his shop, you see. I learned the trade from him. And then he died.'

'And Grigor?'

I believe I must have known what I was doing. It was those reminders I had seen in her reflected face, before I knew who she was. I saw the shadows return, and realized that I had expected this, in a way had willed it, because there was something more I had to discover.

'After the war, he went to search for my father.' She looked at me with a curiously dispassionate emphasis. 'Did I tell you anything about my father?'

'A little. He fought the Bolsheviks, you said.'

'His name was Mikhail. He was Uncle Grigor's younger brother. They both fought, in a Don Cossack brigade, in the civil wars. Afterwards, after they had lost, they came to England. And then I was born, and soon my mother died. And the war came, and my father went away, to fight the Bolsheviks again. Uncle Grigor did not wish him to go.'

Her black eyes studied the table-top.

'To fight the Bolsheviks,' she said very slowly, 'he had to join with the Germans. Many of our people did.'

Her words seemed to have drifted there, between us. I realized I was not surprised by them.

'I remember the day of the blackberries,' I said. 'I remember that you told me you didn't like soldiers.' It was easy, now, to understand.

'He was rounded up at the end of the war, in Yugoslavia, and put in a camp. An allied camp. Uncle Grigor heard rumours. He went out to find his brother – to find Mikhail. It must have been a desperate journey, in those times.'

'I have heard a little of this – of what happened. But what *did* happen, to Grigor, to your father?'

'They were sent back,' she said, with a flat, tired bitterness. 'Not just my father. Uncle Grigor too. And they were British and Americans, who did it – men like Hank and Stuart. They must have muddled their paperwork. They sent them both, to the Gulag.'

'They didn't know,' I said, thinking of those humane and civilized soldiers who had treated two undeserving children with such kindness.

'It makes no difference, now. It was many years before I heard – but they did not live long. The Gulag was a ring of fire they could not survive.'

Nor had Sascha, nor Sigi, survived theirs, I thought: a vision of smoking chimneys. But the image was altogether too convenient.

What wrongs had been done. And how irrelevant, how almost shoddy, now, seemed my bittersweet memories, beside the depths of fearful experience I had seen scored on those twin faces, which time had superimposed, one upon the other.

No, not rings of fire, but black holes in the earth's fabric – cosmic letter-boxes into which were posted people, visions, guilts; the soul of our century, sucked into oblivion, swallowed up. It was a desolate picture I saw. A deserved desolation. There was nothing I could say to Tasha, no excuses that I could offer. The memories, after all, were too insistent.

* * *

While I breathe, what is left of my hair will continue to grow – that is a tolerable certainty. Another, less tolerable, follows from this. There will come a time, three or four months hence, when I shall have to decide where to go to have it cut. Even if it is Tasha's daughter, returned from her holiday, and not Tasha herself, can I go back to that little shop below the churchyard; can I ever bring myself to face that mirror?

Another decision is easier. I think, as I lay down my pen this evening, the story at last finished, that I must take up my flute; and play something for Mrs Wilhelmsbach.

It should be Schumann.

The Sound of the Sea

Henry Saloman Spence, better known to me and one or two others as Harry Spence, stood on the shadowy periphery of my first published (and now long forgotten) novel; and appeared in two other novels and some fragments that remain unpublished – an oblivion that I suspect Harry, who has had a hand in most of what I have written, would agree with me is, if not entirely deserved, at least on balance probably for the best. From this it might be deduced that Harry holds a rather special significance in my life; he has been a preoccupation of mine for a great many years. Therefore it was on the cards that somewhere in this series of stories he was going to find a place. Now, I feel, is the moment.

If, in some of its detail, this one should seem to contradict facts already aired publicly, and others known only to me and a few faithful and private readers, that is not a carelessness on my part, but purposeful. A writer, it seems to me, assumes a pseudonym with every character he creates. However actively the yeast of the imagination is allowed to assist the fermentation, he is always to be discovered inside his own creation, looking out with his own eyes, at the world of his story. I suppose Harry is my most sustained *alter ego*, the one into whom I have put most of myself. A consequence of this is the bewildering degree of internal contradiction, already hinted, that would emerge if all I have written about him, published and unpublished, were put together. I explain this to myself as evidence of Harry's essential reality, for nothing is more uncertain or contradictory than what we stumblingly define as real. It is only in fiction that, mistakenly in my view, we expect consistency. So Harry Spence is a repository not just of my memories but of my imagination too; and over more than thirty years I have changed my mind about him, and myself, a good many times.

'You can also pick up an old day, like a shell, press it to your ear, and hear the sound of the sea.'
 I am no longer sure if it was I, or Harry, who first came across this illuminating sentence in one of Paul Scott's Indian novels, and showed it to the other. Whichever way round, I treasure the discovery because it fits so happily my own apprehension of the nature of memory, and the dimension this gives to what we call reality. To remember is to reinvent the past, which is why memories lend themselves so appositely to fiction.

The Avebury Rings, sarsen stones and earth banks, stand as sky-swept as their own old beech trees in the landscape of Harry Spence's private mythology. When he was six years old it was under the greatest stand of beeches, high on the southern bank beside the main road, that he learned his parents were to return to India without him. Harry was born in India; but at an earlier age than he could remember, he had been brought back to England by his mother, following a mysterious and alarming attack of rheumatic fever. Infant mortality in India, even within the European community, was very high: England, Wiltshire, home, seemed safer.
 Mr Spence was in the Indian Civil Service. He had opted for the judicial branch and served as District Magistrate in a small hill station in northern India. When Harry was five, Mr Spence took home leave, overdue by some eighteen months; so Harry and his mother moved from his grandmother's house into a trim cottage in the same village, and for a year, for the first time in Harry's memory, they lived as a complete family.
 In an unemphatic way, his father was not one to favour idleness, and for most of that year he pursued his study of the law, sometimes away for days at a time in London. But also he was often at home and Harry began to learn the ways of masculine companionship. Mr Spence, lean and

tanned, his sparse hair already grizzled, was a quietly sardonic companion, gravely considerate except in his marked reluctance to stoop to Harry's age, and even in this there was perhaps a kind of deliberate consideration.

As for his mother, it may be that a little of her fear for Harry lingered from his infant illness – certainly she could at times be demonstrative, could still baby him. But she had a serenity too, that to a child less secure than Harry then felt himself to be, might have seemed almost to amount to unconcern. Harry knew better. She had taught him to read, and calculate, and wash behind his ears, but it was for other less elementary lessons that she fixed her character in his mind: she painted skilful, dreamy water-colours, and encouraged Harry to paint; she knew the songs of birds and the delicate colours of their eggs; she was familiar with caterpillars and could predict, unerringly, their mysterious metamorphoses; she took him, unselfconsciously, into her bath; she nurtured in Harry her own love of music, which excluded tone-deaf Mr Spence, but he didn't mind this too much, making dry jokes about it at his own expense. The one tune he claimed to recognize was the national anthem, and that only because of the drum roll which preceded it on ceremonial occasions.

And then the year ended.

Mr Spence drove a 1935 Austin Seven. One day in July a picnic was proposed, and with some misgiving the little car's leaf-springs were persuaded to accept the combined weight of a picnic hamper, Harry, and three adults: Mr and Mrs Spence in front, and – to supervise Harry and the hamper in the back – Mary, a girl from a neighbouring village who had been engaged a year before as nanny. Mary was sixteen when she first assumed her duties, but assumed them with such effect that Harry, if he had been asked, would honestly have supposed her nearer sixty. They drove to Avebury.

And on that high bank, under those old beeches, beside the allusive shapes of ancient anagogic stones, Harry was told things he could scarcely comprehend.

'But I should come too!' he cried, stumbling against a dread perception of their withdrawal, their desertion.

'It's the climate,' his mother gently said, but as though for a moment lost, herself, in labyrinths of regret or uncertainty. 'You are too young. You were so ill, before. It is so hard for us all, Harry. But it's for the best.'

I hold that shell to my ear, and her voice whispers to me over the years; and now I can hear, as Harry was too young to hear, the doubts she couldn't exclude, and her own dismay. For Harry, it was despair: he saw doors closing on past and future, on life itself. He couldn't imagine the world that was being proposed.

'It will only be for a year or two,' Mr Spence said, but Harry couldn't read his voice or make sense of his words. 'There's a war coming. Everything will change.' For this was the July of 1939; around the time, I remind myself again, of Harry's sixth birthday.

Briefly he sought refuge in tears, but they brought him no solace. A year or two, Mr Spence had said – an enormity of time, of emptiness. And in that void he began to see himself, perhaps for the first time, as an entity, a separate rounded and authentic shape, isolated and integral as those arcanal standing stones; different, because divided, from the people he loved. There, on the rim of a lost world, he saw himself whole, unique, alone. It was an unformulated knowledge, in no way dependent on words, but something he felt, images he saw with a child's eye. It was from this moment, I think, that Harry seemed to subsist for all his life as if in a dimension removed from the world of other people, so that everything and everybody existed, could exist, only in relation to himself, in relation to his observation of their phenomenal nature. If this sounds purely egocentric, it was eventually to be tempered by his adult belief that existence is the same for all; that there are, in a profound sense, as many worlds as there are people in them.

Mary, who had withdrawn, tactfully or under instruction, during this brief exchange, now approached with a large white handkerchief for Harry's face; but his few tears had dried already. Presently the picnic was packed up, and then they packed themselves again into that picnic-hamper car, and drove away – from the Rings, past Silbury Hill and the forgotten Sanctuary, over sunlit downs sprinkled with grey wethers and brooding tumuli. Presently, Mr and Mrs Spence left for India; left Harry with Mary and his Wiltshire grandmother. Presently – or precisely, six weeks later – the war began.

Harry was taken only twice to the Avebury Rings in his earlier years; at least (so he tells me) he remembers only the two occasions. The first, to learn that his parents were sailing to India without him. The second, a little less than a year later, to be told that he was to sail for India to join them. So he worked it out: Avebury meant very bad news, or very good news.

This time it was his grandmother, accompanied by her two spinster sisters, who took him for a picnic. When he learned their destination, did he have premonitions? It would be reasonable to suppose some sort of emotion in him – hope, or dread, or simply resentment at being reminded. Again the news, when it came, seemed to splinter his vision. Harry had no recollection of India, and even the faces of his parents had faded rather desperately in his mind, so that they seemed to have certain existence only in the framed photographs that furnished his grandmother's house. He was puzzled, too, by a reserve in his grandmother, not knowing that this was a reflection of her anxieties. Belgium and Holland had fallen and, after Dunkirk, France. German forces were on the Channel coast, poised for invasion. Undoubtedly this was what had decided Harry's parents, far away in India. Whatever the perils, to health in India, to life on the long voyage out, the possible alternatives could not be contemplated. They wanted him with them.

None of this could be told to Harry, whose excitement was, perhaps deliberately, fanned by the gentle enthusiasms of his great-aunts. Blinded by sunlight within and without, he could see Avebury now as a shimmering, mythological promise, an ageless affirmation of life channelled out of the prodigious sweep of time and space; and himself as a part of this, mysteriously at one with its design; with its designers. His manifest, impassioned surrender to delight perhaps for a moment hurt his grandmother, who was graver, quieter than her sisters.

But: 'It will be a great adventure,' she said. For Harry, in his mind, it had already begun.

I have to lend Harry pieces of myself, of my memories.

It was his Welsh rather than his Wiltshire grandmother who accompanied him to India. They sailed from Liverpoool in the SS *Strathmore*, a P&O liner converted to troop-carrier. Over the Mersey, where they lay at anchor three days awaiting escorts, the restless searchlights every night probed the skies, and bombs fell on city and port. When they did sail two destroyers kept them company, buried in white seas, until they were through the Bay of Biscay. Then they were alone, left unescorted to outrun the U-boats. These, like invisible sharks, lurked somewhere in Harry's mind, but as a purely theoretical presence. He could imagine the night-time impact of torpedoes, the regimented panic of people scrambling for lifeboats, the icy clutch of the sea; but this *was* imagined, it was not real, or in a real sense conceivable. It was a story he had made up. From this, his first brush with fiction – a dangerous balancing act, as I have already remarked in one of these stories – he emerged unscathed. After six weeks at sea, innocent of all alarm, the ship reached Bombay.

It was a peculiar arrival, a landfall with no apparent land, for the ship anchored outside the harbour in thick fog. For two hours they lay there, the engines stilled, and out of the fog came hundreds, thousands of gigantic butterflies, fluttering wetly round the steel shrouds, impossibly large, far larger than Harry's hands that reached towards them. This, he supposed, was India – mythic, a glittering fantasy of exotic colour strayed from the pages of Sinbad. The image remained, printed with vivid clarity on the retina of

SOME MARLBOROUGH INVENTIONS

memory, but it was a memory, all the same, that he was never quite to trust, that despite its clarity seemed by its very nature to have the quality of a waking dream.

The fog lifted; the ship moved into the port. From the ship's shop, as a memento of the voyage, Harry bought (aided in this by his Welsh grandmother) a small box containing the materials to construct little pine-cone owls. When put together, for weeks they smelled powerfully of glue, and refused to stand on their legs. But by then, they (Harry, his father, his mother, who had come to meet him) had made the long railway journey from Bombay, northwards across India to the distant hills. Harry had now to consider his new home.

They lived in a long white bungalow of many rooms, with a narrow strip of half-wild garden, all terraced into the side of a steeply plunging hill. House and garden seemed filled with servants; whom Harry came to know, one by one, name by name. Anton, the bearer, was in charge indoors; Gupta, the *mali*, ruled the garden. There was a cook and a boy and a sweeper, and there was Old Man, who seemed to have no other name and was very old indeed, and shared with Ayah the charge of Harry. They all seemed to Harry, as he picked up a few words here and there of the two or three languages they spoke among themselves, more friends than servants. Their quarters, behind the bungalow, mud-walled and thatched, smelling of charcoal fires and strange spices, became familiar to him; once it was established that the Sahib and Memsahib had no objections, he was made welcome there.

Slowly, Harry began to learn India – but through a child's eye, uncluttered by adult apprehensions. His responses were often below the level of conscious thought, so that they sank completely out of sight and only returned, like surfacing logs, ten or twenty years later, to clutch him unexpectedly with that vivid mixture of grief and elation that India imprints on the European psyche.

These memories belong elsewhere. I have written some of them down, and soon I must pull a few of them out of the drawers, not unlike those other compartments of the mind, where I have stored them away. It is Harry's story I am telling now, but only a small part of it.

While India drew him ineluctably into its magic compass, there was still a counter force, that often haunted his dreams. In India, a part of him always yearned for England; as later, in England, he would yearn for India. The two poles of this telluric magnet tugged at his consciousness: somewhere between them, the equilibrium that he sought. I have come to see this as a metaphor for his life.

So he dreamed of England, and always of that corner folded into the North Wiltshire downs. Of windy skies and skylarks, of browsing sheep and brooding mysteries – earthworks and standing stones and burial chambers. But mostly of a house, fading a little in memory yet sharply etched in the night-scapes of his dreams: its mellow friendliness, the four eyes of its dormer windows, a stone bird-bath, an ancient yew, the steep drop over a brick wall into the paddock; a thatched summer-house, an orchard. River and water-mill; the rustle and shimmer of willow. Dreams.

Harry started school. Every morning four sweating, straining coolies hauled him in a rickshaw half a mile up the incredible slopes of the hill above the bungalow. Harry, his fair hair hidden under khaki topee in summer, leaned back against the jolting wooden seat, slightly scared of the angle, innocent of the image he presented (the *chota sahib*) in these ember-days of the Raj. Every afternoon, the same rickshaw waited for him, the coolies patient in the shade of a tree beside tilted shafts – but Harry generally preferred to walk, down that vertiginous hill; it seemed safer.

At school he wrote stories, and counted in French up to a hundred, and wrestled with simple divisions. In spare moments during the school day, and at home, he liked to read: Henty, and Masefield, and Buchan, and some strangely sophisticated tales (in Harry's eyes) about a man called Simon Templar, alias The Saint.

I have to ask myself if all this, or most of it, is not prevarication. Too much, or too little. I am trying to set out Harry for you as he was, as I remember him, at a particular moment in his history, to give him a context, and flesh and blood and bones. This is important, or what follows will make no sense.

Harry had been in India for a year. He was eight. And then his mother went for a month to Darjeeling, to stay with her own mother, the Welsh grandmother. Harry would have liked to go with her, and this was discussed quite seriously for a while; but in the end circumstances prevailed.

'It would mean missing a month of school,' his mother said. 'I'd love to have you with me, and in a way it would be good for you. The change. The chance to see more of India. But there'll be time for that. And school is important, Harry. You're doing so well, Miss Florian says. A break would set you back.'

Harry fretted. There was much about school he liked, but he didn't like the way it loomed now (and would again) as an imperative rather than a choice.

'You could teach me,' he argued. 'Like you did before, when we were in England. Or I could go to another school while we're staying with Grandma.' He saw this with such clarity; it seemed so reasonable. Wasn't it? 'I don't want you to go away,' he said stubbornly, when it became apparent his reason and theirs did not match. He knew the selfishness of this, but what he really meant and couldn't say, except silently to himself, was more frightening: I don't want to lose you again.

'You'll have me,' said Mr Spence hopefully, puffing quietly at his pipe, 'for what it's worth,' his eyes smiling gently; 'and Old Man, and Ayah, to keep us both in order. We'll survive.'

Harry was not so sure that he would.

The day came. They went down the hill together, to the clustered town and bazaar, and the station which was terminus to the little ratcheted single-track mountain railway that wound down steep foothills to the blue haze of the plains below.

'What have you forgotten?' Mr Spence asked anxiously of his wife. 'You must have forgotten something. If I were you, I should certainly have forgotten something.'

'Nothing,' she said serenely. 'Don't tease.'

'He always teases,' Harry said; distracted, as Mr Spence no doubt had intended, from his misery. There was only a minute to wait – another of Mr Spence's calculations. Whistles were blowing, the diesel engine blared a klaxon.

Harry clung to his mother for a last desperate kiss and then she was gone, climbing up into that shiny aluminium caterpillar, to reappear at an open window. She leaned out and down, stretching out her arms.

'Goodbye. Be good,' she said, to either or both of them. The platform was only inches higher than the track. Reaching up, Harry could no more than touch her fingers with his own. With a shuddering of engine acceleration, the two coaches began to slide away; their fingers were left to hold the air.

'Goodbye!' It was Harry's voice, hollow in his ears.

More than thirty years ago now, when I was living on a high plateau in the Horn of Africa, among hills that revived fleeting images of remembered hills in India, I wrote an earlier, rather different version of this story. The difference was partly of perspective, but also I covered some very different ground. That book was never published; a fat bundle of typescript, it has lingered, as I have said, with other accretions to the saga, in trunks and drawers while I travelled my life and the world, but always in my mind; perhaps, I thought, to be brought out one day and dusted off; given a new presence. At one point that distant work meets this other story so clamorously, with such a vivid appeal to memory, that I knew weeks ago I would have to open the drawer, take it out, brush it down: use it again. I have reached that point. So, for the next two or three pages I return, a long journey, to what I wrote all those years ago. I'm not sure what the consequence and outcome of this may be, for myself or my fiction. But I have to follow where the trail leads me.

One afternoon in August Harry and Mr Spence went by

rickshaw down that steep dry sandy lane to the station, half a mile below the bungalow. There was a small bazaar, then a street of more solid-looking shops, then the road followed the side of the hill for a few hundred yards, overlooking the oval of the race-course on the valley floor, and then they reached the station. There was a sleepiness about the little station with its single platform, stretched out under the afternoon sun, that tempered and lulled even Harry's excitement. Time slipped obliviously by, measured by drowsing scurvy dogs and clustered flies and the occasional lazy, unmotivated ringing of a bell in the station-master's office. Harry didn't notice Mr Spence's wry patience slowly give place to puzzlement, to a formless unease.

'Women,' said Mr Spence, 'are the very devil. Never expect, Harry, that they will ever fail to keep you waiting.'

Harry was accustomed to his father's rather complicated sense of humour; but he felt it was a bit unfair on his mother to blame her for the inefficiency of the railway company. She might have missed the train, but he didn't see how she could possibly have contrived to make it late, even to accommodate Mr Spence's ideas on the unpunctuality of women.

'She'll come,' he said. 'I'm thirsty. May I have a fizz, or a *nimbu pani*?'

An hour later the train still had not arrived, and they went home.

Harry had a late tea, drank iced lime-juice and read ten pages of a book called *The Outlaws of Sherwood Forest*. He shied away from speculation, or kept it so firmly at the back of his mind that it was almost invisible. The train had been delayed; he would see his mother in the morning. His father had disappeared, Old Man had gone out, grumbling, into the night, Ayah was somewhere being busy; it was Anton the bearer who came to tell him it was time he went to bed. Harry lingered in the bathroom, waiting for his father, but: 'He has gone out too,' said Anton. 'He will be back later. You go to bed now.' Harry gargled a strong solution of TCP, stinging his mouth and his throat which had been sore since tea-time. He let down the mosquito net, patrolled the room for scorpions, snakes and green crickets, finding none; and filled the air with a fine cloud from the Flit-gun beside his bed. He climbed carefully under the net, tucking it in after him, and called for Anton to turn off the light.

The bearer stood in the doorway, his face comically screwed up.

'Pouff!' he said. 'Harree sahib, you will die of all this Flit, I am always telling you.'

'But Anton. There's so many mosquitoes. And a huge cricket that sits on the net and looks at me. And anyway, it says "Harmless to People and Animals", on the tin.' A thought struck him. 'Anton, is a cricket an insect or an animal?'

'An insect, I should think.'

'So that's all right,' Harry said, disappearing under a sheet.

'Goodnight, Harree sahib.' Anton switched off the light.

When Harry woke up, the light was on again. He didn't know what time it was – it was timeless night. His father had pulled up one side of the mosquito net and was sitting on the bed. Mr Spence didn't seem to know what he was doing; or didn't know, perhaps, that he was not doing anything. His face was very quiet, just a little wrinkled, and he looked at Harry in a way that was oddly detached. His left hand, which had touched Harry to wake him, lay on the sheet; it fluttered almost imperceptibly, a small nervous betrayal that he could not control. He moved the hand and hid it from Harry.

'She's not coming.'

His voice was quiet and firm; stronger than his hand. And then: 'Ever.'

Harry never knew when he first understood. Certainly not at once; he looked anxiously at his father.

'It's not her fault,' he said. 'It was the train.'

Mr Spence seemed to smile, and he nodded slowly.

'Yes. It was the train.'

Intelligence struggled with sleep. Harry suddenly sat up. 'What – ' he said, 'what do you mean – ever?'

But Mr Spence was slowly standing up; his hands wanted to touch Harry, but they were afraid, or ashamed.

'It's too late,' he said. 'I shouldn't have woken you up.' And then, at the door, out of the darkness when he had turned out the light, 'We'll talk in the morning. Go to sleep, Harry.'

Probably Harry already knew when he woke up next morning; sleep could easily have brought understanding. Certainly, when a week later he and Mr Spence went down to the station once again in a rickshaw, a second rickshaw following behind piled high with luggage, certainly by then he knew. This time the train awaited them: the two glittering aluminium coaches and the engine. There were four soldiers on the platform, all carrying rifles, and before the train started they boarded it, two to each coach, and unslung their rifles. Some of the windows were still broken, and there were lines of bullet holes in the aluminium. Harry saw all this without surprise or curiosity, in silence. The holes that had been torn in him, unlike those in the aluminium, seemed to be self-sealing; his mind had swiftly closed round the dreadful scission of understanding, and trapped inside him all the things he could not look at.

That is how the story was first written. I didn't feel I could write it over again. It will have to serve. I have changed very little – a word here or there, some punctuation shuffled, a spelling mistake corrected.

Harry travelled most of the length of India, first with his father to Bombay, and then on with Mrs Graham to other hills in the south, to another school. All that is another story, the one I wrote a long time ago, and have briefly plundered here. A year later he was sent back to England. That was all of India he ever knew.

Harry, I like to think, sailed home in that third year of the war in the SS *Strathaird* – sister ship of the *Strathmore* which had brought him out. I like to think this, because it was at the same time and in the same ship – and at the same age as Harry – that I sailed home myself. We didn't meet; but we might have. I was sent home for much the same reasons as Harry – principally for what my parents considered, now that I was nine, a safer and more appropriate education than India could provide. I have been left to reflect on this for a lifetime, and I still can't decide whether they were right or not.

For company I had David – yes, the visitor from Porlock – and his younger brother who, I believe, had just learned dangerously to toddle. My uncle and aunt had recklessly offered, since they were going, to see me home.

I remember behaving rather badly on that ship. The captain was heard to mutter, darkly, that it was high time that boy was at school. I bring myself and a very real ship into my story now, not for any phantom shade of Harry Spence that might have flickered about the decks where I played so carelessly, so foolishly; but for memory of a little girl I encountered just once, as I remember it, when we were only two or three days at sea.

I think she was no more than five years old, which would have been David's age too, at the time. Her hair golden, tied in a scarlet ribbon. A white cotton dress, and ballet shoes – my memory insists on those. Her face was composed, but not solemn – a face, and eyes, that smiled easily. It was before I had begun to run wild. We met – I have no recollection now of how or why – on an upper deck, lined with lifeboats, behind the after funnel, where hot air and soot were sometimes blown down, scorchingly, on games of deck quoits. I don't think we played – I think it was just a conversation, and there is only one part of it that I can remember, across the arch of the years. She asked me where my father was, or perhaps I told her unasked, unwitting, out of something else we were saying.

'He's still in India,' I said. I expect I would have added that he was in the Navy.

SOME MARLBOROUGH INVENTIONS

'My daddy's up there,' she said. (Did she have a name, ever, for me? I don't remember.)

I followed her pointing finger, puzzled. It seemed to indicate the top of the mast. I looked, sensing I am sure the absurdity of this, for a sailor in the crow's-nest or at the masthead.

'Where? I can't see him.'

'He's in heaven,' she said, and danced away from me across the deck, her feet brittle and light and, I will swear, happy too. I never saw her again. Or if I did, the memory has vanished.

But I did, not much later, hear an explanation. I think it was at table, probably words spoken between my uncle and aunt.

'Such a pretty child. So awful for her. Her father was killed, in the Simla train.'

Just before I left Simla, the mountain train had been shot up, and several people killed: by bandits, by political dissidents, I still do not know. But I remember, when I took that train with my mother, on the first leg of the journey down to Bombay – I remember the lines of bullet holes in the metal, and the armed soldiers who escorted us.

Fiction, I insist, is as near as we can get to truth. If this one seems twisted, I have yet lived with the reality of it for more than thirty years – in a sense, for forty-five. Seven years after Harry's mother died in that mountain train, my own mother was killed in an accidental explosion in Ceylon, when I was far away in England. I have drawn the strings together – that is all.

We landed in Glasgow, sucking oranges, and travelled slowly overnight, sitting up to sleep in blacked-out carriages. At Paddington I was put into the charge of a GWR guard, and said goodbye to David and his family. I ate a spam roll which stuck in my throat, because I had nothing to drink. The train clattered west, the compartment full of elderly, kindly, inquisitive women. They were all going to Marlborough too; one of them was a friend and WVS colleague of Da, my grandmother. I basked in their admiration of my insouciant globe-trotting – all the way from India, through a world at war, and on my own.

When Harry arrived home, there were things he had to see – things that had haunted his Indian dreams. They began with the house, and spread outwards. His room, from which he could see the ash tree when he lay in bed. The lines of the garden, remembered after all. The summer-house, to celebrate which in that school in southern India he had written his first poem; only to see it betrayed, presently, by Judy who was his friend but who discovered it in his desk, stole it, exposed it to laughter. Time heals, and the summer-house itself knew nothing of his shame.

The river. The Mill. Above the hatches that deep slow reach, rippled at evening by a line of rising trout. Whistler's pool, a shrine of sunsets. The valley ascending through arable to the windswept downs, tracked by prehistoric paths. The woods, a carpet of bluebells in spring.

The Avebury Rings, and Silbury. The Wansdyke – Great Wall of Wiltshire. Evocation merging into invocation, for this is a land of mystery more than chronicle. It grew into Harry's bones.

There was also another lesson to be learned.

In the first spring of the war, shortly before he left for India, Harry and a friend had, somewhat joyfully, made their contribution to the war effort. In the paddock below the garden they had dug an air-raid shelter – a shallow ditch, roofed with sheets of corrugated iron and then turfed on top to fool enemy aircraft; it was just large enough for Harry and his eight-year-old friend to crawl inside and lie prone and squashed in the damp darkness. This, too, was a memory he had carried to India and back, and one of the first things he did on his return was to go and look for it. The air-raid shelter had vanished; subsumed by the percipient soil.

Undeterred, but now single-handed, Harry set about its reconstruction. He had done no more than remove a rectangle of turfs one afternoon, as nearly as he could remember on the spot where they had dug before, and rested from his labours, when he was summoned by his grandmother.

'Harry! What have you been doing in the paddock? Uncle Theodore is furious.'

'But we did it before,' Harry said. 'Geoffrey and me. Before I went to India. Nobody minded. We built an air-raid shelter, and it's disappeared. I only wanted to put it back.'

His grandmother sighed helplessly.

'Oh Harry. Why didn't you ask? And why did you want a shelter – were you frightened? But we don't get air-raids here – we're quite safe. And besides, we have the cellar.'

Impossible for Harry to explain. Building air-raid shelters had nothing to do with fear of air-raids. But Great-Uncle Theodore, back for some fishing leave from the war, was certainly to be feared. A small, remote, leathery man he seemed to Harry, who found him on the bridge over the Mill-pool hatches.

Uncle Theodore looked at him grimly.

'What do you mean by digging holes in the paddock?'

'It wasn't a hole. It was for the air-raid shelter. Like the one me and Geoffrey did before.'

But Uncle Theodore hadn't seen that one. He had been in North Africa patching up wounded soldiers. The hole in the paddock was a wound in the property he loved, and his love was not like Harry's, or of a kind Harry could understand. Nor could Uncle Theodore understand Harry.

'You deserve a thrashing,' he said. 'If you ever do anything like that again, I'll thrash you myself.' And Harry thought he probably would. He struggled with a sense of injustice. He had not intended mischief. Nobody understood him.

Uncle Theodore turned away, perhaps awkwardly aware of his own inexperience of children.

Many years would pass before Harry really understood the

lesson, or that it was not quite the one Uncle Theodore had intended. And even when he understood it, he could never really be said to have taken it to heart: that it is dangerous, if not impossible, to attempt to relive the past.

Stories from a Foreign Country

*in grateful memory
of
Charles Wrinch
who read all these stories, some of them
at the time they were written,
and who encouraged me through many lean
unpublished years*

A Preface to
Stories from a Foreign Country

The 'foreign country' is L.P. Hartley's: these nine stories come from a quite distant past, written in the late 'fifties and early to mid 'sixties. They are all previously unpublished – were not even submitted for publication, except for two. *Blackwood's* had taken a couple of my travel articles, and I sent them 'Moonlight Sonata'; but my aim was poor, or I had chosen the wrong target. I can assert my abiding faith in the story without a blush, because the best of it was not written by me, but by Christian Tual. That is the truth. I am only co-proprietor, so for what it's worth I make this public acknowledgement, and give it back to Christian. (I calculate the twelve-year-old I first met must now be nearing his fifty-fifth birthday.)

I have arranged the stories, as nearly as I can remember, in reverse order of their composition – this seems to me to give the whole double collection an abiding symmetry. Earliest of them all, then, was a novella: *The Athenians*. This was the other piece I tried to place – there were publishers who were backing me with some enthusiasm at the time; but it was considered too slight to stand on its own. At the very least I owe another public acknowledgement, here, to Peter Calvocoressi – with Chatto & Windus in those years – whose wise and patient guidance over several unpublished novels helped sustain my faith in myself as a writer. *The Athenians* is a very youthful fantasy, written when I was twenty-three – and it shows. But I still regard it with some indulgence; and even with a certain pride, that I evolved its theme a decade before the arrival of hippies, and flower children, and the fashion for dropping out.

A PREFACE TO STORIES FROM A FOREIGN COUNTRY

The five Italian stories were all written when I was living in Rome, between 1963 and 1967. The two very short pieces, 'La Parolaccia' and 'At Porta Portese', were the first in what I planned as a series of vignettes, perhaps to sell as a weekly column in one of the English Sunday newspapers; but the project died, before any were submitted. 'Il Traforo' was written well before the era of mass packaged holidays, so that Lawford and Margie must be seen as unusually daring examples of their kind; it is not, I think, a story that could be written in quite that manner today. Those who are curious about 'Dr Danakil's' odd pseudonym, and who don't already know its origin, will find the answer in L.M. Nesbitt's *Desert and Forest* – written by the first European, so far as I know, to travel in Danakil country and emerge alive and intact; or in Wilfred Thesiger's *The Life of My Choice*.

'The Flight from the Eagle's Nest' is, to my mind, the least satisfactory of these stories, but is included because its theme is one that has haunted me since earliest childhood. 'The Myth of Belamor', which would bring on a nervous breakdown in any competent PC's Spell Check (but not, I hope, in any of my readers), represents a different kind of haunting. It was written in the late 'fifties, at a time when nuclear holocaust seemed at least an outside chance among the several scenarios confronting our world. The threats today are different, but sufficient to keep the story topical, whether it is read as optimism or pessimism.

Together, these nine stories represent all that I wish to preserve of my short fiction from those years.

Marlborough – February, 1999

Anniversary Letter

Villa Borghese, the gardens. The spurious rebirth, said David Gamble silently to himself – for he had become adept at such secret conversations which his English urbane face, equally adept, concealed from the world – the spurious rebirth, spring, *primavera*, its false promise of beauty and hope revived, an annual and ingenious cheat. Crimson-beaked a blackbird, first perched, then hopping restlessly, pretending unconcern for passing feet across trim paths, sang the lie. Yet this natural and universal conspiracy failed to touch his chattering companion.

'And you know, *caro* David, my passion for speculation. I cannot let things rest – I have to know. So you must trust me. You must at least indulge my curiosity. I need to return, this morning, to that extraordinary scene. Curiosity,' he repeated with impish pleasure, 'compels me.'

Reluctantly David Gamble forced his mind to consider for a moment the urgent aberrations of his friend.

'What exactly did you see, you say?'

'A priest, *caro* David. A priest, who for certain inaccuracies of costume, among other things, I judged was *not* a priest. And a boy. Indubitably a boy, of perhaps thirteen years. In a boat – here, on the lake.'

'But that is not very extraordinary. In Rome?'

Giacomo danced on his little feet and his arms flew round him, beating the air impatiently like the wings of a humming-bird.

'You are too stupidly English. But wait – forgive me! I have not yet come to the extraordinary part.'

I am always, David thought, waiting for the extraordinary part.

Nine years ago, he remembered: also waiting, also in these gardens. Waiting for the extraordinary part, with a ring in his pocket. His face younger, he supposed, by many more than nine years than the face that accused him this morning when, from force of habit, he shaved it – but even then, nine years ago, slightly faded, slightly tired, with that distinguished Weltschmerz of the well-bred Englishman he once was, but which he already suspected might be a mask for a more essential, mortal weariness. Preened, groomed, looking the promising young diplomat he secretly hoped to be mistaken for, David Gamble, junior Representative of the British Council, had waited for an appointment with the extraordinary.

'Your imagination, *caro* David, or I should say your lack of imagination, is sordid. I shall describe the scene.' Giacomo sketched the air with fluttering fingers, turning every few steps as they walked to tap David's arm or the bottom button of his waistcoat or a quarter of an inch in front of his nose. 'I have read somewhere that nine Englishmen out of ten – that is, Englishmen of your education, shall we say? – are shut into dark cupboards when they are six years old, by their nannies; or are shown something disgusting by the gardener, in the tool shed. A theory which I doubt for certain of its premises but which the results, *caro*, force me to believe *en principe*. Therefore, attend. This priest who was not a priest, was rowing the boat. He was decidedly hot. I mention this first because it was the most noticeable thing about him – except of course for the cardinal fact of his imposture, and that in any case was not so very noticeable, *unless* to an expert eye. To me it was, as you say, a sore thumb. He was sweating – whether from unaccustomed clothing or from unaccustomed labour, I would hesitate to say: but probably it was for both these reasons.'

Pessimism, in those now distant days, David reflected through this chatter, had not yet become a habit. There could still be something voluntary, something of a choice exercised by intelligence, in his belief in the essential treachery of the world. Or he could at least suspend that belief, that terror, for long enough to take a step that seemed to contradict it. He could commit himself to love. Surely he had not married Teresa in the absolute certainty of disaster.

His mind strayed over that spring of nine years ago. They had indeed walked this very way, treading he had said exultantly the roof-tops of Rome, because whatever else he doubted one thing was too certain to be assailed: his love found the proofs it craved in a heady sensation that somehow the whole city had crept inside it, had become a part or a share. And she, Teresa, had flashed his ring on her finger, as her teasing eyes had flashed more secret messages. It was his Englishness that had conquered her, he knew – so that he too was able to laugh at his own carefully cultivated public image. His very sober dark suit, his stiff white collar and club tie, for a moment had assumed the office of disguise. The real David Gamble was altogether more remarkable, and unsuspected – so briefly he had seen the world held mesmerized beyond his flickering sword-point; briefly, everything had been possible.

He became aware again of Giacomo, tirelessly bobbing along beside him, Giacomo who was always so intrigued by his own volubility.

'All this of course was yesterday, but I have reasons to suppose that perhaps they will be here again today. And I want your opinion, *caro* David.'

'My opinion?' David Gamble, nine years older, and stouter, but certainly not nine years nearer understanding: a mosaic of fragmentary persons threatening to disintegrate. Opinion, like so much else, had fled him down the alley of the years; but he retained, at least, a professional skill in sustaining conversations from which his conscious mind had secretly withdrawn.

'I have none. You haven't told me enough.'

'Your opinion of that unlikely scene. Come – or at least an explanation.'

But explanations were yet another element in the shifting, treacherous earth beneath his feet, in a world that no longer offered even the illusion of solidity. They had walked by this same avenue, nine years ago, with a surprising lightness – as though the resolution that had ended months of doubts, of hesitations on both sides, had at last changed something in their separate characters, rather than merely in their situation. He had surrendered to an unfamiliar recklessness, daring himself to delight in this. And she? – she had surprised him again, with a strange gentleness folded into her face: a forgiving – not for the past, but for the future. For Teresa's uncertainties had been at least as mysterious as his own, and now she had as mysteriously shed them. 'We are safe,' she had said, and for a space David, who had never believed anything was safe, was able to believe this.

'What a splendid chance,' Giacomo said, 'meeting you here this morning. I could not have hoped for a more impartial witness.'

'It was not chance – that I was here.' David stopped, and seized Giacomo roughly by his fastidious elbow. 'It was not! It was ordained! Everything is ordained.'

Everything is determined, he thought. It is not chance that *I* am here, obeying the implacable dictate of time's prestigious patterns, driven to invest with meaning, or at least with mystery, an anniversary. No, not chance – but that incredible letter, reposing clamorously in his pocket.

Giacomo raised polite, surprised, arched eyebrows.

'*Caro* David, what have I done?' His distress for David's vehemence was unfeigned, but like all his moods elusively comic. There was nothing comic about David's distress.

'The *day*, Giacomo. Didn't you know that a year ago today – '

'?'

'Teresa – '

Giacomo's dancing hand struck his own cheek with more than symbolic force.

'I am a fool, *caro*. A miserable fool. How should I not remember?' His face confessed. 'I remember.'

David Gamble, icily master of himself again, walked on, Giacomo falling into step beside him.

'No, you do not remember. You calculate, or guess, or

know – but to remember, you have to experience.' His eyes and his voice strayed. 'And you never knew very much about all that, anyway.'

Giacomo, who prided himself on knowing everything about his circle and far beyond it, might have taken this as an insult, but instead responded with unusual humility.

'Tell me,' he said. 'Tell me, *caro*, that I may make amends.' The flush on his cheek had begun to fade.

'I was in London,' David said heavily, '– the day when it happened. The day of the accident. As soon as I got back, summoned by telegram, I went there – to the intersection by the *piazza*, where they had told me – where I looked. It was almost as though I were looking for traces, for blood, for some sign of her – of it – on the road.'

Giacomo was subdued, squashed. His little satyr's face was compressed into lines unnaturally sober, ludicrously solemn, sympathetic.

'I felt guilty. Because I was not there, I hadn't been with her.' But why, David wondered, did he find it so easy to tell him this, the small disreputable part of the truth, and so difficult, so impossible to tell him the rest that might excuse him, if he cared? 'You see,' he said, not knowing if this were explanation or confession, 'you see, I loved her.'

Giacomo nodded gloomily. He took a very large, very gaudy silk handkerchief from a tightly tailored breast pocket, and blew his nose – obtrusively, but with nice calculation.

'Would you prefer,' he asked anxiously, 'to turn back? But it is only a little way now.'

If we could carry our symbols consciously, now David Gamble thought: commodities in a traveller's case, to be brought out and displayed at the exact moment, to the exactly appropriate customer. Would he like to turn back? He flinched at the cruel irrelevance of the question.

'We have come so far,' he said, conscious of the irony in this, '– we might as well go on.'

And presently Giacomo took his arm, and held him. 'We have arrived.' His voice was pitched low, aware that it was an intruder. 'And I think – yes, I was right. They have returned.'

The scene was approximately as Giacomo had earlier described it. On the leaf-green water of the little lake floated, dreaming in dappled sunlight, a square tall-sided wooden boat, its paint flaked almost to the bare boards. Black-cassocked a priest sat to the oars, which rested now motionless on the water. He was indeed sweating, his face remarkably red. In the stern, facing the priest, lolled a boy, fair-haired, dressed in a blue shirt and white cotton trousers, one bare slender arm trailing over the side of the boat so that a pointing forefinger cut the surface of the water in a pattern of ripples. There was something in his appearance, either in his clothes or perhaps merely in his languid pose, faintly evoking France – or Elgarian, Edwardian England: something indefinable, hinting at long-forgotten summers, of cool elegance under blazing decadent suns.

A voice from the lake shore, from a group of people incongruously collected there by the water, suddenly awoke this sleeping scene, an intrusion as abrupt and untimely as a stone dropped into the centre of the lake itself, disturbing its dreamy placidity. The priest pulled on the oars, the boat lurched forward, the water parted round the boy's trailing finger, tracing a double line of dancing whorls, a miniature wake soon swamped by the greater motion of the boat. They (the boat, the priest, the boy) in their imposed unity turned towards the shore, towards the group from which the voice had hailed them. But to David Gamble watching them, that unity did not seem true. Something clamoured the illusion, insisting that the picture was somehow incomplete, or that it was only accident or a temporary design that had brought them together. He felt his own interest in that scene grudgingly stir, as though after all there was something for him here – something that might bear upon his private agony.

'Is this the extraordinary part?' The words escaped him, and he realized that the thrown stone of those words splashing in the lake had not entirely woken him from his own odylic and eternal dream.

'Wait,' said Giacomo, with a peculiarly eager patience. 'And look.' He pointed – not to the boat, but to the bank; where the group had parted to reveal, perched on three legs, pointing its black eye like the barrel of some primitive machine-gun at the boat advancing towards it, a large ciné-camera.

David Gamble felt a swift collapse of interest. A film company. Explanations, he thought, are always a sort of surrender: they contribute not to truth but to defeat, adding each time their measure of disillusionment. But Giacomo was still smiling, and hopping again from one pointed shinily-shod foot to the other, mentally rubbing together his neat little hands.

'Look, *caro* David, closely at the priest.'

The boat had turned and was pulling out to the middle of the lake again, so that the priest's florid rather heavy face was turned towards them. David Gamble looked.

At Enrico Vanni.

'Do you know him?' Giacomo seemed very certain of his question.

'Yes. I do.'

And then, to fill the silence between them: 'He has shaved off his moustache.'

Giacomo slapped his thigh triumphantly. 'Of course! I knew there was something, but I couldn't remember. I couldn't place him.'

'I suppose they thought it wouldn't look right. For a priest.' Desperately scrambling up this conversational scree, David tried not to see the abyss below him.

'Let us wait, *caro*, for a word with him when they have finished. My curiosity is a fever, I confess. What does it mean, this scene they play over and over again to their camera?'

On the lake Enrico Vanni rowed and sweated. A middle-aged, tolerably successful film actor of character parts; a man who might have been handsome once; a man of modest ambitions, he would probably claim. His single most remarkable feature was his face – heavy and Englishlooking. David had always been fascinated by that face, because it so contradicted the fluent Italian syllables of its wearer's speech; it had this perpetually renewable capacity to surprise.

He looked at it now, dispassionately; calculating. It was, of course, older. They were all older. Or dead. For it was a long way behind him, the time when he had known Enrico Vanni. Theirs was a *comitiva* to which David had felt secretly flattered to be admitted – actors, artists, writers, mostly of moderate talent, some with over-optimistic ambitions, although one at least, Russo the sculptor, had since made an international name for himself. And Enrico Vanni. And Teresa.

David had liked Enrico. There had been something English in his temperament as well as in his face, a calm that sometimes provided relief from the febrile Latin enthusiasms of the others. His dog, a massively built young Boxer, he called George – the uncompromising English name an extension of Enrico's own image. They lived (Enrico and George) a few miles removed from Rome, in the old imperial port of Ostia, and David remembered an evening party held in that penthouse flat, a summer night soon after he had first met Teresa. There was a wide terrace where they sat under a trellis of vines, the sky hot with brilliant stars. Suddenly, in an excess of mindless exuberance, George had leaped the two-foot parapet, to fall three storeys to a concrete parking lot below. In shocked silence they had peered over the edge, to see the dog, equally shocked but miraculously unhurt, limping stiffly away into the darkness. What had impressed David most, and lingered most lovingly in his memory, was to see, when he turned to Teresa, the tears slowly rolling from her overflowing eyes.

His own eyes withdrew, reluctantly, from the past; he realized they were still fixed upon that face. Was it the face of an enemy? The question floating through his mind eluded meaning. David Gamble no longer had any enemies. A man requires a certain value, he reflected, a certain talent, if he is to have enemies.

'He was a friend of yours, I remember,' said Giacomo. 'I remember you saying, once.'

'Of Teresa's, really.' He marvelled at his cool and steady voice. 'Before we were married. At night clubs, and parties. Afterwards, we saw less of him. Then nothing. Teresa rather gave up that particular circle.'

That was true enough. The retreat had been hers. But it left unanswered the question of his own connivance.

The boat was turning. Along the bank they could hear the camera, and David wondered uneasily for a moment whether it had embraced him in its scope, because the boat was now very close to the spot where they stood.

Enrico had not seen them; or if he had seen, had shown no sign of recognition. David could not risk catching his eye, so when the boat slid past them he looked instead at the boy.

And the boy, at precisely this moment, looked at David Gamble.

The vision of the boy seemed to seize his eye: the placid face leaped to meet him, to fill his sight with its familiar lines. The world tilted, and his mind whirled. It could not be.

'Teresa!' he cried; and plunged away.

Giacomo touched his friend's arm solicitously.

'*Caro*, what is the matter?'

Dear God. Teresa. He choked, his eyes filling with tears. The Council's ex-Representative was in no shape to deal with questions.

'I must get away – I'm sorry – for a moment.'

He walked, blindly, Giacomo beside him, until they came to a wooden bench set between shrubs by the edge of the path, and there he sat down.

'You must excuse my outburst,' he said presently – yet knowing that nothing he said could seal up this calamitous breach in his defences. 'I was taken by surprise. A combination of circumstances that are hard to credit, but nevertheless they occurred. You see, this morning I had a letter from Teresa.'

Giacomo looked, appalled, at his companion.

'*Caro* David, what are you saying? Teresa died. A year ago today, you reminded me.'

David fumbled wearily in his pocket, but allowed his hand to remain there.

'No, I am not mad. I had a letter from Teresa, today. An anniversary letter, I suppose it might be called.' He spoke in a flat unemotional tone that only seemed to increase Giacomo's agitation. 'You remember: I was in London when she died. She wrote to me on the morning of that day – this letter.' It came from his pocket now, but he did not offer it to Giacomo. 'Something very peculiar happened to it.'

Giacomo was listening with the twitching attention he accorded to anything rare and unusual. David Gamble continued, speaking in a thin historical voice.

'The year after we were married, I was posted to Chile. We were there two years, until the Centre was destroyed in the earthquakes and we were moved to Brazil for the rest of that tour. Then we were two years in Beirut, before I was sent back here as Representative.

'I can't explain this – it defies reason – but her letter has been following the same trail all this last year. It went to London. It went to Chile and Brazil and the Lebanon. Now, a year late, or a lifetime, it reaches me in Rome: where it was written.'

David Gamble was no longer talking to Giacomo; his bewilderment was addressed more secretly to himself. He did not know how much Giacomo heard, or understood. He did not care.

For that moment by the lake had seized him, had ground him between millstones of possibility, more terrible even than the letter. And the letter itself had become a part of that moment, reflected in the cool eyes of a boy he had never seen before, nor even suspected.

He had acknowledged, sadly but without questioning it, Teresa's childlessness. Life liked to play him such tricks. So now, his mind in its agony cried out to his dead wife – Teresa, what does your letter mean? The letter, and the boy, and the slightly florid actor once his friend, Enrico Vanni – anonymous in the letter but now, surely, declared?

For a whole year, since she died, he had reproached himself for his lack of faith, only to have that reproach explode about him now. *Dear David,* she had written, *I must go back to him – to them. I am leaving you.* The words were a year old, but they retained their fresh shape. And time had cruelly, lovingly laid upon them its crust of irony. For she had not known how final, how literal her words would prove: within hours of writing them Teresa had, indeed, left him. Forever. Had she, in the instant of death, realized through her agony the truth of her lying letter? He could after all hope, in a spasm of thwarted love, that her last thought instead had been with that still anonymous son.

He would like to have known. The boy must have been already four or five years old when he first met Teresa. Enrico's son, surely. There were so many things he would like to have known; so many he would never know.

The ex-Representative stayed for a while sitting on the bench. Giacomo, ever a man of tact and sensibility when he remembered, had gone back to the lake. Spring continued to put out new leaves, to open flowers, to tell all the old lies. David Gamble sat there, listening to them.

'La Parolaccia'

Alex telephoned one evening last February, a few days after the snow had disappeared and the fountains thawed.

'I think it's time you went to *Cencio's*,' he said.

Expatriates, everywhere, are a proud race, and I wasn't keen to reveal my ignorance.

'I'm not sure,' I hedged, 'if we can, tonight.'

'That's all right, then,' Alex suavely interrupted. 'Nine o'clock at your place. Be careful how you dress.'

He rang off, leaving me to ponder this unhelpful advice.

'Sabrina,' I said, 'Alex has invited us to *Cencio's*. What should we wear? He seems to think it important.'

'Oh hell,' she said (she said it in Italian, but expatriates are naturally adept in the feeling nuances of their adopted language). 'Something very inconspicuous.'

'What – exactly – is *Cencio's*?'

'A *trattoria*. In Trastevere. You'll hate it.' Sabrina was very vague. She seemed disinclined to say more.

At nine o'clock, with a punctuality that was probably intended as a pointed but mistaken comment on my Englishness, Alex was ringing at our garden gate. He was dressed impeccably, with that sober French elegance that we like to pretend is the prerogative of Savile Row. I handed Sabrina into his gleaming Lancia and eased my shabby tweeds and myself into the back seat. Alex whisked us across Rome, nimbly through the traffic, urbanely chatting. He seemed exceptionally pleased with himself.

Now resident for more than a year in Rome, I consider myself an expert on Trastevere. I know which gaudy tourist spots to avoid and which, patronizingly, to patronize. I know half a dozen little restaurants where good food goes for a relative song, and a song or two for the price of a sambuca or a grappa. But until that February I did not know *Cencio's*. Or '*La Parolaccia*' – its fonder, more familiar name.

My unimaginative (perhaps prudish) dictionary translates this: 'ugly word, bad language'. It means, roughly, any four-letter obscenity, and particularly those that derive from the rich vocabulary of the Roman dialect.

Le nostre specialità. In other restaurants when those words occur on the menu, they are culinary; or they might apply to specialities of décor or music. *Cencio's* speciality is verbal: raunchy, raw, and often cruel. The specialists are not the cooks, but the waiters; their talent, and their aim, to insult a masochistic clientèle.

It began quite mildly, as we entered a small, plain, typical Trastevere *trattoria*. A waiter welcomed us with an elaborate bow and a wicked smile. He turned to the tables that were already filled.

'*Signori!*' His voice stentorian, silencing the rattle of knives and forks and tongues. 'We are honoured tonight. A special welcome for His Excellency, Fidel Castro!'

My expatriate beard began to bristle. Alex, beside me, chuckled.

The waiter flicked his fingers importantly to another waiter.

'Quickly! A table – for two and a half.' Sabrina drew herself up to her full height of five dignified feet and two inches. We sat down; and ordered – because *Cencio's* is, after all, also a restaurant.

I realize now that we were lucky. An elderly, cultured and witty Frenchman, a beautiful young Italian, however diminutive, and a shabby bearded Englishman, would normally have been sitting ducks to the agile imaginations of '*La Parolaccia*'s' waiters. But we escaped almost unscathed after that chopfallen and mortifying entrance, because that night they had an even better target. At the table next to us there was a honeymoon couple from Sicily, with a Roman friend.

It soon became clear that this Roman was less than a true friend to his Sicilian guests; he must have brought them there (as Alex had brought me), guilefully, without a word of warning. The waiters were overjoyed. They gathered round the table in ribald conversation; they sang songs that would have brought a blush to the withered cheeks of Catherine the Great. They speculated with bland interest on the bridegroom's capacity and the bride's virginity. They sang eloquent, crude hymns to the delights and pitfalls of matrimony. Every now and then, accompanied by two guitars, the torturers would break exuberantly away to claim other victims at other tables; but they found little sport in the rest of us, it was merely a gesture, a reminder of our vulnerability if we laughed too loudly. There is no privileged class at *Cencio's*.

Afterwards, when we returned to the Lancia licking the wounds to our self-esteem, I turned on Alex.

'It was horrible,' I said. 'Disgustingly cruel.'

'In the worst of taste,' Alex agreed cheerfully. 'I knew you would enjoy it. But I expect there was a lot you didn't understand.'

Expatriates don't like to admit to difficulties with dialect. But all the way back in the car, I had Sabrina retrospectively translating for me.

On the whole, I am grateful to Alex. Since last February I have had somewhere to take all those people I secretly and uncordially dislike. Or, better still, to which I can recommend them with a sanguine enthusiasm, and without risking the thinness of my own skin.

Chacun à la sua dolce vita.

At Porta Portese

It used to be the smart, recherché thing, to go to Porta Portese around *mezzanotte* of a Saturday, and dig about in the rubbish carelessly or lovingly displayed along half a mile of street, like amateur archaeologists given the run of a newly discovered but doubtfully authenticated Pharoah's tomb, picking over the pieces in the hope of uncovering some priceless discarded object (almost anything, be it old enough and odd enough and above all *adaptable*) that might be bought for a beggar's handful of lire.

The smart bought worm-holed gold leafed candlesticks rifled from churches, rickety spinning-wheels, cast-iron coffee-grinders, to convert into lamps and lamp-standards; carved prayer stools to turn into bedside tables; lumps of weather-eroded marble to decorate their penthouse terraces. The recherché concentrated on furniture, with an eye to restoration rather than adaptation. A different kind of imagination was required in these cases – the kind that could see possibilities of restoration in twisted skeletons of age-blackened wood that the ungifted would hesitate to carry home even to feed the kitchen fire.

The most curious thing about this most curious midnight market was that nearly everything came from Naples. There were Roman interlopers who had transported their stuff across a few negligible streets from the antique and junk shops that proliferate around Piazza Navona and the Pantheon. But the initiates, the vociferous, gesticulating genii of Porta Portese, were Neapolitan

They began to arrive on Saturday afternoon: small lorries, groaning under mountains of rope-lashed furniture – little Fiat *cinquecentos* packed to the seams and the ceiling with pictures and porcelain, candlesticks, ormolu clocks, muskets, swords, ploughshares. All evening they would unpack their cars and lorries, and set out this mass of bric-à-brac on the street, in invisibly demarcated squares as precise and inviolable as the lineaments of a cadastral map. In the evening a few buyers would begin to appear, anxious to take advantage of *la prima vendita*.

Neapolitan superstition sides with the buyer only once: for the first sale of the night at any stall, you may more or less name your own ridiculous price – its acceptance without argument or rancour is a sort of *portafortuna*, a handsel offered to ensure the trader's profits through the rest of the night. Thereafter, the bargaining tenacity of these Neapolitans would outcountenance a Merchant of Venice.

All the same, two years ago wonderful things could still be done at Porta Portese after midnight, long after the first sale – if you had a keen eye, and knew what you wanted.

Sabrina's eye was very keen, and she wanted a square and sorry-looking object that might once have belonged, roughly, to the genus table. It was scratched, and black, and crusted with about a century of dust and dirt, and it was worm-eaten (a good point, this, the owner insisted – a sort of certificate of antiquity), and the top opened to reveal a series of sunken trays and compartments criss-crossed with cobwebs. At a hazard, a gaming table. Fifteen thousand lire were asked, and I tugged in panic at Sabrina's sleeve. It was a horrible object.

Sabrina shrugged me off, and suggested to the vendor that his table could hardly be mentioned decently in the same breath as *five* thousand lire. Battle had been joined. There was nothing left to me but to step hurriedly out of the line of fire, and hang on to my wallet.

Some minutes later I found that I had bought Sabrina's table for ten thousand lire, the price including transport to our door.

After a few days, and the expenditure of a further three thousand lire, the table came back from the restorer. I admit that I was shaken. The piece remained unsophisticated, but its quality had been, so to speak, unveiled. The restorer claimed that it was composite, the top half being French, from the middle of the eighteenth century, and the legs a later Italian and nineteenth-century addition. He offered us sixty thousand lire for it.

I am predictably human when it comes to making a quick five hundred percent profit, but in this case I am glad that Sabrina vetoed my immediate mercenary reaction. Our table is much admired by everyone who sees it, and I enjoy their respectful admiration when I tell them airily how I picked it up at Porta Portese for a mere ten thousand lire – I had thought Sabrina might like it.

But we seldom go back there now. Porta Portese is no longer recherché – and much too smart. Everybody goes to Porta Portese. It is not that we object to everybody, but they have spoiled it: the point is that if, for instance, such a table should ever turn up there again, in the same state of horrible and unrecognizable dilapidation in which we found ours, you wouldn't get away with it now for anything less than a hundred thousand lire – not even as a *prima vendita*.

The Human Heart of Dr Danakil

'No, I don't think we have met before. But your face, of course, is familiar to me – to us all, may I say? Permit me to introduce myself: Danakil – Sergio Danakil, *chirurgia* my humble profession. Not that I am altogether unknown – I may make a modest claim to some small successes in my field. But believe me, my dear sir, I do not forget that you are a master in yours – which is my poor excuse for the discourtesy of addressing you thus uninvited and unintroduced. Perhaps you would accept a drink? – a small *aperitivo*, to mark the occasion – a memorable occasion for me sir, I assure you – campari? pernod? strega?

'Ah, you prefer a stronger tipple. From the – excuse me – from the barbaric north. But admirable. A man's drink, and not without medicinal value, or so we can easily persuade ourselves. *Scozzese*, from a cold country, I believe: no wonder their native ingenuity has led them to fire the blood of the world. Chin chin. Yes, a deplorable expression, but I have learned, sir, in my moderately long and modestly successful life to bend, even if I do not bow, to fashion. You are so clearly a man of culture. I feel, unlikely though it may at first sight seem, that we have a great deal in common.

'No – I do not habitually come here. Let me confess: night clubs hardly befit my profession or character – and then, my taste generally tends towards something quieter. Perhaps you would understand me better – you must pardon my presumption, sir – if I admit to an occasional but irresistible urge to *act* out of character. Again, I have in common with a large part of the human race, its capacity for curiosity. This evening, I assure you, is quite an adventure for me. I have, indeed, stepped right out of my familiar world. I would even admit to having felt some slight stirrings of alarm, when I first entered – to see so many famous faces of your profession, sir – and then, most distinguished of all, your own! Even those that were not familiar to me were somehow, unmistakably, famous. What, I asked myself, is Sergio Danakil doing among such glittering people? Where did he find the courage for such a ruffle? (You must excuse me, sir, if my English is imprecise.)

'You flatter me, sir. I am too well aware of my limitations (as a man of the world, shall we say?) to suppose that the conversation of a middle-aged surgeon can be of more than the most passing interest to a person of your quality. But I am grateful for your kindness – believe me, sir, I am. Dare I hope that you, too, may find a momentary stimulus, a renewal of strength (shall we say?), from an hour's contagion in an unfamiliar world? That much of an excuse I will allow myself. You are indeed kindness itself, sir.

'But your glass is empty. Another whisky? No, sir, I protest – this evening I am your host – you will grant me that pleasure? You are, after all, a guest in my fair city – I think I may call it fair with confidence.

'I beg your pardon – I said that I have long been an admirer of your work – yes, I use the term advisedly, in its artistic sense. Indeed, sir, you are an artist, even if your modesty does not permit you to claim that title for yourself – an artist: I insist. Ah, the silver screen! Yes, I know that I date myself by that admission – to your generation, sir, the screen is more often multicoloured. Yet somehow, I feel you are a man of sufficient discrimination and taste to share at least a little of my regret – my wishful nostalgia for past glories. If you will permit me an epigram – silence is silver, or so it used to be. Perhaps I might be bold enough to add that it is rare in your profession, my dear sir, rare to encounter a real artist. But in you I recognize, unhesitatingly – yet now I do hesitate, for you will doubtless mock my presumption – I recognize a fellow artist. Yes, sir, I dare repeat the claim: a *fellow* artist – for surgery, in its small way, is surely also an art. I too, through such skill as I may have acquired in my profession, in my humble way, am an artist. Indeed, let us drink to that. To art, sir! To those frail and enduring monuments of human aspiration, our separate works of art – yours, sir, and mine!

'I feel that our evening – you will permit me to call it *ours*? – is going to be a great success. Would you care to move from the bar to a table, where we can be more comfortable? I will order a bottle – that we no longer need to interrupt ourselves, so tiresomely, in calling for a waiter. But certainly, sir, I leave the choice of table entirely to you. No, please, I am indifferent – it is of no importance to me where I sit – make your choice, sir, I will take the other chair.

'Aha! I see that you like to place yourself where you can survey the rest of the room. I trust you will not take it amiss if I say I can appreciate your choice. The elegance of the women here, to say nothing of their beauty, is extraordinary. But alas! sir, I am not as young as I once was; staid middle-age dampens the most ardent of fires in the end. I can still allow myself to admire, but my heart, I must confess, no longer follows my eye. Not that I hold myself, if we are considering women, in the smallest way unfortunate: on the contrary, I am a lucky man – an unbelievably lucky man. My wife, sir, some years younger than myself, is as beautiful, I may claim without prejudice, as any of the women in this room. Yes, I am indeed lucky. Do I look the sort of man to be married to one of the most beautiful women in all Rome?

'Ah! – honesty, you see, compels you at last to be silent – you cannot pretend not to be a little surprised. Or perhaps your silence politely signifies your disbelief? But I have no motive for lying. You must believe me.

'Allow me to refill your glass. And a little ice? Yes – I suppose a man in your profession, particularly one as handsome as yourself – I insist! – must meet and no doubt conquer a variety of fascinating women. Something tells me, sir, just to look at you, that your *galanteries* must be irresistible to the fair sex. I confess, I feel a little retrospective envy – if I had had your opportunities, my dear sir, at your age! To be able to look round a roomful of beautiful women, and take your pick in the certainty of being accepted. No sir, you are too modest. I do not believe there is a woman here who would refuse you.

'Another drink. No, I insist – the pleasure is mine. Entirely.

'Speaking, if I may for a moment, as a medical man, I would hazard that you are feeling just the least bit run down? – a little lassitude? headaches, perhaps? Yes indeed, I do understand the demands of your profession: overwork, undoubtedly overwork is the cause. And what better physic could I prescribe for that than relaxation? My dear sir, it is nothing – it is not even, except in the most general way, within my field: I am a surgeon, not a physician. But I am delighted to be of such service as I can. I assure you, a little indulgence – even a little over-indulgence – is often actually beneficial in such cases. The stimulus of contrasts, my friend – may I, without offence, call you my friend? Indeed? I feel that the brevity, the chance nature of our acquaintanceship, is somehow irrelevant – I have the warmest of feelings for you already.

'I suppose you must have many friends here tonight – or at any rate colleagues of your profession? Really, I find it most flattering that you should elect to pass your time with me: most flattering, in the circumstances. I must admit that I would be feeling very lost if I had not had the good fortune to fall into conversation with you. I should probably, long before now, have taken myself disconsolately home.

'My wife? Alas, my friend, my wife has been gravely ill. She is – away, the house is empty. My evenings, particularly, when the day's work is done, I find *sadly* empty. But my troubles are no concern of yours – I am boring you. Enough. Let us fill our glasses, let us return to that spirit of celebration in which we began our evening.

'This is such an unusual experience for me that I am determined to taste it to the full.

'But my dear fellow, are you feeling all right? – you look decidedly unwell. My behaviour is unpardonable – I sit here chattering away and all the time you are ill, suffering – no, you cannot hide it from me. The whisky, you say? A trifle *allegro*? But I blame myself, indeed I do. You must allow me to make amends, to see you home. I insist. No, I insist. I have a positive duty, I might even presume to say a right. Waiter! *Senta!* – a taxi please, this gentleman and I are leaving. And the bill, *per piacere. Grazie a Lei.* My friend, I have an absolutely brilliant idea. We will go first to my surgery, it is only ten minutes away, where I happen to have a small quantity of what I might describe as a Bacchic panacea; it is miraculous stuff, I promise you. Indeed, I believe you will feel so revived by its properties, that you will be dragging me back here to open another bottle. Shall we go? Please feel free to take my arm without embarrassment. For an establishment whose *raison-d'être* is the sale of alcoholic stimulants, this place has a tactless profusion of badly lit stairs. Come, we ascend from the Underworld. A sop for Cerberus, *mille grazie, buona notte*, and here is our taxi waiting for us. Allow me. After you, my friend.

'You are comfortable? Excellent. And what a beautiful night it is! I wonder sometimes why what we call night life insists on burying itself as far from the night as it can? Ah yes, driver: Via Nessunonome Tredici. Yes, thirteen. You know it? Good. Then we can relax, my dear friend, and very soon succour will be at hand.

'I cannot apologize sufficiently for my thoughtless behaviour. Of course, in my stupidity it never occurred to me – that you might already have been celebrating, before – before we met. How thankful I am that I should have the means to make such practical amends. You must allow me to make you a present of a small phial of my panacea, for no doubt there will be other occasions – ah, youth! my dear friend, youth!

'But here is the street, already. On the right-hand side, driver – the house with the white-painted gate posts. If you would drive in: you will find there is room to turn. No, don't wait. I have my own car here. I shall escort my friend presently to his hotel.

'Please, my dear friend, put an arm round my shoulder –

I shall endeavour to support you, although I am somewhat small and you so remarkably well-made. One moment while I find the key. There. And now the passage light. Ah, that is better. These rooms on the left comprise my surgery and offices. Naturally, as a rule I do no more than conduct consultations and make my preliminary examinations here – any surgical work I would normally undertake at the hospital. But I am proud of my little surgery – it is equipped for emergencies and those minor operations that would not justify the expenses of a hospital. There, against the wall – you see a small sterilizing plant for my instruments – anaesthetics – specially installed lighting –

'But my poor friend, forgive me! My thoughtless enthusiasm. Sit down – yes, there on the table, it doesn't matter. How can I expect you to feel interest in my surgery, when there is only one thing in it at this moment to engage your interest? My panacea! But here it is – I can lay my hand on it at once, you see! Now, a glass. One drop only, added to a little water, and there you are. Drink, my friend; for in this glass is the cure for half the ills of bodily appetite.

'You feel a little more relaxed, now? You would like to lie down for a moment? But certainly, my dear friend. It is only the action of the drug; do not fear it. Relax. Sleep, if you feel like sleeping; sleep, my friend...

'My friend ... You cannot hear me now, can you? A pity. I should like you to hear me now, my handsome friend. But I shall imagine, as I prepare you, that you do still hear me; because in spite of all I have said to you this evening, there are more important things as yet unsaid. Dear me, how crudely muscled your handsome body – simply to remove your clothes is, for me, quite an undertaking. But you will understand presently that this is an operation I have to perform unassisted. Not that you need have any fears as to the outcome: I foresee no complications, although it is an unfamiliar task I have set myself.

'I never showed you my knives. But you were scarcely in a state to take an intelligent interest. Can you hear them now, boiling and clinking, bathed in steam? My little moment of *grand guignol*. In other circumstances that would earn your professional disapproval, I am sure – the incurable ham, I can hear you saying, in his absurd, ridiculous melodrama. But it all seems very logical to me.

'This is what might be called preventive surgery.

'You were so young, and handsome, and famous. You could have taken any woman in Rome – didn't I tell you this? So why, *why* did you have to take my wife?

'Alas, my friend, I no longer know for what cause, in the name of what justice, you lie here so lustless on my operating table; but the knife, at least, knows its job.

'And the hand that holds the knife is an artist's hand – it will not slip or falter. I shall give you all of my skill. But I think that when you wake, you will not be here, and you will not be *whole*. Nor will you be able to question me: but perhaps you will remember enough to penetrate my disguise – to savour (forgive me) the irony of my chosen pseudonym. Perhaps, with everything else you feel, you will even find room for a little surprise?

'My poor handsome friend, you never knew – did you? – what a rage dwells in the human heart.'

'Il Traforo'

Margie leaned from the wide-open window of the Mini Minor.

'It's a real swelterer – a sizzler! I wouldn't have imagined it like this.'

And all those oranges, she thought. 'And all those oranges, Larry – just look at them!' The torrid air tugged at the flesh of her cheeks and her tightly curled hair, and fluttered her eyelashes. The lower slopes of the mountains were intricately terraced and the oranges – 'Millions of them,' said Margie – grew under roofs of matted straw burnt to a dirty brown by the sun. But the oranges glowed: they shimmered in a brilliant cascade that fell from far above them to far below, where the mountains plunged over the black-shadowed Sorrentine cliffs to the sea.

Lawford changed down, and the car sidled round a sharp steep bend, unrolling a sun-drenched view of Sorrento itself.

'And the sea,' sighed Margie, stumbling against a sense of unfamiliarity, finding only familiar words: 'It's like a mirror.'

Lawford brought the car to a halt beside a low parapet. Dust blew and settled in the road behind them, and the air filled with the hot smell of the engine. Margie opened the door and climbed out. 'I was absolutely sticking to the seat. In a puddle,' she said, laughing, and stretching her arms and shoulders. Her arms were rather plump. Her cotton dress was damp, and clung to her plump comfortable body. 'My goodness, though – what a view.'

Lawford joined her beside the parapet. He had a small moustache and gentle eyes, brown and humorous.

'Well, Beauty – glad we came?' He found a packet of cigarettes and lit two, passing one to Margie. 'What price

England now, eh? Doesn't it make you feel a little ashamed for Margate?'

'But we know better!' Margie half chanted the words and they laughed comfortably together, as they had a thousand times: it was a private incantation.

Across the water, a shape melting into shapeless haze, Capri crouched, inscrutable.

Margie and Lawford had turned to look at the view again, and a silence crept between them, an insertion of the surrounding pervasive silence.

Lawford felt this silence as a shadow falling across the plane of his perceptions. It stirred in him a momentary uneasiness. The mountains and the sea grew and grew in his eye, filling him with a sense of their presence. He tried to analyse his uneasiness, and found that it seemed to lie in a curious optical illusion: under that blazing, blinding sun, the earth seemed to assume a formless instability (produced, he told himself, by the heat and the great light). The mountains and the sea, filling his vision, appeared to shift in a movement that always, at the last moment, escaped him; but traced on the edges of his sight, the movement was ever there – a fragmentation, hinting (he laughed inwardly, silently, at this fancy) of a further dimension, as though the earth might at any moment open and reveal – and his mind paused, startled. Reveal what? Another level of existence? – a world behind, beneath the world he knew?

Beside him, he felt Margie shiver.

'It's funny,' she said, 'seeing how hot it is; but I think I'm going to sneeze.' She did.

'Bless you, Beauty.' Lawford spoke absently, still preoccupied with his thoughts. Margie sneezed again, and blew her nose roundly into a small lace handkerchief.

Lawford was thinking of those poems he had sometimes almost written. He knew he was a sensitive man, but he had a saving sense of humour, which he liked to turn against himself. 'Me writing poetry!' he used to say, preferably to a large circle of acquaintances, and Margie there too, in the local: 'I just can't see it, somehow.' It was generally good for a laugh, and underneath the laughter there was a kind of seriousness that pleased him.

'What'll you have, then, Lawford – a dry Shelley? a Browning ale? Drink up, old man, it's all inspiration.' The banter was always good-natured, responding to his own good nature. They were a popular couple, and they enjoyed their popularity. It showed, Lawford was thinking now, that they belonged. 'We fit in,' he told himself, amused and lightly mocking his own self-satisfaction, 'pretty snugly.' And if the price for fitting in included those unwritten poems, well – he was content to have paid it.

On the other hand, it was disturbing to feel how little they fitted in here. His mind chased down an elusive word, and suddenly pinned it: *alien*. But was it really they who were alien, or was it this alien scene? The heat, the sun – to be practical, those oranges – seemed scarcely real, seemed to threaten his own, and Margie's, reality.

'It's all a bit like one of those films,' said Margie, suddenly breaking the silence, 'with the sun, and all these colours. And then when you come out of the cinema, you find it's raining – or even if the sun *is* shining, it's never quite the same – but here it is the same.'

Lawford squeezed her arm above the elbow, affectionately.

'Trust Margie,' he said, 'to put it in a nutshell. That's just what I was thinking. I'll tell you something, though: that picture-postcard chappie was absolutely right – I'm going to put on those sunglasses after all.'

'A good thing we bought them, even if we didn't want to at the time. I don't know – in that dark little shop it seemed somehow a waste.'

'And me with my bald head,' said Lawford – 'they must make me look like King Farouk. But all the same – I can hardly keep my eyes open. With this glare.'

The sunglasses, if anything, heightened the sense of illusion. But now Lawford became aware that what had seemed silence was not really silence at all. The air was filled with the dream sounds of insects, like the hum of a distant, buried dynamo. It was alarming, in a way, because it corresponded so nearly with the sense of visual vibration that he had noticed before. And then he could hear other sounds – and probably they had been there all the time, his ears untuned to them because of the overlaying silence, but there all the same, on another level: the soft plunk of a pick striking the dry earth, distant voices, fragments of song and sometimes laughter. It was strangely difficult to tell where these sounds came from – from further up the orange-packed slopes, or further down.

There were people on the mountainside, Lawford thought, and wondered why this should seem disconcerting. For all its unreal beauty, the scene before had seemed somehow enervated, but now – now Lawford's thoughts formed words, like one of those distant unwritten poems: *Alien vitality. Crouched beneath the dazed surface.*

'Beneath the surface, a mythologic lion half asleep.'

Without meaning to, he had spoken these words aloud. He laughed, a bit awkwardly. 'Trying out a line of poetry – we poets can never take a holiday, you know.'

And then: 'But seriously. It seemed so – sort of peaceful. I didn't notice the voices at first. And someone digging the earth. Come to think of it, these chaps can't be such a lazy lot after all, if they go out and work in this heat. All the same, I'll bet there's a lot more vino and siesta and you-know-what going on out there, than hard work. You couldn't blame them, either. With a climate like this.'

'Sort of Garden of Eden,' said Margie, sighing. 'But maybe it wouldn't seem quite the same if you actually lived here.'

And that, thought Lawford, was another of Margie's nutshells. Bless her, she was a comfortable sort of person to have around – her busy feet so firmly planted. He threw his cigarette away and turned back towards the car, the weight of all his fancies falling from him. Poetry, after all, was for others; he was sensible enough to see.

'Come on, Beauty – let's go and take a look at Sorrento. See if it's all that it's cracked up to be. See if we can find those seagulls.' He was feeling hungry, too. And Margie was always ready for a bite. 'After all,' she was fond of saying, 'I've a fair bit of strength that needs keeping up.'

The road, empty before, had filled with traffic – small white or red Fiats snarling round the corners, motor-scooters driven by youths in brilliantly coloured shirts, tourist coaches tearing the air with the trumpet cry of klaxons, lorries belching oily smoke. And Sorrento, too, when they reached it, was alive with sauntering people, wearing their holiday suntan with a relaxed lazy pride. The streets were splashed with smiling colours and pools of cool shade. Margie and Lawford walked hand in hand, instinctively downwards by winding alleys, to the sea.

The port moved to its own slow rhythm, matching the scarcely perceptible glassy heave of the swell. A grizzled fisherman sculled a brightly painted boat. Children swam from the rocks of the harbour mole. A speedboat, towing a skier, made wide circles in the bay. Two or three bars spread red and blue and green umbrellas across the pavements, their tables crowded with people sipping from frosted glasses. Young men strolled in groups, eyeing the women.

'Be careful, Beauty – you'll have your bottom pinched again!' said Lawford, laughing. 'These young rakes – Italians.' His laughter trailed away in wistfulness.

But Margie was watching the children swimming, sun-blackened and flashing, the water streaming from their necks and arms and shoulders.

'We should have had some kids, Larry,' she said quietly. 'While it was still possible.'

Those unborn children, like Lawford's unborn poems.

Lawford was never very sure that he knew how to deal with this. After a suitable pause, he took her hand and swung it jovially. 'Margie, I'm famished,' he said.

There was a small restaurant, with a terrace facing the sea, and more of those umbrellas spreading shade.

'Spaghetti,' said Lawford when a waiter appeared. 'For two – ' he held up two fingers, 'and some of your best vino. The red'll do nicely.'

'IL TRAFORO'

The waiter grinned, shrugging inoffensively. Lawford settled back into his chair, smiling and pleased with himself.

'It's wonderful how you can always make yourself understood,' he said. 'You can go anywhere with a bit of English and a bit of patience. Though I wouldn't mind knowing what some of these things on the menu mean. We'd better stick to steak, even if they do slice it like paper. I don't want to find another octopus on my plate, like yesterday.' They both laughed at this. 'That was a good one on us, if you like. "Fish," he said. Well – I suppose it is, in a way.'

'The things they eat here,' said Margie. 'I wouldn't have believed it, really.'

'But we know better!' Lawford saluted her with his glass – the wine had already arrived.

They crumbled bread, and sipped their wine. 'This is the life, eh, Beauty?' Lawford stretched out his legs so that the sun fell across his bare knees. They were red from yesterday, but this time he had covered them with lotion. He refilled their glasses and they drank again. Presently the spaghetti arrived, glistening coils under a red sauce spattered with clams.

'I still haven't got the hang of this stuff,' said Lawford. 'More of it seems to come out of my ears than goes into my mouth!' He called the waiter for more wine, and ordered their steaks at the same time. They wound spaghetti onto their forks and drank the wine and laughed a lot. There was, after all, a lot to laugh at: if their own efforts at eating spaghetti were pretty comic, so in a way was the spaghetti itself. 'Foreign countries are an education,' said Lawford, 'if you take them with a pinch of salt.'

When they had eaten, they ordered coffee. 'Though you could stand your spoon up in this stuff,' said Margie.

And the waiter brought two glasses of a transparent liqueur they hadn't asked for.

'Drink up, Margie. It's on the house.' It tasted of liquorice, which Margie had never liked. She made a face.

Afterwards they walked arm in arm up the brick-walled street, feeling comfortably dazed by the heat and the food and the wine. It was difficult to think of plans with any sense of urgency, but: 'Come on, Beauty. Back to the car,' said Lawford presently. 'There's an awful lot of these kilometres to put behind us yet. Even if they are only a lazy man's mile.'

From Sorrento towards Massa Lubrense they were never far from the sea; and then the road turned inland and climbed through many curves to cross the peninsula by way of Sant'Agata. From these heights it curled down towards the same blue shimmering sea on the southern coast, still keeping to a vertiginous altitude. The traffic had thinned again, but there remained enough to make Lawford approach each bend in the sinuous road with sober caution, a sobriety exaggerated if anything by all the wine he had drunk.

Presently the mountains began to elbow the road further out, to hang like a ledge over the sea still far below them. These were stony mountains, the palest grey and pink, and sparsely overgrown. Small fishing villages huddled beneath steep-sided valleys, the houses washed in white or pale colours, lemon or pink or faded blue, the churches glinting dulled gold from weathered cupolas. And then for a stretch there was nothing, just the road, the sea and the sky, and the empty mountains.

'If those AA fellows haven't slipped up,' said Lawford, 'we should reach Amalfi about now.'

But the road curved inland again, following the broad flank of a mountain, and traffic signs proliferated: graphic representations of falling rocks, of skidding cars, of hairpin bends – and then, as they entered one of the sharpest of these, a picture of an inverted or 'closed' horseshoe and beneath this, on a crosspiece, the word 'TRAFORO'. Before the road could begin to unravel they were plunged, abruptly, into a tunnel.

The bend continued into the tunnel, so that almost immediately Lawford found it necessary to switch on his headlights.

'What a lark,' said Margie. 'But they could have put some lights in. It's a long one.'

'IL TRAFORO'

It was cold in the tunnel, and Margie closed the window beside her. Water splashed from the roof every now and then, onto the windscreen.

'I expect we've entered the Underworld,' said Margie cheerfully, drawing on distant recollections of mythology.

'I can't say I remember seeing any three-headed Cerberus at the entrance,' said Lawford, chuckling. 'Just that sign. I suppose *traforo* means tunnel. Learn the language as you go.' He peered ahead into the pool of light cast by the headlamps. 'I hope we don't meet another car in here; there's precious little room for passing. Seems to be narrowing a bit.'

And then: 'Come to think of it, there hasn't been any traffic for quite a stretch.'

Margie lit a couple of cigarettes, and passed one to Lawford.

'Larry,' she said presently. 'We must have been in here a good five minutes now. I've never known such a long tunnel. Except that one in Switzerland. Can't you see the end yet?'

'No, Beauty. There must be another curve further on. Cheer up, ducks – there can't be much more of it.'

Lawford slowed to a crawl. The tunnel had narrowed so much that there was little space on either side of the car, and he found that the hallucinatory effect of the advancing rings of light on the walls and ceiling of the tunnel made it very difficult to hold the car on a straight course.

'It certainly is a queer case,' he said.

'It doesn't make sense,' said Margie. 'I mean, if there was another car coming the other way. You'd think they'd have put in traffic lights, or something.'

The car nosed on into the tunnel, the sound of its engine thrown back by the rock walls in a reverberating echo.

Presently: 'Larry. Do you think we might have made a mistake, somehow? Maybe this isn't the right road – maybe it isn't a road at all. Maybe it's the entrance to an old mine, or something?'

'I don't see how it could be,' Lawford objected. 'After all, you saw how it came, slap bang in the middle of the road like that. There simply wasn't any other road to take.' He stopped the car. 'Tell you what, though. We'll have a look at that map.'

He switched off the headlights and turned on the inside light. The black night of the tunnel closed in until it seemed to be pressing against the windows of the car. Lawford spread the map and began to study it.

'Seems you were right, after all,' he said presently, his voice preoccupied. 'There isn't any tunnel marked on the map, not of this length. Look, there's that last village we passed, Praiano. And there's Amalfi. No tunnels.'

Lawford sat very quietly. Perhaps he was thinking.

'Larry, we'd better do something. Can't we try to go back?'

'I don't know, Beauty – I don't know. We can try. But we can't turn round, there isn't the room for it. And there's two or three miles of it behind us, and how can I see to go backwards?'

His voice, to Margie, seemed flat and empty.

He started the motor, and put the car into reverse gear. Then he turned on the headlights again, but he kept his foot on the clutch.

'Margie,' he said, 'I don't think this is going to work. I don't think it's meant to work. There's something in all this – in the tunnel – I don't understand.'

The car began to move slowly backwards. Almost immediately there was the sound of metal grating against rock. Lawford turned the steering wheel, but the car stuck, imprisoned, vibrating, the rear wheels spinning.

Presently Lawford stopped the engine again. 'It's no good,' he said. 'We aren't going to get out backwards.' (The thought had seized him again: we aren't meant to.)

'But we must, Larry. We can't stay here for ever.'

Lawford lit another cigarette.

'No, we certainly can't stay here for ever. We must go on. Or if we don't want to go on, we must get out and walk back. But that would be a bit ridiculous, and – Margie, I don't know how to say this, but I'm not sure we'd find our way out, even walking, even if we tried.'

'I don't believe we could, either.' Margie shivered. 'Not in this dark, and without a torch or anything. But Larry, if we go on – it might just come to an end, in the middle of the mountain.'

Or it might, Lawford was thinking, just not come to an end, ever. Suddenly he had to consider this as a rational possibility – a hidden fold in reality. It had been with him, he was reminded, since the morning. Planes had shifted; the material world had teetered there on the edge, it had seemed, of poetry – a gulf opening beneath his feet. Had they fallen into it? He was wondering how he could explain it to Margie, this idea he was contemplating with such curious calm. But Margie was very quietly crying there beside him, and through her tears she said: 'Oh, Larry – I know what you are thinking. But it doesn't matter. Really, it doesn't matter.'

'I don't know,' said Lawford. 'It seems so absurd. Why should this happen to us?'

Margie was drying her eyes on her lace handkerchief.

'It's all right, Larry. I'm all right now. Shall we go on?'

Lawford started the engine once more. 'I think we'd better,' he said.

The car moved slowly away from the wall, metal briefly scraping on rock again, the wheels holding. Lawford reached out with one hand and found Margie's hand resting in her lap; he closed his fingers over hers. 'Maybe we'll be out the other side in a couple of hundred yards,' he said. 'You never know your luck. Maybe we're just a couple of old ninnies.'

But we know better, he was thinking – his bitterness touched by wonder. When it came to the pinch, we always did know better.

They sat, their fingers quietly touching, while the car forged on, deeper into the tunnel.

Moonlight Sonata

A few years ago it was my joy, and my privilege, to teach English to a French boy called Christian Tual. It happened at a time when, in a hypnotically fictional manner, I found myself declining, if not actually falling, into those ranks of gentlemen ushers who still staff so many of our private preparatory schools. Christian, and his twin brother Jacques, celebrated their twelfth birthday almost exactly halfway through the year when I taught them.

   Before it goes any further I had better come right out and admit that this is, in all of its essential details, a true story that I am writing. I haven't even bothered to disguise Christian's name; but I don't think he will grudge me this unprofessional candour. And perhaps I should also take my chances with a personal plea, here, in defence of my rash claim that, irrespective of its truth, this account deserves the dignity and title of a story. On the whole I feel I had better not be too insistent about this; the first three-quarters of the piece may appear to be a bit shy of events, of narrative excitement. The last part, I hope, will be sufficiently, shatteringly dramatic to make up for any apparent reluctance on my part to be rushed into reaching that moment; at any rate *I* think it is, and I have more than half a hunch that Christian himself, who knows a good story when he sees one and has written a few too, would agree with me.

   I see that I have twice in my first short paragraph claimed or at least implied that Christian learned his English from me; I wish that this was even partly true, but I realized afterwards, in certain moderately cool moments of self-examination, that all I ever did was to sit back and watch with awe and admiration. I don't believe anyone, except

Christian himself, can properly claim the credit I would so much like to appropriate. Less than three years before I met him he did not have a word of English; but I am inclined to assert that almost from the day he was born he must have been nurturing the style, the wit and irony, the impassioned poetry, and that breathtaking flair for words, which even the unfamiliar medium of a foreign language could not disguise or defeat.

The school where I discovered Christian and his brother (notice my choice of words – I indulge myself again with that extravagant 'discovered') was remarkable, among other remarkable qualities, for its tolerant recognition of a world beyond the English Channel, a world that most preparatory schools keep firmly imprisoned in the history and geography lessons. This school, Dane Court (having taken the plunge, I become reckless with real names), welcomed foreigners with the enthusiasm lesser schools reserve for the sons of dukes and cabinet ministers. It was a sensible policy – 'inspired' might be the truer word – because these children gave as much in education as they received. The Tuals were an outstanding example of this. Make due allowance, if you must, for my prejudice: they seemed to me an abiding lesson in civilization to their English barbarian companions.

Jacques and Christian were almost identical. Jacques had a small scar beside one eye – even now I forget which eye – and Christian was a little fatter. But often I was not entirely certain, when talking to one alone, which one it was. This didn't seem to matter very much; I felt that, in a curiously indirect and frankly mysterious way, whatever I said to one, whatever *rapport* was established at any time with one, was said to and established with the other also. There is a mystique of identical twins I have noticed in other examples, but never more strongly than in the Tuals. In one way, however, I did presently learn to distinguish them fairly easily: in their writing. I could never make up my mind whether I was glad or sorry for this; I suppose it would have been altogether too confusing if Jacques had produced stories indistinguishable from Christian's. Literature, perhaps more than any other art, needs to be attributed: we must believe in Shakespeare *or* Bacon. I never for a moment confused even Jacques' best work with Christian's. For all its diversity, Christian's was stamped with a style that was unmistakable – a unique signature.

It is more than possible that the day will come when, from desperate necessity, I have to seek employment again in private schools. So, to protect my interests, I must be slightly reticent about my unmethodical and optimistic approach to the teaching of English. But I should at least mention, here, a warm memory of my own childhood delight in creative writing – a delight I am convinced all inspired (and therefore normal) children share. In my English classes there was a maximum of imaginative writing. So it must have been very early in my acquaintance with Christian that he wrote a story called **SHIPWRECK**. It began unremarkably, for these were early days and Christian was feeling his way still, like any untried genius, towards his full powers:

> It was a stormy night and the steam-liner 'Knight of France' was forcing his way through the night and I, W.S.J.M. Willsonborough was sleeping peacefully in my cabin when suddenly the ship gave a rending crack and immediately the alarm bells started clanging. I had just time to grab a suitcase and stuff in all my personal belongings...

He hadn't quite found his touch; there was (I still feel this) something a little laboured in Jake Willsonborough's four initials. But it would pay to keep an alert, unprejudiced eye on that suitcase, so innocently, so cunningly introduced. The story continues with Jake's discovery, when he rushes up on deck, that all the lifeboats have gone, and 'the waves like monstrous whales were sweeping over the ship'. Undismayed, Jake leaps into the sea, still clutching his suitcase, and supported by a log and his life-jacket, is swept for miles through the night to be washed ashore at dawn on an island –

which I calculated was about five miles long and two miles wide. And so immediately I landed I sat on the soft sand and opened my suitcase and this is what I found: an alarm clock still working, two packets of cigarettes, a lighter which is very useful, a shirt, two pairs of trousers, a book, a knife, my browning which I always carried when I travelled, two boxes of cartridges, some pennicillin, a wad of bank-notes and one of those 4" × 2" big new portable american radios. So I didn't think it was too bad after all.

Nor did I. I can't remember now with any certainty which predominated in my mind when I first read that paragraph: the general and detached pleasure of the teacher stumbling across someone who could write with such casual mastery; or a particular, a more personal pleasure in that very dashing satire (I soon established that it was deliberate) on the Swiss Family Robinson and all their serendipitous descendants. I wondered if this might be no more than a flash in the pan, an unrepeatable accident; but I didn't think so. I looked forward impatiently to the next occasion when I could test what I already believed was a remarkable talent.

My practice was to give my classes a fairly wide choice, of four or five titles; as they became more confident, the titles became more obscure, challenging imagination. But these were still early days. For his second story Christian chose **THE RIVER**.

I am a silly little river that runs across America.

Better prepared, I refused to be discouraged by this first sentence. Besides, being unaware at this time of Christian's extraordinary range, I was looking for satire. Viewed in this light, as an opening it had possibilities, although again I felt that the initial touch was a little uncertain. The next paragraph quickly reassured me:

I start in the Rockies and bounce down-stream over

stones and gravel, run under rough wooden bridges and my gosh! What a fright I get when the sherriff and his men gallop across me in the pursuit of some outlaw.

And this was immediately followed by a paragraph that astonished me; effortlessly changing the mood, Christian had suddenly fused poetry into his story, and in a moment that was likely to prove disconcerting to a youngish man with his own immodest pretensions to be or become a writer, I realized that I was in the presence not of a mere satirist but of a fellow writer, an artist with command of every mood:

I sometimes run across shady woods into lakes where all the little squirrels, skunks, the fearsome wolverine, the majestic stag, the beautiful and frail looking hind, the clumsy porcupine, the cunning little red fox and his mate the beautiful silver fox, the cruel and carnivorous mountain lion, the bouncing little white rabbits, come and drink together of my water at nightfall.

Look at the poetry and perfection of those adjectives. Perhaps some of this defies natural lore; if it does, I can think of no better argument for encouraging nature to imitate art.

After reading **THE RIVER** I could never again, in one sense, be surprised by anything Christian wrote. In another sense, of the constant capacity for surprise in good writing, everything that Christian wrote surprised me; I came to expect that new facets of this flashing diamond would be revealed as he cut and polished his talent. An analysis of style and mood and the human understanding contained in those twenty-odd stories and poems could easily fill a book. Consider the next paragraph of **THE RIVER**:

I then bound out again, and go through Indian villages where the 'squaws' come and take out my water for their 'tepees'; the little 'chiquitos' also come out and play, splashing each other laughingly on their copper-coloured bodies; I flow away still and go through an evil smelling black, noisy town which human beings call St Louis, where I join my great-grandfather the Mississipi, with whom I travel quite a long way seeing river-boats, hearing negroes singing on the river banks and seeing little boys like Tom Sawyer playing about.

This versatile river then jumps out again 'to join my mother the Ohio', and lets itself 'be carried on by her until she finishes her course'.

...then I start running again until I reach the great lakes; when I arrive finally I let myself be carried to and fro from one lake to another but I am too tired to go on any more.

It must be a mean-souled man who would criticize the geography of all this. And the poetry of the last sentence is also too good for mean souls:

In the winter I hibernate, like bears do, under the ice.

Soon an element of mystery began to obtrude in the stories; but with a delicate oblique touch that lifted them from the dimension of mere thrillers to heights of subtle inference and suggestion. I particularly like, in this *genre*, **THE FAST TRAIN IS DUE** – a story which combines Buchan and Dornford Yates with Poe, and a dash of Sax Rohmer:

It was raining, raining heavily as Bill saw his pater's 1936 vintage disappear in the mist; he turned away from the dirty and cracked window.

Observe how the opening has acquired confidence, and an assured sense of direction; the first half of the sentence where satire still lurks, because even mystery stories can admit recondite half-hidden smiles; changing abruptly to the businesslike brief realism of the second half.

The hero, a schoolboy, is waiting for the fast train:

> The wind was howling, and the little waiting-room looked dismal, the small fire had gone out; Bill looked around him, in a corner was an old lady with a basket; in front of him sat a young curate lost in his thoughts, he shifted and a little prayer-book he was holding carelessly in his hand dropped on the soiled stony floor; a chit of paper flickered towards him, he caught it and hastily glanced at it before giving it back to the young man; on that bit of paper were the words 'Sthaffel, non-stop. Beware.'

This is masterly; it is written with the economy of true mystery and terror. The slight ambiguity of pronouns is a carelessness the context, surely, forgives. This ambiguity continues, but now we might suppose it deliberate:

> Bill got up soon after, put his cap on straight, picked up his suitcase and walked on to the platform, he heard the faraway rumbling of the express; suddenly, happening to turn round, he saw the young man coming at him, he side-stepped, the train came rumbling in, there was an awful scream! ...

The climax bursts on us with an explosion of unanswered questions; and before the debris has had time to settle, the story ends on a compulsive last enigma:

> In the little waiting-room the old lady sat in a dark corner, she hadn't seen anything, she hadn't heard anything.

For another example of this skilfully evoked atmosphere of mystery, I will quote unabridged and without comment a little masterpiece called **THE ISLAND**:

On a gay evening of June, Wiks was marching happily on the muddy pavement of a dark, obscure, sinister... No, it wasn't all that sinister, in front of him was a door, on it was written 'The Island'. He pushed the massive door and was immediately engulfed into a noisy crowd of smoke, noisy records, showy dresses, and alcohol. He sat down on a bench and looked. 'This ought to get me a good story,' he murmured to himself. 'Think of it, a reporter in a Soho lair.' Then suddenly everything stopped and there was a dull sound like a bag of sand dropping on the floor.

'It's him!' shouted a voice; all eyes turned menacingly on Wiks.

'W ... Wh ... whaat d'you mean?' he stuttered, and he pressed himself against the wall which was crumbling with moisture.

'Out with him!' another voice cried and Wiks saw a knife flash...

Bobson got the scoop finally, on the murder of his pal, and poor Wiks came out of 'The Island' ... in a coffin.

I have already suggested Christian's versatility; the mystery story was no more a cul-de-sac of style than the early satire had been. Descriptions of compelling realism began to mingle with a dashing use of idiom. Under the elusive title **THE MYSTERIOUS DEATH OF JOE GOLD**, a story began:

'It was an unusual meeting; the man stared into the fiery eyes of the bobcat and then back to the bloody body of his companion, his sweaty hand was still gripping the butt of a smoking six-shooter.'

The old-timer looked at his audience, they were spellbound, he passed his rugged and scorched hand across his lips and spat, the clock over the patched-up mirror was ticking monotonously, he looked at the whisky on the counter and then significantly at the barman.

'Okay, okay,' the barman muttered, 'Here,' and he slid the small glass of 'fire-water' across the glistening wood.

Later in the same story we learn that 'old Joe Gold was very touchy if anyone teased him about lifting the elbow too much'.

MR INCHSOLE marked a new approach to humour; the satire broadened into farce, but without sinking quite to slapstick:

Mr Inchsole is an unbeliever: ghosts do Not exist, crystal balls are ROT, heaven and hell is Non-SENSE, miracles are old women's talk! Only MONEY counts for him, in other words he is a miser and believes in nothing except what he sees.

How admirable the casual confidence of that opening; the cool and arbitrary use of majuscules; the chatty but perfectly controlled style.

Mr Inchsole, it transpires, lives in a house haunted by ghosts which he refuses, with obstinate rationalism, to believe in. This drives the poor ghosts to distraction, and one in particular to suicide. A committee of ghosts is formed to deal with Mr Inchsole; they must face the problem of their invisibility:

of course they could ask a Visible ghost from China to come and help them but the travel expenses would bankrupt the Committee's savings.

Eventually the ghost of old King Alfred hits on the solution: luminous paint. They all paint themselves, with devastating effect. Mr Inchsole, after one look, flees in screaming terror and is 'never seen again; in England, that is'. Here fantasy slides imperceptibly back into satire:

You sometimes might see him dressed as a cowboy in the Californian desert saying:

– 'Hiya pards! don't believe a word about ghosts, no sir, don't believe a word of it!'

Or sometimes you can meet him in the Libyan desert, in the arctic dressed as an eskimo, or in China dressed in the very honourable array of the country saying:

– 'Me velly solly but me, unworthy son of the earth, not believe in spirits, no, me not.'

Sometimes I rather wonder if he hasn't become a ghost himself?

Towards the end of that year a more serious, reflective note began to predominate, though the humour was always there in the background ready to spurt out in little puffs of flame that Christian himself seemed unable or unwilling to extinguish. In **THE NIGHT** the intensity of theme and thought leads to some rare but seductive lapses into unconscious gallicism (I have transcribed all these stories without correcting a spelling or altering so much as a comma):

A white palour reigns over the chaotic shapes of gaping holes, rock, upturned, weedy and rusty gun barrels, muddy shells, dead horses with their harness still on, sloughs, the gentle moans of dying men.

And then! The stillness is broken, the spell has vanished, a detonation, and a green star soars high up in the spangled night, hell has begun once again!

The incandescent light of the moon seems to have vanished terrified, scared away by man's infernal machinery.

When man starts fighting he shows cruelty, courage, ferocity, bravour, nobless of mind...

There is romanticism here, but it is romanticism tempered by reality – courage is balanced by cruelty, ferocity by bravour and nobless of mind. And clearly (and significantly, but that is another question) the war described here is the

First World War; it is the mud of Passchendaele, not the sands of Libya or the snows of Stalingrad, that forms the background; and in dealing with ancient history, a little romanticism is excusable. In the last paragraph there are some sentences I consider remarkable, if we remember the experiences of France at the hands of Prussia since 1870:

> The night [...] also looks into the enemy's lines, sees the newly promoted young officer who, at the trembling light of a candle writes proudly about his hopes for his country and his new promotion; the young volunteer writing to his mother and saying, 'We will beat them yet,' the same young man that might next day be a body on the battle-field among many others. It hears the enemy soldier's family wondering when Fritz or Franz will be back home. It sees all that among many other things; and, when dawn comes, surrenders its sceptre to the sun.

I happen to know that Christian went through a bad period at about this time; the trouble was complicated, private, and is no concern of mine here; it involved a sharp disappointment. Even if I had known nothing of the circumstances, however, his writing would have told me that something was wrong. It became far more personal, and less detached. A story called **ALONE** began:

> He came on a rainy day, a thin, small figure in a stuffy school uniform, he was alone, all by himself; the driver asked for his fare, the boy held out some coins in the palm of his hand, the driver took some, grumbled, and started his engine. The boy was all alone in the courtyard; jeering faces were peering at him.
> Suddenly I heard a splash and a tomato landed on the boy's mackintosh. He never said a word, he just wiped himself and went towards the changing-room door amidst hoots from the boys. This is how he came to Faltington.

I took pity on him, and for the first few days I always tried to help him, he was a foreigner I learned. His name was Jehan.

Again an element of mystery enters the story:

Once, I asked him for his home address; the colour immediately drained from his face and he said: 'No, I cannot.'

Presently Jehan, 'the lonely boy', disappears as abruptly as he had appeared, but less publicly, leaving behind him a parcel (for Christian) containing a gold fountain pen and a sad, brief, enigmatic note of farewell.

And it was around this time, too, that I was presented with a story in two parts: the first was a poem, the second was one of Christian's shortest pieces of prose. **THE CHASE (I)**, subtitled 'The Last Speech of the Hunted Man', began like this:

I am sick of life
Of its shouts of its strife
I am sick of this world of pity
   With so little purity
I am sick of its unkindness
Of its injustices, of this mess
Of joys, sadness, hope,
Of its faded glory, which, like a rope
Has burnt its way to the knot.

THE CHASE (II) develops the same theme, in more fantastic terms:

He looked out of the window and he saw the bloodhounds outlined like a nightmare, against the red, evil sky of the evening, THEY had picked up his scent. The sky had turned violet, the violet of a flower, 'flowers,' he thought, 'Ah, HE liked flowers.' Oh, it would all be over very soon, I wonder, what will the rope feel like?'

He pressed his sweaty face against the stony wall to cool it, and suddenly he felt he was angry against the world, even with that wall, the evening, against everything, and yet nothing, and, he turned his face towards the spire...

I have by now, I hope, even at the expense of some slight self-indulgence, conveyed a fair impression of the quality of Christian's writing, of what his writing was when he was just twelve years old, a French boy in an English school with three years' practice in the language. I can now move on to what, at the beginning, I more or less promised: the part of this disjunct account that might be called a story; the dramatic part.

Perhaps I should mention that the Tuals and I left that school within a year of each other (I first), but that though they returned to France and then went to Rome for eighteen months, we didn't lose touch; not only were there letters, generally written by Christian (they would be worth publishing too, I can promise you) but always signed by both: we also met on three occasions, once in England and twice in Rome. And then, about two years after that last meeting, I found myself in Africa.

If I become deliberately vague at this point, it is not because I hope to emulate Christian's evocations of mystery, but for more personal reasons; and so it must suffice if I place myself, evasively, 'somewhere in Africa'. I was making a journey of nearly a thousand miles in a battered, deceitfully optimistic Land Rover, accompanied by three Africans. One night, camped beside a dry water-course in empty bush country that had almost hypnotized me into believing it endless, after a day when twelve hours' driving had advanced me barely a hundred miles, Christian Tual, aided by the BBC, came to my rescue in a way so profound and so elusive I knew, even then, that only this tribute, these pages that I am writing at last now, could begin to pay off the debt I owe to him. For reasons that had little to do with the circumstances of my journey, I was that night plunged into a depth of personal anguish and depression which, fortunately, I have seldom experienced in such desolating, deadening measure. I knew all about Christian's 'world of pity, with so little purity', and his 'faded glory, which, like a rope, has burnt its way to the knot'. I too could see those blood-hounds, 'outlined like a nightmare against the red, evil sky of the evening'; I knew exactly what it was to feel 'angry against the world ... against everything, and yet nothing...'

THEY had picked up my scent. Even there, in the remote distance of the African bush, THEY were implacable, they could not be shaken off.

My companions had lit a large fire; this was not lion country ('the cruel and carnivorous mountain lion'), but they liked to dramatize our situation, and for myself I welcomed it – there were other things than lions on my mind, and I felt perhaps a primitive confidence in the protective power of fire.

And then I switched on my transistor radio (Jake Willsonborough's 4" × 2" big new american portable): across two continents, with marvellous and fortuitous clarity, breathed into the air around me, triumphant affirmation of creative man, Mozart's *Requiem Mass*. I experienced a sudden release, a lifting of my spirits; Africa, and with it my loaded apprehensions, retreated into the night. At first I thought that the music alone had achieved this; but suddenly I realized the music was not alone – it had served as a trigger for memory, and something else had come out of the night to heal my spirit. To put it as precisely as I feel capable now of putting it, this visitor in the night was a man; a man called André.

> I knew André, he was a tall 'svelte' powerfully built priest; he chose to become a missionary.

With these words, which I have come to regard almost as

an incantation, so momentous has their effect on me been, Christian began one of his last stories for me, a story called **MOONLIGHT SONATA**.

> I met him at Holywell in Scotland, he was a novice then, he liked organ music; being a musician myself I took to him immediately, I liked him, he liked me and it went on for many years, even when he was in Africa; I went to see him once or twice, he had changed a lot, fever was ruining him. The first time I went to his mission I arrived at dusk and I will always see him standing there in shorts, a white shirt, and a hunting rifle slung on his shoulder; he had negroes all around him, they were singing, shouting, laughing; then he suddenly quietened them down, lifted me from the coach and in a booming voice he said, 'Salut mon fieu! ça gaze la-bas?' Rather shaken I answered back a bit shyly but politely. In the evening we dined with the darkies in the great hall he had built with his own hands and sweat. He had gone back into his white tunic and looked much smaller now, he wore on his breast an ivory crucifix. Then suddenly I asked him, 'Dis donc, vieux, et la musique ça marche?' He answered in English with a twinkle in his eyes, 'You wait and see.'

Scene by scene, image by image, eventually word by word, as memory caught fire, it came back to me. And I knew then why Mozart, played in the middle of the African bush, at night, should have so certainly, so inevitably evoked the man called André, so that for a time I believed I was with them in that jungle clearing, seeing in reality what I had seen so often in imagination:

> We had a cup of coffee and some jam after that, and then we rose up. He led me along a row of 'bananiers' as he called them, which is French for banana trees, and we came to a clearing and guess what I saw ... an enormous steam organ!

The negroes were sitting all around with bright shiny eyes. He jumped on the seat and started to play, he played ... well, he played, I have never heard such playing, not even at Nôtre-Dame or St Paul's have I heard such beautiful organ playing; when the last dying notes echoed through the jungle I jumped from my seat and embraced him with joy, he just smiled and said, 'D'you want something else?' And he played, he played Mozart, Schubert sonatas, operas, he played all night long, the negroes were wild! When he finished he turned his face to me, he was sweating abundantly, his face was white, he smiled and said, 'Viens, petit.'

From my camp-fire, from my three Africans, from a time and a place whose reality was dissolved in a dream, I had slipped away, it was André I saw, it was his music I listened to; and I had been brought there by Christian, who had had a cup of coffee and some jam after that, and who could pause to explain patiently to me what he meant by 'bananiers', although his soul was already reaching forward towards André's music: 'Dis donc, vieux, et la musique ça marche?'

Oh yes, it did – it marched all night, and we, and those shiny-eyed negroes, marched with it. And only time stopped marching, because when it was all over at last, and we were perfectly at rest, the night after all was still not finished, but it no longer held any terrors. THEY had abandoned their pursuit, and we were safe.

And as we walked back in the dead of night arm in arm, we could hear the wild beasts in the distance howling.

Let them howl. When there are tall 'svelte' powerfully built priests like André around, ready to take my arm in the dead of night, or play Mozart and Schubert, on a steam organ, in a jungle clearing, with such inspired insouciant skill, then you can be fairly certain that I, for one, won't even hear the howling.

The Flight from the Eagle's Nest

As a child Alexis Jaye was oppressed by a feeling that he was unlike anybody else. On the face of it, this seemed hard to explain. He was small for his age and rather thin, with short dark hair and sharp aggressive features. At school he was attentive and intelligent, at home he was friendly and easy to please. When he was six years old he came to the top of the stairs in their narrow two-storey house and, instead of walking or running down as usual, launched himself gently into the air and glided, floated to the bottom.

Such a dramatic event gave him much to think about. He was aware that normal people didn't have this ability to fly, and he doubted if so strange a talent would be welcomed by those who didn't share it. On the whole, it might be better to keep it a secret.

At the same time, he now had convincing proof of his difference; and although he enjoyed flying, he didn't at all enjoy feeling different. Each time he flew, down the stairs or through his bedroom window into the back garden, he felt guilty: as though he were practising some forbidden indulgence. To make up for this – to salve his conscience, because he was quite unable to avoid the occasional lapse – he threw himself with exaggerated ardour into all the more normal aspects of his life. As a result, he made remarkable progress at school, so that his father began to plan seriously for his future.

Mr Jaye was largely self-educated but, perhaps for this very reason, attached considerable importance to the opportunities he had himself been denied. When Alexis was twelve, he was sent to the local grammar school. There, in his determination to achieve some sort of normality, he joined the school troop of Scouts. But destiny can't be ducked: this gesture gave him his first chance to test his secret capacity in a wider context. During the summer holidays the troop went camping for ten days in the Lake District, and one afternoon Alexis found himself alone on the high fells, standing on a steep rocky outcrop.

The wind ruffled his dark hair and the sun warmed his face, as he stood there looking down over a wide deep valley, struggling with his conscience. In this crucial moment there was nobody there to see him, nobody whose simple presence could have balanced the awful longing of his soul, and held him to that rock in the sunlit, safe, material world.

He spread his arms and half closed his eyes, breathing the wind, the rush of air, the freedom of space. The broad floppy brim of his Baden-Powell scout hat shaded his puzzled features. And then he sighed, and pushed gently with his feet against the earth, and a moment later that earth was no longer under his feet but far below him, and he slipped strangely through the air, looking down on the valley wrinkled like a map, on the green and purple heather and the glinting of a hundred moorland streamlets tumbling towards the river that meandered the valley floor. A mile away another hillside floated towards him. He turned in the air and willed himself to pause. Now he was concerned that somebody might wander into the valley and see him. His longing for the firm, safe earth became as overwhelming as his previous longing for the freedom of the air: hurriedly he sank to the ground, landing in a wide patch of heather near the river. For some time he lay there, trying to calm his turbulent emotions. Then he stood up and began the long walk back to camp.

The next afternoon he climbed to the same spot and then flew all the way across the valley and back again. He saw, even more plainly than six years before, that this was something he must always keep a secret – but he knew, now, that it was also something he could not deny himself. He could lament his difference, but he couldn't escape it.

When he was seventeen, Alexis fell in love.

Rosalind was a year younger than Alexis, with fair hair and a soft pouting mouth and eyelashes that were given to fluttering. In the early summer they began walking out, which in effect meant one evening a week and occasional afternoons, because Rosalind was an usherette at the local Odeon. Alexis was extremely proud of her. Mr Jaye was less pleased, because recently the headmaster had been talking discreetly of a scholarship to the university, but now Alexis showed more interest in Rosalind than in his exams. Mr Jaye spoke doggedly to Alexis of the advantages of a university degree, and Alexis listened and nodded and concurred, and thought all the time of Rosalind's pouting, inviting lips, and the way her eyelashes fluttered, and the plump hidden curves under her summer dresses. That summer Alexis didn't go camping. It was the first time in five years he had not returned to the hills and the wide valley where he could fly in solitude.

Towards the end of that summer Alexis lost Rosalind to George Rowley. Rosalind found it difficult to explain this to Alexis. Her eyelashes fluttered more than ever, and she was careful not to blame Alexis for anything. But George had certain undeniable advantages, such as his twin-cylinder Norton and the twelve pounds a week he earned as a house painter. Alexis listened to her in angry silence, knowing he must never show her how deeply she had hurt him, he must never reveal what a terrible mistake she was making. For she could put ten George Rowleys together, and they still wouldn't equal Alexis Jaye: they wouldn't be able to fly. So he clung to his silence and his angry grief. He could not tell her this.

All the same, the affair with Rosalind was important, because it gave Alexis a new resolve. He accepted once and for all his difference, and no longer regretted it. The world was wide, and in that tremendous width possibilities awaited him that neither Rosalind nor George could ever dream of. All through the autumn and winter he worked with single-minded vision, winning with perfunctory ease, next year, the top scholarship to a northern university.

To mark this success, Mr Jaye (a frugal man) gave him twenty-five pounds, and Alex went to Scotland for a holiday before the beginning of the university term. In the desolate expanses of the Cairngorms he found plenty of opportunities for flying.

At the university Alexis studied biology and joined the rock-climbers' club. He was a little under average height, and thin, but he had a wiry strength and a physical stamina that by themselves might have made him a climber. His still secret capacity, when added to these qualities, made him something altogether amazing to the mountaineering fraternity. In his first two years he climbed all the most difficult routes in Wales and northern England and Scotland, and pioneered others that nobody had dreamed possible and where few dared follow him. The mountains were his kingdom: he walked where men had never walked before, and when there was nobody there to see him he stepped into that other kingdom, of the birds; into the free and liberating spaces of the air.

In his third year he spent the Easter vacation in the Dolomites, climbing in snow with two Italians. In the summer he took a double first and decided to stay on at university for two more years on a research studentship. He was specializing now in biochemistry, directed into this new field by a curiosity about his own nature. He carried out laboratory tests on himself late at night, secretly and unobserved – and when he could escape to the hills he began to study the practical aspects of his singular endowment. He noticed that it required no physical effort: after the first gentle moment of launching himself into the air, he seemed to move and turn by the power of his will alone – almost as if in some mind-directed dream. But one result of his observation and analysis was oddly insinuating: ever since that first revelational moment at the age of six, when he flew down the stairs of their back-street semi, his flights had always started from a height and either continued on that level or taken him downwards. He had never flown *up*. Now that he realized this, he was eager to experiment.

He soon discovered that he was unable to gain altitude. He tried several times, in a remote valley on the Yorkshire moors, but there seemed to be some mental block inhibiting him. He came to the conclusion that it must be something psychological, a crucial failure of the will. For a time he was disturbed by this discovery, and impatient with a limitation that hadn't bothered him before he became aware of it. He considered psychoanalysis, but discarded this idea because of the manifest impossibility of being sincere with the analyst. Presently he decided to shelve a problem which time, after all, was likely enough to solve.

The two years of his studentship passed, and Alexis was offered a fellowship, which he accepted. The life of the university suited him, and his solo ascent of the north face of the Eiger had established him internationally as a mountaineer, so the university authorities were indulgent towards his long absences. In the Alps he met Gordon Strathallan, a young Scot who was also a prodigious climber. They made several difficult climbs together and then projected an expedition to Alaska, where the next year they scored a number of first ascents. Alexis enjoyed company in the mountains, but there were also moments when he had a consuming need for solitude. In all his relationships now, since Rosalind, he was aware that his secret difference was a dividing element, a gulf that could never be bridged as he could bridge the gulfs between the mountain tops.

Gordon invited him one Christmas to his family home in Ross. Alexis was twenty-six, physically hard but socially at ease in a world that long ago he had known could not be half as strange as he was himself. Within a very short time Gordon's sister Alison was in love with him, and although Alexis no longer trusted his own capacity for love, he experienced an answering tenderness that passed, on the surface, for much the same thing.

Alison was the very opposite of Rosalind – dark and quick and vividly intelligent. Perhaps she sensed something inexplicable in Alexis. At any rate, after one over-eager confidence, she never spoke to him of marriage. Instead, at

Easter, she came to the university town where Alexis worked and took a small house in the same street as his faculty. They lived together, more or less discreetly, for a year – Alexis was practised in secrets. It was a year in which Alexis, without exactly planning this, neither climbed nor flew.

This was a decisive period for Alexis: in moments of lucid objectivity, he saw it as his last experiment with normality. Possibly it was this very lucidity that defeated him, although afterwards he was inclined to see it as something inexorably determined by his nature. The morning after Whit Monday he returned to his faculty rooms and found a telegram from the Midlands town where he had been born. It was quite short, telling him only that his mother and father had been killed in an overturned coach on the bank holiday roads.

Alexis sat for two hours in his rooms, thinking about his life and himself and sometimes about Alison. Then he telephoned the Dean and explained briefly that for private reasons he must ask for a four months' leave of absence, starting immediately. He wrote a short note to Alison, and caught the afternoon train to London.

There, he spent a fortnight talking with various editors and company directors, because he needed sponsors; and at various embassies arranging visas and climbing permits. At the end of the fortnight he left London in a BOAC jet for India – the first time in his life he had flown by mechanical means. He found it, by comparison, an uninteresting experience.

The story was in most of the newspapers even before he left. Alexis Jaye was going to Everest, to make the first solo ascent.

This was something that had occupied his mind for many years. But he had always hesitated, not because the mountain dismayed him but because his mind recoiled from a future where this was already accomplished. He was afraid of a world where there were no higher mountains waiting to be climbed.

His decision had been made in those two hours after he read the telegram. He had made it almost in desperation, realizing he must climb the mountain as a gesture of final renunciation, and so at last to confront himself exactly as he was, as alone as any man must be alone on Everest, but lonelier still. As for the afterwards, he would accept it: as indeed he had already accepted it years ago – as perhaps in his heart he had accepted it from the first, when he was six years old.

Alexis climbed Everest. He planted a flag that stood out like sheet metal in the wind, and photographed it. And in a more private ritual, standing on the roof of the world, he launched himself into the air and flew out over half a mile of the terrifying Himalayan wasteland, through that roaring wind, before returning to the peak. But presently he knew he would have to leave this particular solitude. He was tired, and disinclined to simulate. Gathering up his equipment, he pushed himself once again into the air, and floated down over two miles of ice and snow to the camp where he had left his Sherpa porters. Hundreds of miles away, and then thousands of miles away, people were waiting for him: the febrile world of earthbound people. Alexis went back to that world.

In his rooms at the university another letter was waiting for him, this one from Gordon Strathallan. He congratulated Alexis. He wrote that Alison had returned home briefly and then gone away again, abroad. She had left no word for Alexis. He wondered if Alexis would like to come up to the west coast again at Christmas. Alexis accepted.

He was fond of Gordon. He knew that Gordon was an exceptional mountaineer, and exceptionally courageous. Courage was a quality Alexis had never needed in the mountains: the physical courage that Gordon possessed to the point of recklessness.

They climbed several of the Ross mountains, mantled in their winter snow. One day, scrambling on crags that overlooked the sea, they came to a rock tower with a deep forty-foot overhang. It was known locally as the Eagle's Nest, Gordon explained. In summer it could be climbed quite easily from the eastern side, but the overhang in any season was formidable, needing ropes and pitons. In winter, he said laughingly, it was impossible, even for a single-handed conqueror of Everest.

They sat down beneath the overhang, on a narrow ledge, their legs dangling over a precipice that plunged two or three hundred feet to snowy screes. Alexis looked up, at the overhang. Gordon followed his eyes, and grinned. They could work round to the other side, he suggested, and try the east face; but even that would be very difficult to climb in ice. Alexis shook his head, still looking up at the overhang.

'You would have to be a bird, to get up from this side,' Gordon said. 'It's well named the Eagle's Nest. You'd have to be able to fly.'

Alexis sighed.

'I can fly,' he said.

Gordon laughed. 'I could almost believe you. It would explain so much.'

'I *can* fly,' Alexis repeated. 'But I have never allowed anyone to see. And I've never been able to fly *upwards*.' He circled his knees with his arms, and gazed out over the sea. 'I wish I knew *why*. Perhaps because there has never been sufficient reason. An *aim*.'

Gordon looked at him curiously. 'You're an odd chap,' he said. And then: 'Why did you leave Alison?'

Alexis shook his head again, confused. 'I don't know. Because I am different. Because I can fly, I suppose.' He stood up. 'I'm going to try, Gordon. Perhaps this time it'll work. You see, this time I really want to go upwards – I *must*.'

'Don't be an idiot,' Gordon said lazily.

Alexis looked up into the sky. It was a cloudless day, with a thin wintry sun. He breathed in the sharp cold air, deeply, spreading wide his arms, straining towards the buttressed Eagle's Nest above him.

After all, he wasn't sorry that he could fly. He smiled, always looking upwards; and pushed himself gently into the air. Perhaps, as he fell, it still seemed to him that he was flying.

The Myth of Belamor

Michael Julianus, Sir: in the thirty-eighth aion of his proemial sempiternity: formerly, formally to remind you, Sir, novitiate of the Schools, *scholasticus praestans* by your sapient favour, student of All-the-Arts.

You Sir, esteemed Professor, inscrutably perceived promise in the tentative fervours of Michael Julianus: praised and encouraged his subtil and muscular intellect: gently nourished the fire of inchoate curiosity flooding his [veins]: took him indeed most especially to your [heart]. He was grateful.

Among his condisciples was one Belamor: whom Michael Julianus perpuissauntly, as will be disclosed, favoured above others with his friendship. They were of an age, each having entered his third aion: they each were under your tutelage. Yet in all else there seemed nothing they had or held in common, and therefore their friendship was frequently remarked. You yourself, Sir, remarked it with an impression of regret. You will remember, even now, your reluctant concealed distaste for Belamor.

He was a mistake: an oversight: an intrusion in the Schools. Perhaps once in a sempiternity it happens: the delicate trembling balance of Selection fails: but Selection is irrevocable.

Sir, for thirty-five aions truth quiescently has maintained an ambush: (not once but) twice Selection failed you – not Belamor alone, but your favoured Julianus: Michael Julianus also, infranched Selection: entered the Schools, unaware at first and even innocently, but like the cuckoo's egg of his own mythology.

It was no accident that Michael Julianus and Belamor achieved their fast friendship: only at first neither was aware of the causal nature of their association. Their studies threw them frequently together. And from the first Michael Julianus was made conscient of certain excentric qualities in his friend Belamor. To be precise: Belamor was manifestly unsuited to the Schools. His mind was deviational, it explored and lingered beyond the fringes of lucidity: timid of knowledge or unconcerned, it dabbled in the dark primitive territories with-out intellect. He was ill-equipped to make a Scholar. He lacked the qualities to recommend himself to other Scholars. And yet, perversely, he recommended himself: to Michael Julianus, archepitome of Scholars. Sir, this occurred. All-in-a-flash, Belamor revealed himself: shewed himself strange, terrible, beautiful: O Belamor, your secret dark power.

Michael Julianus, favoured neophyte of Knowledge: Acolyte-of-the-Truth, intellect serving Intellect: became in a single moment bounden to the wheel of Ignorance: thrall of Belamor.

His bland clever [face] never betrayed him: was never shadowed by the cast of Belamor's deceit. They were an insidious pairing. Belamor was suspect: you, Sir, suspected him: but the mien of Julianus smoothed suspicion from his friend, where-as their association should have reflected suspicion on himself. Michael Julianus was praised for his redoubtable unflinching spirit, that he should be undismayed by the task of reforming Belamor. In secret together they concerned themselves (not with the reform of Belamor but) with the slow unwilling ineluctable re-forming of Michael Julianus.

The secret of Belamor was a resurrection: of an infinitely old defeated and forgotten Art. Belamor contained or had dis-covered, Imagination. Sir, even its extinction was never whispered in the Schools, so thoroughly had Knowledge and Intellect triumphed. But Belamor knew. And in Michael Julianus and Belamor, Intellect and Imagination cohabited: they did not contend. Perhaps the Schools had buried that conflict too well. Intellect and Imagination, they struck sparks from each other.

Michael Julianus for his pre-eminent superexcellent qualities, Belamor for the protection Julianus afforded his strangeness: were most acceptable to their many con-disciples. Their friendship did not exclude them from the pleasures of esteem and popularity. In the Halls they were much frequented: they were sought-out for their opinion on every matter of significance. It would be exemptible to affirm: in a manner they were the most celebrated novitiates of their millennium. Therefore everything that was secret between them, they perforce ex-cluded from the Schools: in private colloquy they evolved a private life, far from prying and inquisitive [eyes].

Sir, Michael Julianus crowned his most exceptional per-excellent career at the Schools, with a Thesis: the fruit of research: which you yourself were pleased to honour with many awards and commendations: not least the place of distinction you gave to this Thesis in the hierarchy of the Library: now housed among all the treasures of the Schools.

On the remote peripheries of Space, Michael Julianus discovered, chronicled and impeccably documented, the long-forgotten overlooked creation of a minor Deity. It was considered an absolute model of Research: became firmly established in the curriculum of the Schools: was expounded and extolled, Sir, in your own lectures on Primitive Intelligence.

Now in repentant memory of the many great favours that you Sir, esteemed Professor, once graciously shewed one Michael Julianus: this Footnote is written to his Thesis. On his own authority – and in this he is the only authority – the essence of his confession is this: the Thesis is a forgery.

*

Michael Julianus and Belamor [walked] together with-out the Schools.

In terms of eternal Truth it would be hard to describe their surroundings, but the manifestations were these: arbors tinkled and flashed against the sky, supported by firm green undulations: there was light before and behind them: the channels of communication were uncluttered, limpid.

THE MYTH OF BELAMOR

Belamor [said]: 'The Schools should shew a greater interest in personal manifestations.' 'Belamor, you are very-critical-of the Schools.' This was but an idle exchange, preparing a way to the particular: which Belamor very quickly approached. 'For an ensample, Michael Julianus: I will now manifest myself in a shape I have recently imagined.'

Belamor with-drew: and presently shewed himself in a strange fashion: there was to his [body] a [head], limbs grew from his body, two [arms] and two [legs]. Appended to these arms, were intricately contrived [hands], to his legs [feet], to his hands [fingers], to his feet [toes]. His body delicately was clothed in white. His head was featured: two blue sparkling exstatic [eyes], red curving mobile [lips] of [mouth], fair moulded [chin] and [cheeks], smooth [forehead], sculpted [ears]: in glinting golden curls this head was crowned with finest softest [hair]. He stood, silent and achieved, his eyes a-light: with the merest smile upon his magic face.

Michael Julianus was dumb-founded.

He, O esteemed Professor, whom your arts had trained and constrained, channelled into the hierographa of intellect: in that dreadful moment stripped of understanding, in-comprehending: was assailed and instantly was vanquished: by Beauty.

Belamor softly spoke: 'See, the power of Imagination.' 'See, the defeat of Intellect.' 'Not the defeat only: but the triumph of both, of you and I conjoined.' Michael Julianus looked at Belamor, and had only one wish: but it was hard. Slowly, arduously, the transformation was made: not by his will unaided, but in conjunction with Belamor's will. His body grew in similarity to Belamor's. When it was done, they were not the same: Michael Julianus was dark to Belamor's gold: stronger and less graceful: compact, containing and displaying a force, an energy. But he too had limbs, arms and legs, a featured head: he felt his hand taken in another, and knew contact. 'Michael Julianus, this is a secret between us: it is not for the Schools.' 'It is a secret, Belamor.'

So-it-began.

*

Michael Julianus patiently, incessantly applied himself to the task of comprehending the nature of Belamor: and the nature of himself in the light of Belamor. Michael Julianus and Belamor remained Intellect and Imagination, but now con-mingled. His task was to apprehend Imagination by the power of Intellect. In this the Schools could not help him: the Archives were silent on the subject. Finally, he must resort to Belamor himself, unique repository of Imagination, for the resolution of his problem.

With-out the Schools they walked together privately, in their new manifestations: Michael Julianus warily approached the substance of his porismic agony. And always looking with wonder upon that wonderful form.

'Belamor, tell me again: what is your secret?'

His secret smile. 'Look at me, Michael Julianus: that is all of my secret: I created.' 'Created what?'

'Beauty.'

Michael Julianus reeled. That word had touched-him, as surely as a hand. But this was nothing they knew-of in the Schools.

He returned to the Archives: sifted them down to their residual dust: and dis-covered: nothing. Creation had ended, sempiternities ago. It was all documented: a necessary impetus to Evolution. But Beauty, it seemed, had never had this meaning. Or it was forgotten, even by the Archives.

'O Belamor – what is Beauty?'

Sir, Michael Julianus unexpectedly had stumbled on the boundary of boundless Intellect: the paradox dismayed him.

Belamor secretly smiled his secret smile. He impassively waited. Drawn ineluctably against his rational nature, Michael Julianus reached-out his manifest hand: reached out and at last touched: the golden head of Belamor: his fingers touched that manifest head. His hand trembled.

Belamor [breathed] softly on the air, and his breath warmly delicately pulsingly enveloped Michael Julianus: so that a whisper of it subtilly touched-at his manifest ears.

'I have imagined a Vision,' whispered the breath of Belamor. 'O Michael Julianus, this manifestation which we have created' (that he had created) 'is not whole: it requires completion.' Belamor had conceived an idea, O esteemed Professor: that the Soul is a severed being, seeking totality. And he thereupon projected for Michael Julianus his idea, shewing him the principle of [male] and [female].

'Do you understand, O Michael Julianus, do you now understand?' 'I understand: with my senses, with my manifest body: but my mind is dark with it.' 'This is a new understanding. Ex-cept the Schools: this is an understanding with-out the mind.' Belamor gently inclined his head: to Michael Julianus this seemed a singularly fugitive submission.

So-it-continued.

So for a millennium did they successfully hide their secret knowledge. Sir, no rumour of it reached you. Michael Julianus, esteemed Professor, continued to in-cite your favour: his Intellect was always unimpaired. He assiduously exhausted the learning of the Schools: his irreproachable perscrutations were the wonder of all: his perexcellence as a Scholar was a by-word: his fleet fluent perspicuous mind, nothing could make to flinch. But Belamor was the-very-opposite. Belamor continued-to-be remarked: you, Sir, continued to remark him. But having infranched Selection, he was accepted by the Schools for the lustre reflected on him by Michael Julianus: he was considered merely a poor Scholar, and only different from others of his kind in his imperscrutable indifference to failure. His condisciples were of a mind to pity him: and to envy him his evident friendship with Michael Julianus. On-the-whole, the dichotomy of these feelings did neither alarm nor imperil that sodality, of Belamor and Michael Julianus: generally, when they were alone, they were left alone.

Sir, as the millennium approached its term, Michael Julianus approached the matter of his Thesis. This was to be the crown and seal of his academic career. What subject might be worthy of such a scholar?

*

Michael Julianus worked in secret: he worked in the Library and the Archives: none knew the nature of his work, the subject of his Thesis: ex-cept Belamor. You, Sir, would closely question him: yet trusted him. He was *scholasticus praestans*, by your sapient favour. He must be allowed to work alone. You indulged his whim of secrecy. The Thesis was finished: submitted: lauded and infallibly acclaimed. Took its own place in those Archives from which it had putatively been scoured.

For your refreshment, Sir, this conspectus of his work:

Primo: (primordial postulate): a hither-to unchronicled planet: situate in the Seventh Peripheral Universe, its existence inferred from documents appended for your scrutiny. This planet referred-to for convenience by its indigenous name: Earth. On doubtful evidence the Seventh Peripheral Universe had been provisionally attributed to a minor Deity of the Age-of-Creation: Yah-veh. This, Michael Julianus seemed to confirm and prove in a brilliantly reasoned and documented exordium to his Thesis.

Secundo: closely chronicled and ex-posed, a definitive history of Earth from its in-ception. This was the bulk of his Thesis. He used the Archives as they had never been used before: impossible to track him in his course: but the documents were there at every point to confirm his every assertion. In ten thousand closely-written [pages] he expounded the physical laws that governed Earth: this was a necessary proem to his formidable task. Earth, he discovered, had been populated by various manifestations of Life. These were on-the-whole primitive manifestations, for Earth had existed early in the Cycle of Creation: Yah-veh was yet unpractised. His account of Life-on-Earth, and its most completely evolved manifestation, Man, was the remarkable subject of his Thesis.

Michael Julianus chronicled Man-on-Earth from his genesis: nothing escaped his scrutiny. A curious and interesting aspect of these primitive manifestations was their elaborate mythology. Yah-veh had given them inklings of their origin:

they always were avid embroiderers. Michael Julianus faithfully recorded their mythologies. He collected and collated languages, literatures, sciences. He appended to his general history, biographies of a million Men: millions more of lesser interest attracted passing mention each in a brief hundred [pages]. Each tentative advance in knowledge was intricately plotted: the social, the economic, the political, the artisitic, the philosophical: minutely were ex-posed. There was not a stone left unturned in his search, not a particle of dust unexamined, not an echo of a word passed unheard across the sempiternities. Earth revealed its last secrets to Michael Julianus. Ex-cept one mystery.

Tertio: to its abrupt conclusion. Michael Julianus could offer no explanation: others from internal evidence claimed to infer a resolution, but he explicitly maintained an open-mind. There in the chronicle it stood: Yah-veh himself fatefully revisited his Creation: incredibly but two millennia then passed and the-planet-Earth was ex-tinct (suddenly extinguished). Imperforate occlusive darkness circumscended the Seventh Peripheral Universe.

Esteemed Professor, remorsefully Michael Julianus now discovers the Truth: it happened like this:

Michael Julianus and Belamor in their secret manifestations secretly associated as often as they could escape the Schools. And their association, their secret, demanded some explicit endeavour: they searched for consummation.

'Michael Julianus, this manifestation that we have dis-covered' (that he had dis-covered) 'this body with head and arms and legs, with hands, feet, fingers, toes: this divided creature, male and female: this featured head with hair, with eyes, mouth, ears, nose, lips: this intricate and marvellous mechanism: deserves reality.' 'But it is not real.' 'But it could-have-been real.'

A seed ensowed. O Michael Julianus, O Belamor: whose mind first conceived? Belamor's, of extreme Imagination – Michael Julianus', of perexcellent Intelligence? Undoubtedly it was, it must have been, of Belamor. 'To create a world to match, to frame, this manifest Beauty.' Undoubtedly, Imagination was the in-ceptor: undoubtedly, only the disciplines of Intellect could achieve the geniture of that in-ception. One-without-the-other, could not have done it. Michael Julianus, with Belamor, did.

Michael Julianus worked in the Archives: Intellect demanded that the work should be perfect, the ends perfectly buried beyond the possibility of ex-posure. Belamor's leaping Imagination was his impetus. Earth, so-to-speak, was born: Man was created. A place was made where-in their secret manifestations could walk, un-secretly.

Sir, this is the Truth of it: the Thesis is a forgery. With such cunning did Michael Julianus work on it, with such marvellous invention did Belamor assist him: it was a perfect, a too-perfect forgery. Sir, appended to this confession are the proofs: the Archives which proved the Thesis, will prove the forgery: Michael Julianus has now un-buried the tortuous paths of his pre-sumed research.

There remains the hither-to unresolved mystery of that abrupt conclusion: and another matter of some importance. Sir, some further explanation is necessary.

Michael Julianus and Belamor quarrelled: the consummation of their secret friendship was to destroy their friendship: ultimately Intellect and Imagination would confirm their ancient incompatibility. It was like this:

Belamor postulated and described the manifestations of Earth: all that he imagined was good and beautiful. But Michael Julianus could not forswear Intelligence. Intelligence demanded corollaries: into the chronicles of Earth, even against his will, evil and ugliness were assigned a place. Intellect bent and corrupted the fine Vision of Belamor: Logic was too strong for Michael Julianus.

With sadness, they recognized their gradual estrangement. (The episode, Sir, of Yah-veh's return to his Creation, was Belamor's penultimate vain assertion of his will against Michael Julianus.) Thereafter was a rapid deterioration in their understanding.

But upon the thresh-hold of disaster, Michael Julianus

paused. For love of Belamor, or for the memory of his love: you, Sir, shall judge. He saw with horror the swiftly approaching destruction of Belamor's Earth: destroyed by the inexorable logic of his own Intelligence. Indeed, he was touched-by Belamor, -by the memory of Belamor: and yet he smiled a little at his own concern. For was it not all-a-dream: of no existence, ex-cept on [paper]?

But he stopped. Because Belamor was gone.

Sir, Belamor as you will remember, had fled the Schools. Michael Julianus presented his mysteriously un-finished Thesis. Thirty-five aions since have passed.

*

Thirty-five aions. And Belamor returned: presented himself to Michael Julianus in his old manifestation: sadly.

He had only a few words for Michael Julianus, and they were strange enough to suggest insanity: 'Michael Julianus, I have dis-covered a Truth: there is reality in manifestations: Earth exists.'

Sir, Belamor has gone-away again. To the Seventh Peripheral Universe: looking-for Earth. He has a theory that he will find it exactly in the condition of the conclusion of the Thesis: as Michael Julianus had left it. He believes he can still save his Vision from destruction.

Michael Julianus, Sir, knows that this is madness: that Earth has no existence with-out the Thesis. It is a forgery. Belamor is with-out Reason.

Not now for memory of Belamor: nor for apprehensions about Belamor's vain search, esteemed Professor: but for reasons of personal shame, and in the name of the Truth to which he would return, he ardently desires and requests: that you, Sir, as a measure of your sapient favour once shown to one Michael Julianus, formerly novitiate of the Schools, *scholasticus praestans*, student of All-the-Arts: should acknowledge that this displaisant incident has gone too far: and therefore, swiftly upon receipt of this Confession, ex-tract from the Archives, and [burn]: his Thesis.

The Athenians

PROEM

I

In a Greek Orthodox church the altar is hidden behind a decorated screen which follows certain inexorable laws of design. On each side of the doors are tall painted icons, the first on the left a picture of the Virgin Mary, the first on the right a picture of Christ. This is invariable. And in the centre, exactly above the arch of the doors, is painted a single eye, the eye of God, the All-Seeing Eye. Because it sees everything, into all hearts and into all kinds of men, it is in turn seen as many things – grotesque, menacing, fearful, loving, beautiful, haunting.

Above the Eye, crowning the doors, at the highest point, are two letters – Alpha and Omega: the beginning and the end.

II

Of all accidental creations, since the turning of the first wheel, the most implausible is the idea of the beginning and the end; of alpha and omega. For the Church, no doubt, they have a peculiar and special significance, but this story does not particularly concern the Church – it lives and lived in a curious realm of its own, somewhere between art and life.

But to be practical, I must all the same begin: I must make an appearance of beginning. I must break into the flow that is the small world of my story, like a swimmer who plunges into a river. I hesitate. The water is cold. I look each way, standing on the brink. To my right are the distant mountains and snowy Olympus – aloof, disdainfully remote; the river comes from those mountains, but I cannot see it beginning. To my left is the fat and lazy valley, where the river broadens and sinks to the level of wide soft fields, and meanders to an ocean I cannot see: let us suppose, to wine-dark, Homeric waters. But I am not concerned with extremes. All I know of the river is what I see: it flows – it does not begin, it does not end. I can choose my spot. If I don't like it I can climb out and try again, somewhere else: it will still be the same river.

I can feel the sun now. The river reflects the sun a thousand times. The water invites me.

I plunge.

* * *

This is not a beginning, and it cannot end.

THE PHILOSOPHY OF WEALTH

The Story of the Millionaire and the Five-Hundred-Drachma Note

I

Visitors to Athens are drawn irresistibly and immediately to the Parthenon. It is something they cannot escape, any more than a needle can escape a magnet. The Acropolis is the Mecca of *tourisme*, the ultimate fate of the globe-trotter. They come, most of them with no true idea of what they are going to see, and leave an hour or so later with no idea of what they have seen. Voluble and inexhaustible guides encompass thousands of years of civilization in a phrase and a sweeping gesture, and the crowd sways helplessly before a vastness that moves each individual to the most secret centre of his soul, but which few can define because few are familiar with those shrouded contours of the psyche. The Parthenon stands in wounded majesty against the sky, defying their anxious admiration. It is a challenge they don't know how to meet. They look at it, and wonder what they ought to see, and some think what a shame that it was ever destroyed, and others wonder what there is in a heap of marble that can inspire such uncertain and profound belief.

The American Millionaire was no exception. He stood in a haze of doubt, a little apart from the quietly docile crowd of which he was supposed to be a part, reflecting that here was something which had no dollar meaning. Even if he wanted to buy it, even if they wanted to sell it, how could anyone ever fix a price? It was worth everything, and it was worth nothing: a cent, a million million dollars. *He wanted* it. Or he wanted to remove it, an affront to reality, from existence.

Sometimes, behind his doubt that was always at the front of his mind, he heard the harsh persuasive voice of the Greek guide, explaining the Parthenon in fervent French and English, with a wholly fascinating dexterity.

'Ladies and gentlemen, the Parthenon ... *Messieurs et Mesdames, le Parthénon* ... the most famous building in the world ... *l'édifice le plus célèbre du monde* ... the highest achievement of all civilization.'

Kostantios the guide removed his brown felt hat, mopped the beaded sweat from his bald head, and took a deep breath. Twenty minutes to go. He looked at his submissive audience, and chose his words with the deliberation of Zeus selecting a thunderbolt. But thunderbolts could not touch the American Millionaire.

A cent: a million million dollars. It's too big for the garden. Have to move the swimming-pool. *I want it.* Or put it *round* the swimming-pool.

He groaned. It's no use – you can't have the Parthenon without the Acropolis. You can't have the Acropolis without Athens – the Parthenon *is* Athens. And he couldn't have Athens.

Even an American Millionaire must face facts. Athens won't go into a garden.

'My friends, you will not believe me ... *mes amis, vous ne me croirez pas* ... but there is not a single straight line in the Parthenon ... *pas une seule ligne droite au Parthénon.*'

Sun-bleached marble; scarred columns; a shattered roof. A ruin, simply a ruin – a junk heap of broken stones tossed up by history on a high rock. It would look the same in California.

'*Ici vous voyez l'homme, l'art et la nature, travaillants ensembles à produire la perfection* ... art and nature, working together to produce perfection.'

It would look the same anywhere. A scrap heap. Worthless. Why bother with it?

I want it.

'Ladies and gentlemen ... *Messieurs et Mesdames...*'
Kostantios flicked up a sleeve to look at his watch. Five more minutes.

'The Parthenon was at first a Greek building ... *autrefois le Parthénon était un édifice grec* ... but it is no longer Greek ... *mais ce n'est plus grec.*'

The Parthenon was silent, heavy with time, anchored by centuries of endurance to its rocky foundation; but the sky seemed to move, the pure depth of blue seemed to gather protectively against the thin edges of those immortal proportions, and the sun struck a clean, echoing light from chipped Pentelic marble.

'*Il appartient à tout le monde; il appartient à moi, il appartient à vous...* It belongs to the whole world – it belongs to me, and it belongs to you.'

Diogenes P. Brandt looked again in astonishment, and looked away. He slipped on the worn rock and stumbled awkwardly. An arm held him where he swayed, and a pair of sympathetic brown eyes found and held his own for a moment.

II

He saw a young man, bronzed by the Athenian sky.

'You all right, sir? Too much sun perhaps?'

'I'm all right. Yes, I'm all right. These rocks – I guess I slipped – the sun on that thing – ' ... his voice trailed away, and he gestured helplessly towards the silent reproach standing in radiant marble behind him. He looked at the young man again. He saw dark hair and a pleasant face; a dirty white coat, a torn, stained shirt; and a few yards away, on the rocks, an angular wooden tripod crowned by a black cabinet of miracles that had an air of hidden mystery, and all the sinister possibilities of Pandora's Box.

'You want photograph, sir? Very nice photograph, you and Parthenon?'

'No. No, thank you.'

But he felt curiously weak, uncertain even of the will to resist. He allowed the young man to turn him again, to seat him on a rock, and then watched listlessly while he spread the tripod and disappeared under a thick black cloth. Presently the smiling face reappeared.

'Very nice photograph, sir. You take it back to America, you see – surprise everyone.'

The face disappeared again. The voice went on, muffled by the black cloth.

'You ready, sir?'

Back to America. To the security, the safe familiarity of his Californian house and estate.

A long brown arm reached round the camera and fumbled for a moment. Everything was very still, waiting for something. Two epochs, two civilizations, had come together briefly, and the camera, as if it understood its responsibility, stared thoughtfully at Diogenes P. Brandt – fat, hunched, haunted, framed by the Parthenon. There was a faint click.

'Five minutes, sir. You wait five minutes, look at Parthenon, look at lovely buildings, I soon have photograph ready.'

The Millionaire sat, contained in his own world of silence. He didn't see the brown triumphant face plunge back beneath the enveloping black cloth; he didn't look at the beautiful buildings. The blue sky he saw was half a world away, as blue, as clear as this sky, but without this sky's strangeness. He saw the trellised white walls and the gently sloping roof of a house which was his; the wide, tidy garden with its well-drilled semi-tropical vegetation, the cool avenues between obedient palm trees, the swimming-pool with its two fountains and the glass pavilion at one end.

He pulled fretfully at his collar, loosened his tie, and felt the sweat trickling against his spine and down the insides of his arms.

California. Safe, new, submissive California. To a millionaire, homely California; to Diogenes P. Brandt, home.

'Damn and blast! Damn, damn and damn!'

The head had reappeared, curiously changed.

'This bloody camera! Socrates understood it, but I'm hanged if I can. The third time this week. I'm sorry, the light's got in. Ruined it.'

The Millionaire felt the astonishment seeping into his confused, bewildered mind. He was aware of the change, but not yet aware of its significance. He looked at the young man, who was waving a piece of white paper disgustedly in front of him.

Then he traced the origin of his astonishment, and found words for it.

'But you're English. I'd know that anywhere for an English voice. For Christ's sake, what are you doing up here – dressed like a local, and peddling photographs?'

In his excitement the American forgot his own personal anguish. Afterwards, he could never be certain how much had really happened to him, how much was due to a sun-worked imagination.

The young man smiled apologetically.

'I suppose I *am* English. As much as I am anything.'

'But what are you doing here?'

'– Peddling photographs –'

There was a note of simplicity in this reply that quelled the American's rising exasperation. He looked thoughtful.

'A fool question,' he said – 'and I don't make a habit of asking fool questions. What's your name?'

'Julius,' said the young man.

The American had a strong feeling there was nothing more to say about this; so he said nothing. Silence stretched between them. Then suddenly he held out his right hand and gripped the brown hand of the young man.

'My name is Diogenes,' he said.

Solemnly they shook hands.

Again silence crept between them, but this time it was an easy silence, for the American had forgotten his own perplexity.

'You are a long way from home,' said Julius presently.

'And you aren't?' The American was beginning to understand. He screwed up his keen eyes against the glare of the reflected sun, and spoke quietly, more to himself than to the young man.

'Yes,' he said. 'A long way from home.' And then, with something of a sigh, 'And I must be getting back.'

Julius nodded.

A boy appeared, hovered a few yards from them, watching curiously. His feet were bare and baked brown by dust and sun; his clothes were ragged but they had a rinsed cleanliness about them. On his head, sizes too big for him, a Panama hat of incredible age reached ludicrously to his ears. He balanced on one leg, scratching a shin with the big toe of his other foot.

The American stood up. He fumbled in his pocket, and brought something out.

'Thanks for the picture, Julius, anyway. Even if it wasn't so good.'

His hand went to the young man's shirt pocket, there was a faint rustle, and then he was gone: a lonely figure picking his careful, heavy way down the rock steps.

Julius watched him go.

Thoughtfully his hand felt into the shirt pocket, and he pulled out a five-hundred-drachma note. He looked again at the retreating American. The Millionaire was still within shouting distance, but Julius didn't shout. Instead he turned to the boy, and called.

'Look, Plato. What shall we do with this?'

The boy scrambled lightly to his side, and looked. His eyes sought the other's, doubtfully, his forehead crinkled in thought.

'There is my grandmother,' he said – and then stopped. 'No,' he said.

'No.' Julius smiled at him. 'I have a better idea. Come with me.'

Together they climbed the rocks, passed between the Parthenon and the Erechtheion, and reached the highest part of the Acropolis, overlooking the sprawl of the city. They stood together at the wall, gazing over a jungle of rooftops to the distant haze that covered the mountains. Julius began to fold the note, carefully, as he had folded paper when he was a child. When he was ready, he gave it to the boy.

'You do it, Plato. I am too old for such games.'

The boy took the note, which was folded into the shape of a dart, and leaning out over the wall, threw it. Together they watched it float out into the emptiness of the sky, growing smaller in its gentle movement, until at last it was lost against the pattern of houses.

'It has the wind behind it,' said Julius. 'It should go far.'

The Innocence of Julius

I

In April, a year ago, nobody noticed the flight of the five-hundred-drachma note over Athens. I was in Athens myself, and *I* didn't notice it. I climbed the Acropolis in the evening, but Julius and Plato had gone, and even Kostantios the guide had abandoned the Parthenon to the night. He was somewhere below, somewhere among all those houses that stretched in three directions to the lap of the distant mountains, and in the fourth to the sea; somewhere down there, conducting a party of tourists round the more innocuous nightspots of Athens, with a nicely modulated version of his afternoon's enthusiasms. It was between sunset and moonrise, and for a brief moment all that marble was allowed to rest: mine were the only intruding, inquisitive eyes.

You may wonder what I am doing on the Acropolis, since you left me after that first cold plunge into the river. I explained about the Acropolis. It draws people, irresistibly, and I was drawn like everybody else. But perhaps it would be better to return to the river. After all, when I stood that evening on the Acropolis I knew nothing about Julius, or Plato, or Socrates; I had not yet heard of Kostantios or Nikolaos; Sappho, I thought, was a poetess who lived on Lesbos in the distant hellenic past; Diogenes and Dulcibella were unknown to me. For me this story did not exist; it hadn't begun.

And yet, like the river, it was going on all the time.

I think I'll join you for a moment on the bank. The water is very pleasant, once one is in, but I chose the wrong place. We must walk – upstream. There is a spot I know about a mile (or a year, maybe) from here – we'll try again there, together.

II

Julius climbed stiffly from the train, dragging three suitcases.

'You want taxi?'

A beaming, enthusiastic face shoved itself close to his own; he looked down at it. He tested the platform with his foot. It felt unconvincingly solid after three swaying days in the train. So this was Athens. And this crinkled, monkey face belonged to an Athenian.

'Yes please,' he said.

The taxi driver seized one of his suitcases, the smallest, and Julius staggered along the platform behind him with the other two. Outside it was dusty; looking at the white flat houses, Julius felt himself more than halfway to the Levant. A battered car received them and the three suitcases with cheerful optimism, and lurched furiously away from the station. The taxi driver spoke little English, and Julius had no Greek. Julius showed him the label on one of his suitcases, and sat back limply in his seat. He had not slept for three nights.

'Hotel, sir.'

Julius sat up, fishing in his pocket for some money. He took out a fifty-drachma note and gave it to the taxi driver, hoping it was enough. He knew at once, from the expression on the monkey face, that it was more than enough, but it was too late; he was left standing in a swirl of dust on the pavement with his three suitcases.

His room was on the fourth floor. French windows opened onto a balcony overlooking the city. To his right the street followed a line ruled straight towards the Acropolis. A mile away the inescapable Parthenon stood high above the avenue of houses. He closed the windows and shutters, and looked at the bed. He was three-quarters asleep, and wanted nothing better than to accomplish the other quarter. But the letter in his pocket wouldn't let him alone. He took it out, and read it for the thirtieth time.

'Here are your tickets, darling, and a hotel reservation. It's only for a single room, but of course when I arrive we'll change that. If you need any more money, you can draw twenty thousand drachmas (whatever *they* may be) at the Bank of Greece. Naples is simply *heavenly*, I do wish you were here' – then why the hell did you send me to Athens? – 'I can't wait to see you, darling, you know how I feel.'

Yes, he knew how she felt; he *ought* to know, after two years. Yet even after two years there was so much about Dulcibella that he didn't understand – as for instance her long-range management of his life, sending him chasing around the world, always in front of her, for her to catch him up: New York, Singapore, Rio, Berlin, London – and now, Athens. He shrugged his shoulders; that was Dulcibella. And Dulcibella was money: she paid the bills. He took off his coat and shoes and lay out on the bed, feeling the luxury of it; the letter dropped from his hand to the floor. A moment later he was asleep.

III

The morning sun struck a dazzling glare from the hotel steps. Julius screwed up his eyes against it and walked slowly down to the pavement. A shoeshine boy came towards him, whistling cheerfully, his box slung from one shoulder.

'You want shoeshine, sir? Clean shoes?'

Julius hadn't known clean shoes for four days. He had put them outside his bedroom door last night; in the morning they were at least still there, but untouched, untended.

'Yes, please,' he said.

The shoeshine boy grinned, swung his box to the pavement, squatted on it and went to work. A young man sidled up. He was dark, his face was thin, and he had a scar under one eye – it looked to Julius like a knife scar. When he smiled, his whole face seemed to reflect the Mediterranean sun.

'You pay him three drachs, sir, only three drachs.'

Julius looked at him gratefully. The money was Dulcibella's, and seemed comfortably inexhaustible, but even so he always had an uneasy feeling, in countries where he couldn't speak the language, that he was being swindled.

'Bier?' said the young man, tipping an imaginary bottle – 'want bier? Quite near here. I know nice place.'

'All right,' said Julius.

'You American?'

'No. English.'

The young man withdrew; and bent to tie his shoe-lace, which he did with great elaboration, while he waited. The boy finished, and Julius gave him five drachmas, secure in the knowledge that he was overpaying him freely, of his own will. The boy looked at him with grave and disconcerting eyes, his smile gone, and then turned abruptly and disappeared before Julius could pin the curious expression in his face. The young man straightened up and joined Julius; he walked him swiftly along the pavement.

'What is your name?' he asked.

'Julius.'

'Tsulius.'

'No – Julius.'

'That's right – Tsulius,' said the young man complacently. 'My name is Nikolaos. Now we know each other.'

He seized Julius by the elbow and led him rapidly across a street, threading the hurtling traffic.

'This way,' said Nikolaos.

Presently, as they pushed along the crowded pavement, Nikolaos turned and grinned at Julius.

'In Athens,' he said, 'is better not to be English just now. Is political. You be American or German; that better than English.'

Julius smiled.

'That's all right,' he said. 'I'm an American.'

Nikolaos slapped him delightedly on the shoulder. 'Good, Tsulius, good – we good friends. Now this way, down here.'

Abruptly he led him down narrow steps into a basement bar. They rushed through two small rooms into a third at the back. Julius wondered why his guide seemed in such a hurry. They sat at a little three-cornered table against one wall. Light filtered in through a grating from the street.

Julius took out a packet of cigarettes and offered them across the table. The Greek selected one carefully and lit it. Julius took the match and lit his own.

A waiter appeared and Nikolaos broke into a spate of Greek. Julius relaxed, and thought of Dulcibella; in Naples; who couldn't wait to see him again. It was nearly a month since they had left Berlin and she had sent him on to London.

'I'll write soon, darling, to tell you where. Somewhere new for us, somewhere exciting. I feel – I feel I want *history*.'

There is really only one thing you want, Julius had thought: luckily for me. And now Athens. Perhaps she was serious. Perhaps she was making a subliminal attempt to reach back, to rediscover the past. Did she feel her youth deserting her? And yet she didn't show it – she could still disguise the years.

The waiter returned with two filled and frosted glasses. Julius took out some money, and felt a restraining hand on his arm. Nikolaos managed to look shocked.

'No – no, Tsulius,' he said, 'not yet.'

Idly Julius wondered where he had gone wrong. He must have transgressed some odd local custom in proposing to pay at once. He sat back and drank deeply from his cool glass; Nikolaos sipped his beer, and made a face. His cigarette was in the ashtray, scarcely touched. The waiter had gone.

Suddenly Nikolaos stood up.

'Now you give me the money,' he said decisively. 'I pay.'

Julius fumbled in his pocket and brought out two notes. He saw that he held thirty drachmas.

'That is enough,' said Nikolaos swiftly, and took the notes. He swept out of the room with the same nervous energy of movement he had displayed in the street, and Julius found himself alone.

Ten minutes later he was still alone, and the cigarette in the ashtray had gone out. He finished his beer, and thoughtfully filled his glass from the other almost untouched bottle. After twenty minutes, he decided that Nikolaos wasn't coming back.

The waiter hovered near his table, and Julius concluded he had not been paid. He finished his beer, stood up, and walked across to the watchful waiter, who shrugged his shoulders at an unspoken question and wrote the bill out on a paper table-mat. Julius paid him and found his way out into the street, still half expecting to meet Nikolaos on the way. But Nikolaos was the other side of Athens, hunting up other business.

The Story of the Panama Hat and the Camera

I

Julius was bored. He had exhausted Athens, and in the process Athens had exhausted him. He had made the acquaintance of Kostantios and the Acropolis, and was if anything more impressed by the first. He had explored all the ruins and sampled most of the likely-looking tavernas. Three days after his arrival he stood in Constitution Square, and knew that he was bored.

'Constitution Square ... *La Place de la Constitution*,' Kostantios had called it, but in the demotic it was *Plateia Syntagmatos*. Julius had not heard the Greek name, because he worked from a French map of the city. Personally, I find it easier to write it in English.

Julius sought distraction, and couldn't find it, in the façades of hotels and tourist offices. He was pestered by street vendors. He wandered into the middle of the Square. He saw a box camera perched awkwardly on a tripod, and behind it an old man asleep on a deckchair. The old man was bearded, and as much as could be seen of his face was gently lined, even in sleep; and he had a hat.

In every other detail his dress was unremarkable, it approximated to the dress of every other street photographer in the Square; and there were many. But his hat was astonishing, and it was the hat that made Julius pause. A wide straw brim shaded his shaggy grey eyebrows; the dome was dented, the straw was worn to holes in several places and the ribbon, which had once been a smart shiny black, was a frayed stained grey. Yet it was unmistakably a hat of quality, an aristocrat of headgear, even if it had come down in the world. It was bent and battered and faded, but it still proclaimed its lineage: a genuine Macey's sixty-dollar Panama.

II

Julius poked the old man experimentally.

'Excuse me – but where *did* you get that hat?'

The old man opened one reluctant eye.

'Go away,' he said crossly. The eye closed. Julius saw that he had started badly. He poked the old man again.

'I want,' he said in a loud voice, 'to have my photograph taken.'

Both eyes opened.

'You do?'

'Yes.'

The old man showed no enthusiasm. The eyes threatened to close again.

'Good heavens!' said Julius, 'don't you want to take my photograph – don't you want to make some money?'

'Not much,' said the old man, and this time the eyes did close.

Julius stood perplexed, watching him. Here was something as mysterious as the Parthenon, a street photographer who didn't want to take photographs. The old man was not asleep. Presently one eye opened, and when it saw that Julius was still there, was joined resentfully by the other.

'You want a photograph?'

'Yes,' said Julius patiently.

The old man grunted and stood up slowly, the fingers of one hand lost in the white curls of his beard.

'All right,' he said. 'I will take it.' The blue eyes softened as he looked at Julius.

'There are others,' he said. 'All over the Square there are others. Why did you choose me? Didn't you see I was happy to sleep?'

'Your hat,' said Julius. He offered this as an explanation.

'Ah yes, my hat.' The old man was busy with his camera. Suddenly he seemed to forget his annoyance, and his whole face was moulded to the secret and smiling delight of a memory.

'It was given to me, nearly twenty years ago. At least, not exactly given to me.' He chuckled.

'It was about this time of the year, I remember, and the city was beginning to fill with visitors – though there were fewer of them then, and not many of us. One day a man – just a moment, please; turn a little; no, to your left; that's good, now look over there, towards the Parliament – one day a man, an American I think, or it may be he was from the south, from the Argentine perhaps – keep still, please – woke me from my sleep, just as you have done,' he looked reproachfully at Julius, 'because even then I would sometimes sleep in the afternoons – and demanded a photograph. So I took one.' Again he chuckled.

'He was fat, this man, and ugly – as some might say I am fat and ugly myself. So naturally, because I am a good photographer, my photograph showed a fat and ugly man. He did not like it much. He stood where you are standing now and screamed at me. He took off his hat and stamped on it. He spat – oh, he was disgusting – he spat, and went away without paying me. But he forgot his hat.'

Julius looked at the hat, fascinated.

'I hope your camera is kind to me,' he said.

'My camera is the All-Seeing Eye,' said the old man simply. 'It does not lie. But it is too late to consider that now. I have taken your picture.'

III

'You must wait five minutes,' said the old man.

Julius nodded, and sat down on a bench beside the camera. The old man talked while he worked.

'You are English,' he said, and Julius did not deny this.

Nikolaos had said: 'In Athens is better not to be English, just now. You be American or German.'

But the old man had not asked a question: he had stated a fact.

'What is your name, Englishman?'

'It is Julius.'

'I understand. Julius.'

The old man had disappeared under the black cloth of his camera. Presently he folded it back and said: 'What are you, Julius?'

Julius was perplexed. What was he?

'I am nothing,' he said. 'Nothing much – in particular.'

The old man looked at him searchingly, and then at something in his hand.

'No, you are wrong,' he said. 'Each person,' and his hand swept slowly round the Square, 'is something. *You* are something. You cannot say you are nothing. Besides, there is the photograph – look!'

Julius looked, and at first he saw a stranger. He didn't recognize the eyes looking back at him for his own. The Square had faded into the background, leaving only a face and the outline of shoulders that seemed to blur into transparency. It was the face that held his attention – a face of unseasonably raddled discontent. Slowly he recognized it, after all, as his own face.

'Such a person,' said the old man, 'is more than something: he *has* something. What have you, Julius?'

Julius opened frustrated hands. 'I don't know,' he said. 'Money, I suppose. Sometimes.' Dulcibella's money.

'Yes, I can see that.' The old man was dusting his camera. 'And you have something else; something else is heavy on you.' He turned to look at Julius. 'I have nothing,' he said, 'but I couldn't say that I *am* nothing.'

Julius felt sharply criticized. There was a lurking sting in the old man's words, even though he had spoken gently.

'You do have something,' he said angrily. 'You have two things – a hat and a camera.'

'You think so?' said the old man quietly.

Julius was silent.

'What are you doing, Julius?'

The question broke distantly against a swirl of dreams. What was he doing: in Athens?

'I am waiting.' That was true enough.

But there was still a question in the old man's quiet face.

'I have seen Athens,' said Julius doubtfully. 'The Acropolis, the Agora, the Temple of Zeus – the Tower of the Winds, the *tavernas* – the Theseum – the Pnyx – '

'You have not seen Athens,' said the old man dismissively. 'You have tried too hard, you have been too busy. Go into the Gardens, over there,' he pointed, 'and sit there a while. Then you may be ready to see Athens.'

Julius had not noticed the Gardens. In his unorganized haste they had eluded him.

'How much do I owe you?' he asked presently.

'I don't know, yet,' said the old man. 'Five drachmas will do.'

It seemed very little, but Julius didn't dare offer him more.

'Now you will let me go to sleep again,' said the old man, tipping the hat over his eyes.

'You want shoeshine – clean shoes?' said a familiar voice.

Julius looked round and saw the sun-dark face of the shoe-shine boy.

'Go away,' said the old man crossly – 'you are a nuisance. Take the Englishman with you, Plato. I want to sleep.'

The boy laughed, and pulled the old man's beard teasingly. He chattered a moment in Greek, and then towed Julius away. At the side of the Square Julius suffered his shoes to be cleaned.

'Free, this time,' said the boy. 'Last time you pay me too much.'

Julius was beyond astonishment. He looked at the photograph in his hand, and then put it away very carefully in a coat pocket.

'Last time you cleaned my shoes,' he said, 'there was a young man – a Greek – who told me to pay you three drachmas.'

'Yes,' the boy agreed, 'he was right. That is Nikolaos.'

'Then you know him,' said Julius eagerly. 'Do you know where I can find him?'

'But I not know him,' said the boy, and he looked up and smiled at Julius.

Julius shrugged. He didn't understand these people. The boy gathered his things together and stood up.

'You go to the Gardens?' he said. 'Perhaps we meet again soon. Goodbye.'

Julius stopped him.

'Just a moment,' he said, and gestured across the Square to the distant figure sleeping peacefully in a deckchair, the ancient Panama tilted almost to its nose. 'Who is the old man?'

'The photographer?' said Plato. He smiled. 'They call him Socrates,' he said.

Le Jardin National

Julius consulted his French map of Athens. He crossed the wide street and walked to the right. *Le Soldat Inconnu* slept peacefully below the steps of the Parliament building; Socrates slept peacefully in the Square. The Gardens lay behind high iron railings, and the wrought-iron gates were flanked by kiosks and boys selling pistachio nuts and bootlaces. He went in.

Julius delighted in the strangeness of the Gardens, just as Diogenes would have delighted in their familiarity. But Diogenes never discovered the Gardens, and this was a whole year before Julius and Diogenes met on the Acropolis.

He wandered down labyrinthine paths, shaded from the sun by orange trees and palms, bordered by slender marble columns and half-hidden statues – until, climbing a short rise, he came to a trellised arcade hung thickly with sharply scented wistaria. He paused to explore the cool depths of a cave, and found a spring in the shadows at the very back; he reached up to it and sprinkled water over his face. He drank the cool air. He came out into the sun, and wandered on down branching paths, unhampered by decision, with no desire to choose his way. Presently he found himself beside a long shadowed pool, spanned by a little wooden bridge. He sat quietly by the edge of the water, and watched. He saw comfortably Englishlooking ducks swimming about on the water and grey, unfamiliar peacocks picking a delicate path round the edge of the pool. He heard low conversations and the light shuffle of passing feet. He relaxed. He saw Nikolaos.

He saw Nikolaos standing at the other side of the pool; and Nikolaos had not seen him. He stood quietly, and crossed the bridge, approaching him from behind. He touched the young man's shoulder. Nikolaos turned, and Julius almost laughed at his dismay. The young man made a movement, as though he would break away, but Julius tightened his grip. He smiled.

'That was a very quick thirty drachs you made out of me, the other day. Don't you like beer?'

Nikolaos hesitated, and then his face broke suddenly into a broad smile of welcome.

'Tsulius! I not expect to see you again.' There was a

sincerity in this that Julius could appreciate. 'No,' he went on regretfully, 'I not like bier very much.'

'Come and sit down,' said Julius. 'It's very pleasant here. Have a cigarette.' He offered one.

'Please,' said Nikolaos, with a laugh. And then: 'We go out together, see Athens?' he suggested.

But Julius was content. 'We will stay here,' he said.

'So you like Greek cigarettes? Me, I like American cigarettes. All American things is good.' He grinned at Julius, his eyes expressing a huge and secret joke.

'Today, I am English,' said Julius gravely. Nikolaos shrugged his shoulders, accepting this.

'I am Spartan,' he said. 'You know – I come from Sparta. I not know Athens very well.' He dug in a pocket and brought out some papers.

'I am sailor, Tsulius. Look, this is me.' He showed Julius a thin document that looked rather like a passport. Inside was a photograph. Nikolaos in seaman's uniform smiled irrepressibly from the page. Above it were several lines written in Greek letters, and then some words in English: GREEK MERCANTILE MARINE; and further down the page: APPRENTICE SEAMAN.

'My ship is in Africa – ' this sounded improbable, but Julius didn't argue. 'My family in Sparta, so I all alone in Athens.'

Julius returned the document and Nikolaos pulled out a sheaf of photographs. He extracted one.

'This my girl,' he said. 'German girl – she live in Vienna.'

Julius looked.

'Very nice,' he said. 'A girl in every port.'

'I think Vienna not a port,' Nikolaos said reproachfully. He stood up, stretching, and threw away the last of his cigarette.

'I go now,' he said. 'You not come?'

'Not now,' said Julius. 'But we'll meet again.'

'You give me your address, Tsulius – your hotel. I come find you one evening, and we go out together. I show you Athens.'

('I not know Athens very well,' hadn't he said?)

Julius scribbled on a piece of paper, and held it out. Nikolaos took it, and paused awkwardly.

'I sorry to ask, Tsulius,' he said at last, 'but I not have much money. Maybe you let me have twenty, thirty drachs? Then I go out tonight, have good time.'

Julius took out a hundred-drachma note and gave it to him. Nikolaos grinned.

'You and me, Tsulius, we good friends. I show you good time, any night you want.' Then he was gone, and Julius leaned back in his seat looking dreamily at a large ripe orange clinging to a branch a few feet above his head. The fountains trickled gently across the pool. The ducks quacked busily, swimming after the bread that was thrown to them. The peacocks continued their elegant procession. An attendant walked round the pool collecting half-drachmas for the seats. But when he reached Julius, under the orange tree, he too was asleep. The attendant did not disturb him.

The Story of Dulcibella and the Neapolitan Lover

I

It was a little after four o'clock. This was how things stood:

Socrates was asleep in Constitution Square. Julius was asleep in the National Garden. *Le Soldat Inconnu*, of course, slept all the time. Plato was polishing tourists' shoes outside the Panathenaic Stadium. The hotel porter was sorting the mail – he pigeon-holed a letter with an Italian stamp for Julius. Nikolaos was on the town, working up towards the evening's good time. Sappho was sitting in breathless concentration in front of a mirror, putting on a deep crimson lipstick.

You must forgive me for a moment, while I climb out of the river. None of this is very interesting. I will walk downstream, just a few yards, and try again there – over there, beside that little bent tree. What tree is it? – I'm afraid I don't know. Never mind. It's a good place: the river is waiting.

II

Dulcibella was in Naples – and that would make a story in itself. Even in Naples her influence could shape the course of events as far away as Athens. In this case her influence took the form of a typically disconcerting letter, which was waiting for Julius when he returned to his hotel.

'Such a charming young man, darling Julius, if you could see his arms – so brown and strong, how he bullies me! I really couldn't face the journey, not now, I find Naples so *exhausting*! I do hope you have enough money, darling, because honestly I can't send any more; you know, you were *rather* expensive.

'Antonio is so sweet, about money I mean, but then he's not used to it. It's simply shocking, you wouldn't *believe* how little they pay their road sweepers in Naples.'

So Dulcibella hadn't waited. The delights of history, after all, were a less potent reassurance than the charms of an Italian road sweeper.

I suppose I was lucky, thought Julius; to have managed even two years; with Dulcibella that must have been some sort of record – he'd had a good run for her money. That money, of course, was a more serious loss than Dulcibella; much more serious. He had enough for the time being, but it might be wise to move into a cheaper hotel.

Next morning, by the time he had finished paying his bills, he was convinced of this wisdom. He left in style, tipping magnificently, but out on the street, alone with his three suitcases, he felt peculiarly deserted.

III

The Hotel Byron was propped between two houses. It was a good thing these houses still stood, because without them the Hotel Byron would certainly have fallen down – for a long time now it had been tired of standing, but it couldn't help itself. It looked down into a street market, and that had been quite interesting at first. In time, however, the kaleidoscopic restlessness of the market grew monotonous, patterns seemed to repeat themselves indefinitely, and long ago the Hotel Byron had closed its eyes to the febrile but unchanging activities of the street. Shutters covered all the windows, and the peeling brown walls had a bored, blank look about them.

Inside, the proprietor had done his best to defeat the sullen pessimism of the building. The stairs, which led up from the street door, were cool and clean. Julius climbed them. On the first landing there was a desk and a bell. Julius pushed at the bell. Presently a head appeared over the banister above him – a small dark head, a brown face, a black moustache that grew like a successful weed. A flow of Greek words descended on him and tangled in his bewildered mind. When these sounds ceased he began, hopefully:

'Do you speak English?'

Brown eyes looked at him curiously. The strange sounds began again – so strange that he couldn't believe they belonged to any language or would make sense to anyone. The head was joined by another, a small fat head belonging to a small fat woman.

'*Que voulez-vous?*'

Oh, Lord, thought Julius – and rather desperately raked together the remnants of his schoolboy French.

'*Parlez-vous anglais?*' It was worth trying.

'*Non. Que voulez-vous?*'

Julius resigned himself helplessly to memory.

'*Je veux une chambre.*'

The small fat face smiled.

'*Vous voulez une chambre. Tout seul?*'

'*Oui. Tout seul.*'

The two dark heads consulted in voluble Greek, and then the woman turned again, and leaned over the banister.

'*C'est bien.*'

This seemed promising; he'd better make sure.

'*Avez-vous une chambre – pour moi?*'

'*Oui.*' The woman nodded reassuringly.

'*Aujourd'hui?*'

'*Nous avons une chambre.*'

'*Et – quelle prix?*' Julius was rather proud of himself, he seemed to be managing quite well.

'*Quelle prix? Moment.*' She turned back to the man and there was another long consultation.

'*Trente-cinq,*' she said at last.

'*Chacque jour?*'

'*Par jour – trente-cinq.*'

And so Julius moved into the Hotel Byron.

IV

His room overlooked the street market. He opened the shutters; they protested, but he opened them. Julius was fascinated by the market. For him each twist of the kaleidoscope was something new, and he sat for a whole evening watching it. Caged birds sang piercingly of their captivity; bananas turned brown in the sun. Flowers bloomed and wilted and died, and brightly coloured fish lay flatly on slabs, turning a blank eye to the sky, until they began to stink. People came and went, and when dusk brought out the neon lighting further up the street, the market was still as full and busy as it had been at midday. Old men leaned against walls selling nuts or bread or mineral water; young men hooted imperiously through the wedged crowds on ancient motor-cycles, their sidecars heavy with oranges or planks of wood or rusty iron. Boys shouted shrilly, billowing huge plastic bags in the wind like giant balloons, satisfied if they sold five in an evening. Children sat swinging angular brown limbs over the boundary wall of the little Byzantine church of St Georges, which stood back on a quiet edge of the street.

Julius wasn't ready to accept his poverty; but for a while managed to forget it.

*

In Naples Dulcibella was wholly occupied with the perplexing problem of introducing Antonio into her hotel. She hadn't sufficiently appreciated that Julius had certain advantages denied to an Italian road sweeper.

THE PHILOSOPHY OF POVERTY

Nikolaos Speaks

Constitution Square has an air of cosmopolitan raffishness at night. The coloured lights are almost convincing. Bars and restaurants seem to spring up where during the day there are only hotels and tourist offices. Julius stood in the middle of the Square and considered his future. He thought that he hadn't much future to consider. He wondered why he had been washed up on this particular shore, and what it was like to be driftwood. He had no experience to build on. Before, there had always been something, even before Dulcibella: his own money, or someone else's. He saw a battered Panama and recognized Socrates.

'Hello,' he said. 'I didn't expect to see you here. Surely you can't take photographs at night?'

'I take photographs when I like,' said Socrates with dignity. 'And when I don't like, I don't take them,' he added pointedly. 'Tonight, though, I am not here to take photographs.'

Plato appeared and put his shoeshine box firmly on the ground in front of Julius.

'You want shoeshine,' he said, and this time it was not a question.

'They've been done once already today,' Julius protested.

'Athens very dusty,' said Plato. 'In Athens you want shoeshine two, three times a day.' He went to work.

'Tsulius! My friend Tsulius, I thought I had lost you.' It was Nikolaos. This place is like the legendary Piccadilly Circus, or Times Square, thought Julius.

'I go to hotel, to address you give me, you not there.' Nikolaos sounded reproachful.

'I'm sorry,' said Julius. 'I had to move.'

Plato had reached the velvet duster stage, and Julius saw that his shoes reflected the flashing colours of the neon signs.

'Never mind. I find you. I always find you,' said Nikolaos. Julius thought that probably he always would. He paid Plato. This time he was careful to give him exactly three drachmas.

Nikolaos pulled urgently at his arm.

'We go for good time?'

Julius considered. 'I'm afraid I'm not as rich as I was when we last met. That's why I've had to move.'

Nikolaos was worried. 'You have money?'

'I still have a little, but – '

The Spartan looked relieved.

'That all right then. We still have money, we still have good time. Come, I show you.' His persuasive hand remained on Julius' arm. 'We good friends, Tsulius, we have real good time.' Julius surrendered.

Socrates and Plato watched them go. Plato looked at the three coins in his hand, selected one carefully, and gave it to Soctrates. Silently, the old man took it.

Interlude – at the Copper Banana

Nikolaos led Julius swiftly down Stadiou Street. Every few yards a kiosk rose like an island from the pavement, punctuating the flowing crowds. Tyres squealed on corners, and people crossed the street oblivious of hurtling traffic. They turned into a small square, where the pavements were dotted with tables. A red and green lighted sign above a small door beckoned with insidious promise. Nikolaos turned without pausing, dived under the sign, and propelled Julius with calm assurance down steep steps into the gloom below.

They were inside the Copper Banana.

After the glare of the street lighting Julius thought for a moment the place was in complete darkness. He stumbled against a table, and felt Nikolaos pushing a chair towards him. Then his eyes began to adjust to the gloom, and he saw that the Copper Banana was indeed illuminated, in its own way. Thin red lights glowed faintly from hidden corners; the walls were hung with a deep red velvet, which absorbed the light and gave it an oppressive heaviness. The bar was the brightest place, because the bottles reflected the light; there was strip lighting over the bar, but only one tube, and it too was red. The place was empty: it was still early, for the Copper Banana.

Nikolaos apologized. 'Little early for good time. Later on music and dancing.' He gestured towards one end of the room, and Julius could just make out a small curtained stage, where three music stands lounged in an untidy row, and abandoned drums waited patiently for the good time to begin. On the first stand was painted COPP – on the second, ERBA – and on the third, NANA.

A waiter stood silently out of the darkness, and Nikolaos said:

'What you drink, Tsulius?' A question, rather than an invitation.

Julius couldn't think of anything, so he said 'Beer,' and noticed the astonishment of Nikolaos and the disgust of the waiter, when Nikolaos translated the order.

Nikolaos drank some unidentified liquid out of a tumbler: it was transparent, effervescent, and deceptively innocuous. Julius knew it was deceptive when he was presented with the bill. Soda-water doesn't cost thirty-five, even in the Copper Banana.

A juke-box was playing Greek music in one corner. Nikolaos, always anxious to please, leaned across the table in the darkness.

'You like American music? Rock 'n Roll?'

'All right,' said Julius.

Nikolaos called to the waiter, and launched into a long and incomprehensible argument. Eventually the waiter crossed the room and fed the juke-box. Abruptly the Greek music stopped, and Frankie Laine tried his voice on the Copper Banana. Nikolaos seemed pleased.

'American?'

'Yes, that's American.'

'You understand American? I not very good at understanding.'

Julius thought even an American would have trouble extracting any kind of sense out of such a battered and overworked machine, but he listened with polite attention. Frankie Laine was followed by a big band, and Nikolaos tapped one foot on the floor, gently rocking the table. Suddenly he stood up.

'We move over there,' he said, pointing to an obscure and even darker corner. 'We see more.'

It seemed to Julius they had already seen everything there was to see, but he picked up his glass and followed across the small square of dance floor to the other table. He sat down facing a door marked WC. Nikolaos managed to suggest an air of excitement and expectation in everything he did. Julius was strangely affected by his optimism.

A girl came in and sprawled over the bar, talking with the waiter. She moved to the juke-box, twisting and turning as she went, in time to the music. Julius watched her, looked at Nikolaos, and saw that he was watching her too. The girl turned and saw Nikolaos, and Julius thought perhaps she recognized him. She came over, still moving lithely to the rhythms of the music, and sat down across a corner of the table, facing Nikolaos.

Nikolaos grinned at Julius, and grabbed the girl's arm. She laughed at him and pulled his hair, and they spoke together with furtive animation. Julius felt that Nikolaos was explaining him to the girl, and wondered exactly what he was saying; he watched her intently. Presently she looked at him, and winked. There was a disguised, mocking expression in her face, and Julius felt the extremity of his disadvantage, without their language. He adjusted his own expression until the girl, he hoped, would see in it whatever she wanted to see, but suddenly she doubled up in involuntary laughter, and turned to share this disconcerting joke – whatever it might be – with Nikolaos: who laughed too, and threw an arm round her shoulder, poking her experimentally and drawing her towards him. He looked over a shoulder, to explain.

'This Sappho,' he said – 'she work here,' and the girl turned a poker face towards Julius. She winked again, and kissed the air with enormous lips, and again her laughter seemed to mock him.

He felt a need to assert himself; to fly some rags, at least, of sophistication. He was accustomed to being taken more seriously by his women. But Sappho, he suspected, was a law unto herself. She seemed to have no English, so he turned to Nikolaos.

'How much does she charge?' he asked, uncertain whether the question was cynical or merely inaccurate, but certain of its brutality. Either way, it should help move things along. It was an initiative.

'You not think about money, Tsulius. We friends.'

Oddly, Julius had come to believe this refrain. Nikolaos, he knew, would take him for his last drachma, if he could; but they were friends.

Sappho was looking sultry. She leaned across the table, swallowing Julius with huge black flashing eyes – it would be easy, he thought, to drown in them.

'I love you,' she said. And with the same intensity – 'I kill you.'

'She like you,' Nikolaos explained. 'See, is as I tell you. We have good time.'

'I lo-ove you. I kill you.' This was, it seemed, the limit of Sappho's English, for she continued the conversation with impudent hands and a sharply-shod exploring foot under the table. Did he want to be lo-oved? Was he yet ready to be killed?

'I don't think I'm enjoying this,' he said to Nikolaos. 'I'm sorry. I don't really feel in the mood, tonight.' He placed a cigarette in Sappho's wide painted mouth, because it seemed to him quite dangerously voracious, and lit it. She drew a deep breath of smoke, and then spat – smoke and cigarette – full in his face.

'I kill you,' she hissed.

'Some other time,' said Julius. 'Come on,' he said to Nikolaos, 'we're leaving.'

Nikolaos didn't understand. 'But we stay, Tsulius. We have good time.'

'I've had my good time, thanks. Come on.'

Nikolaos followed, unwillingly. In the street Julius took out a fifty-drachma note.

'Thanks for the good time, Nikolaos. I must go back to my hotel. Take this – it's not very much, but I warned you I was running out of money.'

Nikolaos stood looking rather sadly at the fifty-drachma note in his hand, and then suddenly he remembered something.

'Tsulius!' he shouted, 'Tsulius! I not know your new hotel. How I find you?'

But Julius had gone.

Interlude – At the Hotel Byron

It was raining; the first rain since Julius had come to Athens, and he felt it with an obsessive melancholy. So much seemed to have gone with the sun, he wondered uneasily what was left to him. The future nagged and threatened his mind: he was alarmed to discover that what he had always thought of as a natural resourcefulness had depended so much on practical resources. Without those resources (without Dulcibella's money, to be thoroughly practical) he was helpless.

Three empty days had passed since he had shaken off Nikolaos. He had searched in vain for Socrates, and his shoes had gone unpolished. Socrates and Plato seemed to have disappeared.

He sucked his pipe until it went sour on him, put it down and spat from the balcony of his room to the pavement. The clouds spat back at him; he withdrew, and closed the shutters. He counted his money.

There was a knock on the door, and here was Nikolaos excitedly shaking his hand.

'I find you, Tsulius. I always find you.' He beamed with satisfaction. 'You come out tonight, we have – '

'No,' said Julius, 'we don't. No good time, tonight. I haven't any more money.'

Nikolaos looked swiftly round the room, and took his point.

'Never mind – I no time really; just come here to say goodbye.' He put his hands in his pockets and rolled on his feet.

'My ship come from Africa, leave finished now.' He looked suddenly sad. 'I go now, Tsulius, I got to go.' He took one hand out of a pocket and held it out uncertainly. Julius found that he was sorry too. He reached out and held the brown hand for a warm moment, and said goodbye. He thought that was all, but it wasn't quite. Nikolaos had turned at the door.

'I not have much money too. Maybe you let me have five, ten drachs?'

Julius smiled, and pulled out a note from his pocket. Nikolaos took it, his face unusually solemn, and went without another word. He didn't even look at it – the twenty drachmas went sadly to his pocket without a glance. He stood in the street, oblivious of the rain, and looked up.

Julius, at the window, saw a bronzed arm flash in farewell, and heard the laughing voice that this time was not laughing.

'Goodbye, Tsulius! You have good time – we always good friends!'

And Nikolaos passed from the story.

Plato Speaks

When he left the Hotel Byron, Julius had one suitcase and exactly two hundred drachmas.

'*Je dois partir; aujourd'hui.*'

The small fat face was sympathetic. '*Ah, c'est dommage. C'est la vie.*'

Several faces appeared over the banisters, many he didn't know, to witness this curious departure. The bill was paid.

'*C'est fait. Les jeux sont faits.*' Julius smiled at his own joke, because no-one else seemed inclined to smile. He shrugged. 'So be it. *Au revoir.*'

The small fat face had found its smile. '*Au revoir, m'sieur.*'

The stairs led him straight down to the pavement. Plato was standing a yard from the door.

For the first time in a week, Julius felt unreasonably hopeful.

'Shoeshine, sir, Julius?'

Julius was amused. 'So you know my name – how did you know it?'

'I listen,' said Plato, 'I hear things.' But Julius hadn't told him – who had?

The boy was busy at his feet, removing a thick layer of Athenian dust from scuffed, neglected shoes.

'You leave Hotel Byron now?'

'Yes,' said Julius. Plato scrubbed briskly at the shoes, and looked up, smiling.

'That is good,' he said. 'You go on now. Where you going to?'

Julius didn't know. Until this moment he had refused, obstinately, to think about the disaster he had contrived. He wondered if the British Consulate would pay his passage home. They took away your passport, he vaguely remembered hearing, and that wouldn't do at all.

'Where are you going?' Plato looked at him insistently, pulling at his trouser leg to attract his attention.

Then Plato spoke.

'You stay here, in Athens. You come with me, I show you Socrates.'

Julius forgot the British Consulate. His mind was filled with an absurd optimism. Plato stood up, swinging his box of brushes and polish, pulling joyfully at Julius' sleeve.

'You come,' he said.

'Just a moment – your three drachmas.' But the boy seemed in a hurry.

'Free today, I not want it.' Then he laughed. 'Three drachmas is a lot of money now, Julius?'

Three drachmas was exactly one and a half percent of his entire capital – Julius couldn't deny it was a lot of money. Plato led him away from the Hotel Byron.

It had stopped raining. Julius hadn't noticed when the rain stopped, but he noticed the sun now, and the drying streets, and the dust that was already rising and lying in dark corners. The sun had a new strength, a new burning intensity: April had passed, and with it the best of the Athenian spring – this was a summer sun. People slept on the pavements.

'Where are we going?'

It was an idle question, Julius didn't much mind where they went.

'We go to Theatro Dionysou,' said Plato, leading him towards the hill of the Acropolis. 'The Theatre of Dionysus,' he explained. 'Socrates is waiting.'

Socrates Speaks

But unfortunately Socrates had grown tired of waiting. Besides, he was an old man, and the sun, as I have said, was very hot. Socrates was asleep.

It is a pity, because this might have been a very interesting chapter. Never mind. Let it go.

Kostantios Speaks
(in two languages)

Julius sat on a stone seat high up in the theatre, looking down on the mosaic of the 'ορχηστρα. Plato sat one step below him, his feet on his shoeshine box. Socrates slept under a cypress tree on the other side of the theatre. A party of tourists climbed from the road, led by Kostantios. They clustered by the fresco for a moment, and then spread out on the seats of the front row.

'He's going to lecture us now,' said a loud Midwestern American voice. Cameras clicked, Kostantios removed his brown felt hat and mopped his forehead, his audience waited patiently for him to begin.

'Ladies and gentlemen, the Theatre of Dionysus ... *Messieurs et Mesdames, le Théatre de Dionysos.*'

Each word was carried with winged precision, reaching up to the distant height of their refuge.

'Here we have the cr-radle of the theatre ... *ici nous avons le berceau de la drame.*'

'You want pistachio nut?' Plato held out a battered paper bag. Julius took one and chewed it thoughtfully.

'Socrates sleep very much now,' the boy explained. 'He is getting old.'

'That's all right,' said Julius. 'I can wait.'

He didn't know what he was waiting for, but waiting seemed suddenly enjoyable. He stretched in the sun, so much lost in the present that the future had ceased to matter. More than that, the future did not seem to exist.

'It is the same every day,' said Plato, as though he knew what Julius was thinking. 'You will like that.'

'My friends, in this historical place ... *mes amis, dans ce lieu historique* ... famous actors and playwrights, such as Aeschylus, Euripides, Sophocles, Aristophanes, Menander, performed their own plays two thousand five hundred years ago ... *des acteurs, des écrivains célèbres, comme Aeschyles, Euripides, Sophocles, Aristophanes, Ménandre, ont joués leurs propres pièces, il y a deux mille cinq cents ans ...* '

'*They* knew,' said Plato – and for Julius time lost its meaning, the past merged with the future and the present, and he saw the theatre filled with people, and giant masked figures moving on the patterned floor below him. Plato spat, and offered the bag of nuts.

'You like it here?'

'Yes,' said Julius, and felt that such a small word had never meant so much to him before.

'We come here often,' said Plato, and Julius thought that he might have been coming for thousands of years, from the way he spoke. *Il y a deux milles cinq cents ans* – it was possible: somehow that place seemed to have escaped from time, and in it, Plato shared its timelessness. Julius recognized it in himself too, he had known it from the moment when the future had merged so certainly with the present.

'The seats in the front row, my friends, made of mar-rble ... *construits de marbre, mes amis* ... '

Kostantios had embarked upon one of his favourite stories.

'... were reserved for the high priests of all the towns in Attica ... *étaient loués à tous les prêtres chefs des villes de l'Attique.*'

'You listen,' said Plato – 'You hear Kostantios.'

'They were places of honour, in the front row ... *les places d'honneur, au premier rang*... You will notice that there is a lit-tle hole in the front of the seat, those of you who are sitting on them ... *vous remarquerez, vous qui y sont assis, il y a un petit trou à chacque* ... You may wonder what they were for ... *peut-être vous vous demandez pourquoi ils sont là?*'

Kostantios looked anxiously over his audience, and saw with satisfaction that several people were smiling.

'There are two theories ... *il y a deux théories*' – he held up two fingers, and then clasped one of these in the fingers of his other hand. 'Some archaeologists think that they were to hold umbrellas ... *pour tenir les ombrelles* ... because in summer the sun would often be very hot, and in winter it sometimes rained ... *parce qu'en été souvent le soleil était très chaud, et quelquefois en hiver il plut* ... I myself believe...' and here he grasped the second of his two fingers – '*pour moi, je crois* ... those who have suggested that people would bring their children, two, three years old, to the theatre ... *des enfants qui avaient deux ou trois ans, au théatre*... Sometimes the plays would go on for a whole day ... *un jour complet* ... and with children, you can imagine! ... *avec les enfants, vous pouvez imaginer!*'

Quiet laughter rustled through the group like a passing wind, and Plato grinned at Julius.

'He usually say that,' he said.

Down below, the party was splitting up. It was the usual five minute break that Kostantios offered at every stage of the tour, 'to make a little visit.'

'Those who want to take photographs,' he said now, 'I will show you the best place. You see that little tree,' he pointed – 'up there is the best place to take a photograph of the Theatre of Dionysus.'

He took out a cigarette, and lit it with satisfaction.

The tourists surged up to the tree and surrounded it. In the centre, under the tree, Socrates stirred and woke.

Julius Speaks

They walked, the next day, past the ironworkers' shops of the Adrianou; empty-handed, all three, for Socrates had come without his All-Seeing Eye, Plato without his shoeshine box, and Julius had nothing left to bring, except his remaining suitcase, and there was no point in bringing that.

Beside them the wooden trains of the Metro blinked into sunshine for a brief moment, before plunging back to explore the unpromising depths beneath the Athenian crust. Beyond the glistening Metro rails lay the Agora, picked bare by scavenging archaeologists, and – standing a little above, and to the right – the Theseion, humbled by the loftier heights of the Acropolis, but still formidable in its integrity.

'So now,' said Socrates, 'you are like the rest of us: you have nothing. Perhaps I should take another photograph.'

Julius was troubled. 'The one you took,' he said, 'has changed. I can't explain what I mean, exactly, but it has changed. Look.' He took it from his pocket and handed it anxiously to the old man. Socrates looked at it.

'It has changed: and you, Julius, have changed. That is interesting,' he said, and there was an unmistakable note of satisfaction in his voice.

'It's disappearing,' said Julius, 'and yet it's not really disappearing.'

Once, when he was a small child, a street photographer had cornered him on the sea-front at Brighton, and Julius had gone home with a photograph of himself. He had been quite proud of it at first, and showed it to all of his family, but after a week he wouldn't let anyone see it. The photograph was turning yellow, and fading. After a month, there was nothing left but a smudged piece of paper.

This was different. This photograph was not exactly fading – but the background seemed to be growing out of the picture, assuming a sharper definition, while he himself was disappearing into that background, his features changed and blurred, beginning to share the transparency he had first noticed in the shoulders. It was the change which troubled him, the change of expression, because although he was certain of its reality he couldn't define its nature.

'It is the All-Seeing Eye,' said Socrates. 'You must accept what it sees.'

They climbed slowly past the Theseion, and out into the main road. The changing perspective of the Acropolis pointed their progress. The Old Town was far behind them. It was in that district, among a maze of houses clinging to the slopes of the Acropolis, that Socrates and Plato lived. Unquestioned and unquestioning, accepted by all three as a matter of course, Julius had come to live with them. The streets there were cobbled or deep with dust, breaking into long steep steps towards the top. Open drains flowed between the houses, filling the air with a ripe, heavy smell; donkey carts took the place of motor-cycles and sidecars, and all the cats and dogs of the city seemed to have collected in this one small forgotten corner. They lived in two small, clean rooms which grew out of an angle in the hill, shaded by a huge and improbable palm tree.

'We are going, today,' said Socrates, 'to the Pnyx.'

They climbed the hill until they reached a wide, flat rock terrace that sloped gently towards the last line of houses. At the back, against the hill, three steps had been cut roughly out of solid rock, leading to a small platform. They climbed the steps, and sat on top, looking down on the city.

'This is the Pnyx,' said Socrates. 'It is the place where men came to speak. What will you say, Julius?'

'I – I'm not ready to speak,' said Julius.

'It depends,' said Socrates – 'it always depends. For some people it is not even necessary to speak. Plato,' he dug gently at the boy's ribs with one foot, 'Plato says nothing, but he is listening all the time, and that is best for him. But you, Julius, who say you are not ready to speak, are you even ready to listen? – how much do you hear when you listen?'

'I heard you the first day, when you told me it is better to have nothing than to be nothing. But I didn't believe you.'

'And now? Do you believe me now?'

'I have no choice,' said Julius.

The pale blue eyes of the old man turned on Julius in astonishment.

'You think that? Oh, Julius, believe me now – there is always a choice. Always.'

'I didn't choose poverty,' said Julius. 'I was made poor.'

'As, before, you were also made rich. But in each case there is the choice: how you will use your wealth, how you will use your poverty.' Socrates tilted his face to the sky; his blue eyes contained its ageless distance, the great beard, the fine Athenian nose, belonged to all time.

'How will you use your poverty, Julius? What are you going to do?'

'I won't work!' he said violently – obscurely taunted by the unreal sense, the shimmering mirage, of his own words.

Socrates sighed. 'That is not what I asked you. I said, *What are you going to do?*'

Julius was silent.

'It is like this,' said Socrates. 'To have nothing is to see the world with open eyes. The more you have, the more you are burdened, the less you see. And it is like this. To have everything is to want nothing – and wanting nothing is the most bitter of desires in life, for it can never be satisfied. While there is anything lacking there is something to look for, and when everything is lacking there is everything to look for. When a man has everything, when he has ceased to look, he has ceased to exist. The search is wonderful, Julius, it is fraught with possibilities – but be careful of possession: for possession is not a true discovery – it blunts desire. Possession is the beginning and the end, but the search goes on for ever.'

Julius stirred, shaking off his doubts.

'What do you do, Socrates?'

'I live,' said the old man. 'I am growing tired now, but not of living – never of living. I live. I see things, I and my camera. And Plato hears things, but he does not work either, beyond the day. Nor should you.'

'It isn't easy,' said Julius, 'to live.'

'It is the easiest thing in the world; it is so easy that it is always overlooked. But if you know where to look, and how to look, and if you go on, always looking, never impatient to find, it is easy.'

'But I would grow tired soon, always seeing the same things.'

'They are never the same. No day is like another, everything is always new.'

The sun crept across the sky, and far below it Julius felt its progress, and its warm healing strength; his perplexity was washed from him, he was open in expectation. He turned to Socrates.

'I am ready,' he said.

But Socrates was asleep again.

Meditation and Colloquy

Julius, I would speak to you of reconciliation.

I have put aside my camera and my hat, I am simply an old man now. I have never pretended much, but now there is no pretence in me. I would speak to you of reconciliation.

It comes when people are at peace. Most of all it comes when people are at peace with themselves.

Reconciliation is the fabric of a true life, it is woven into the pattern of a true life, it is life itself.

Julius, do not believe those who say life is not good. They have given up, they have ceased to live, how should they know? They fought their battles in the past, they lost their battles in the past; and in that past they still wander, among the ruins of their dreams, in a dead world. They have nothing left but memory, and regret, and a sere and bitter resentment for what is lost. Julius, the past is still with us, there is no need to retreat to find the past.

I would speak to you of reconciliation, of all things reconciled.

I am not a dreamer: I look for reality. A man once said to me:

'If you cannot realize the ideal, at least you may idealize the real.'

He was a wise man, but I do not think these were wise words.

I look for reality, I am no dreamer, I am a realist. I am as stark a realist as ever scratched his head.

'If you cannot realize the ideal, you may at least idealize the real.' But the ideal *is* the real, the real is the ideal – and that is not to idealize the real. It is the final reconciliation.

Julius, love life. Give all you possess to life, and life will repay you a thousand times. There is no secret, no mystery then, which is not yours.

Search your own heart, for in your own heart is both the reality and the ideal. You will not find it in another: not in me, not in anyone else – for we are all alone. We are all alone together. Reconciliation is a man at peace with himself.

The real and the ideal are One.

We have found a quiet place and we live a quiet life, our thoughts are quiet thoughts, and people would say we have withdrawn from the world, we have turned our backs on the real in the search for the ideal. That is not true. I look for reality, but I have never looked for false realities. I look for peace, I search for reconciliation. Reconciliation is a man at peace with himself.

A man cannot be at peace with himself if he is at war with the world.

War is a false reality.

Men fight for riches, for power, with ambition – which are false realities: for ideologies – which are false ideals. I see the world grow weary of its own violence, and I see it breed another generation to violence.

I am an old man, but I do not despair.

I could point to a hundred guilty men, and yet I would not touch the fringes of responsibility. Man bears his own guilt, he is his own responsibility: men are pawns in their own prodigious game of self-destruction. One man is more important than the State.

Julius, do not put your trust in institutions.

It is a courtesy to obey the law: it is folly to worship the law. The laws of God are not God: nor is the Church God.

There is no point in throwing stones at the Church – the most you will do is break a few windows, and often the windows are beautiful. But do not put your trust in institutions. We are all alone: search your own heart: you cannot search another's.

There is no point in throwing stones at the State. It is a courtesy to obey the law. One man alone is always more important than the State.

Reconciliation is the real and the ideal: the real and the ideal are One.

The past is still with us, Julius; there is no need to retreat to find the past. It is there, knocking at the door of today; it will still be there tomorrow.

Look, there – to that wine-dark sea: a ship. That ship has a black sail, and today a king has killed himself because of it. Or it is another ship, perhaps, sailed by a bronzed bearded pirate who dreams of Ithaca; his eyes saw Troy burning. The past is still with us; it is with us still tomorrow.

Look, there – to that distant snow-capped mountain: it is Mount Olympus, the dwelling place of the old gods. Look carefully and you will see them still – Zeus the cloud-gatherer, Artemis and Apollo, Hermes god of thieves, and Athene who gave her name to this city. They were twelve gods, and they were One. The past is still with us.

But I would speak of reconciliation: the real and the ideal are One. Reconcile them in your heart and you will be at peace with yourself.

I do not say that you can do this. But you can try, as I have tried, and will always try. They are One, but the world has torn them apart: this is the mischance, the calamity of life, and this is the eternal struggle, to reconcile them in life, to make them again One. It is a search, Julius, and the prize is peace. But do not imagine that anyone else can win the prize for you. It is your life, your heart, and only you can make the reconciliation.

Do not look to me.

I can only tell you to search, I cannot tell you how or where to search. I am an old man: I have walked my way – you must walk your own.

Plato listens, but then Plato has large ears.

And Plato is a child, and I am an old man: I shall not live for ever. When I am dead he will grow up in the places I have known and to the paths I have followed, but to a life of his own. Plato listens, but Plato is all the while growing away from us; in the end he will reach beyond us, towards the sky. For him one day there may be an end to the search, in him one day the real and the ideal may be reconciled: there is this hope for Plato, that he at last will be a man at peace with himself.

Forget my words, Julius; hold to yourself, and discard the rest. No man can find reconciliation through another; we are all alone, each with himself. Search your own heart: you cannot search another's.

Reconciliation is the fabric of a true life, it is woven into the pattern of life.

Love life, Julius; life is good – do not believe those who would tell you life is not good. Reconciliation is in the real and the ideal. It comes when people are at peace. Most of all it comes when a man is at peace with himself.

My eyes are not for you: there is no-one who can look on your behalf, no other eyes can serve except your own. The All-Seeing Eye is the Eye of God, it is not for our seeing.

Forget my words. Give me my hat and my camera. I am an old man, and I have said some foolish things. Forget my words.

Leave me, Julius: I would like to sleep. I have loved the sun, all my life I have loved the sun, but I am too old for it now. Leave me; let me sleep. Put my camera beside me – there, on the rocks. Sleep is a sort of peacefulness. And give me my hat. If ever I denied hope, I lied: there is a certain peace that any man may find. It is a good hat; it will shield my eyes from the sun, while I sleep.

THE DEATH OF SOCRATES

Alpha and Omega

I

Socrates died as quietly as he had lived. April had passed and May turned to June, unmarked by Julius – the present was all-absorbing and he had ceased to take any account of time. The old man slept more and more, and fell increasingly silent in his waking moments: even in midsummer there was an air of autumn about him, which filled Julius with a secret melancholy. Plato contained his anxiety, but sometimes Julius betrayed his own. Gently the old man turned his questions aside, and he sent Julius out with his camera, saying he had no wish to go himself. Plato disappeared all day with his shoeshine box, but always returned in the evening with enough food for the three of them, which he cooked quietly in one corner, over a charcoal fire. Julius had long since spent his money, but he had spent all desire for it too, and was content to give all he earned to Plato, who bought the few things they needed.

He cultivated a broken accent to delight the tourists, as Nikolaos had once delighted him, and wandered through many hot afternoons, from the Temple of Zeus to the Acropolis, from Constitution Square to the Tower of the Winds. His photographs annoyed many people, but none of them stamped on a hat: the world seemed to have acquired a measure of dignity in twenty years.

II

Sometimes, still, he had doubts: not of the satisfactions of this existence, but of its worth.

'It seems like giving up,' he said one evening to Socrates.

The old man had slept all afternoon, and for the first time in five weeks he seemed disposed to talk. There was an intensity, an air of bridled urgency in him, that Julius hadn't seen before.

'It *is* giving up,' Socrates agreed; but he had taken the words only to twist them in a new direction, away from the despairing incomprehension that Julius had given them. 'It is giving up the unimportant things, the things that don't matter.'

But Julius hadn't meant this, he had posed a different problem, and he was puzzled until he understood what Socrates had said: that there were no problems to be solved – it was as simple as that.

Plato stirred slightly in his corner, and flushed.

'I have made you coffee, Socrates. I thought, tonight –' he broke off, his eyes fixed firmly on the ground.

Socrates looked at him, smiling gently.

'Tonight?'

Plato didn't answer; he hid his confusion behind those downcast eyes.

'Yes,' said Socrates, 'tonight we will drink coffee. Was it hard, Plato?'

'It was an American. They were fifty-dollar shoes.' And then Plato could look at Socrates, and his eyes and his whole face lit up again, in relief, in the sudden confidence of approval. 'He knew it was too much, yet he gave me twenty drachmas. I could see it was a kindness. And you sleep so much now – I took it.' At last Plato's anxiety was in the open.

'You thought, perhaps, that coffee would keep me awake?'

'No,' said the boy. 'It wasn't that.'

'You are right. Coffee will not keep me from sleeping now. But tonight we will drink coffee, Plato, because you wish it and because I like it. We shall drink to your American.'

Plato filled three cups, and handed the first to Julius. Then he held out the second to Socrates, and there seemed to Julius to be a sadness in the gesture. They sat quietly, looking at each other. At last Socrates raised his cup, and his arm was old and weary.

'First we must drink to your American,' said Socrates, and drank.

The coffee was bitter to the tongue, and Julius held it in his mouth for a moment; it was the burnt coffee bean that gave it the curious flavour.

'And now,' said Socrates, 'we must thank Julius: who has brought new light into old eyes, and new sounds to young ears.' His grey eyebrows drew together as he spoke, and he smiled at Plato, pulling gently at one of the boy's ears. The old man and the boy raised their cups again.

Socrates turned to Julius.

'You and I,' he said, 'must make the last offering. It is for Plato. I am old and you are young, yet each of us is younger than Plato.' He raised his cup for the third time. 'This is for the child, who is older than the earth and young under the sky. It is for life, too, because the child is life. The gods have smiled on him.' Socrates paused. 'It is he, too,' he added with a chuckle, 'who provided the coffee.'

Julius drained his cup to the bitter dregs.

Plato took the cups, put them carefully in a corner, and returned to sit on the floor between them.

'Tonight, I have something to say.' Socrates looked at them. 'I have two friends, and I have two possessions. Tomorrow seems a great distance away, and I shall face the night more easily if you listen to me now. For you, Julius, there is my camera. Take it – it is yours. My own eyes will be enough for me tomorrow.

'For you, Plato, for you . . .' the old man smiled inwardly, at himself. 'It is not much, but it is all I have left now. My hat.' He placed it on Plato's dark head, and it covered the boy's ears, reaching in front to his eyes.

'It is good to give, I think,' said Socrates. 'It was not exactly given to me' – his blue eyes twinkled – 'but I give it to you, now. It is yours.'

Plato looked at the floor, he didn't stir. The hat guarded his downcast face, so they couldn't see the pain that struggled in his eyes. The brim cast a giant shadow of stillness over the floor, but the oil lamp was dying even as they sat there.

'It is late, said Socrates, 'and I have spoken ... all that I would speak. I have finished, my two friends.'

The weariness spread from his old eyes to the whole face.

'See, Julius,' he said – 'Plato sleeps.'

And his own eyes closed.

III

In the morning Julius and Plato woke early, but Socrates slept on. They did not touch him, for they knew he would not wake.

IV

Julius and Plato stood in the little church of St Georges. The windows were very small and deeply stained: most of the light came from the altar candles, and the air was heavy with incense. They stood under the dome, in the middle, looking up. The paint had flaked from the walls, and the once splendid frescoed saints had lost noses and arms in the process. The icons were richly intact. There the figures lived in calm resplendent colours, but lost their unity in grotesque extremities, for their hands and feet grew out of the pictures in silver bas-relief. Plato pointed to the door between the icons.

'There,' he whispered, 'is the All-Seeing Eye. It is watching us.'

Julius looked, and saw the Eye, and the Eye looked back at him.

'Look higher,' said Plato, still in a whisper, 'above the door. It is Alpha and Omega – the Beginning and the End.'

SPEECHES AT THE FUNERAL OF SOCRATES

There is not much to this story; only a few words are enough, and it is told. If I have lingered it is because it was a pleasant time to linger, and everything is slow under the sun.

They buried Socrates, and most of the people from the Old Town were there, because they had all counted Socrates for a friend. Afterwards they went back to the Old Town, and gathered in a forgotten square where a secret and unexpected taverna spread its tables beneath the lime trees. Plato and Julius went with them.

At first people tried to talk, but soon they found there was nothing they could say. Each was affected privately, in a way that he could not share. Presently the square was silent, and Julius, looking at all those troubled, expectant faces, knew that the death of Socrates must not pass unmarked. He stood up, and saw that they were all looking at him. He had no idea what he was going to say, and he knew that few of them would understand him because his words were English words, but they had to be spoken. He began his speech:

JULIUS

. . . .

'I am going to tell you about Socrates,' he said. 'Socrates was a man who lived on the hill of the Acropolis. Everybody knew him, but he had only two friends, Plato and Julius. He had a Panama hat and a camera.'

He heard his own voice like a stranger's voice, speaking strange words that were not his own words. He felt strongly that he was speaking as an idiot, in an idiot's language, and he wanted to stop; but no-one there, except Plato, understood what he was saying, and Plato's eyes were urging him to go on.

'Socrates was a simple man. He used to sleep a great deal – at least,' he corrected himself, 'lately he slept a great deal. His camera was not like other cameras. He called it the All-Seeing Eye. He took photographs.

'One day an angry man took off his hat and stamped on it. When the man went away, Socrates picked up the hat and it became his. These were the only two things he possessed. Now Plato has the hat, even though it is too big for him, and I – have the camera. He gave them to us.

'Socrates liked to give things, but his gifts were usually of another kind: he had no other possessions to give away. He had a white beard, and blue eyes, and a fine Athenian nose. He rated himself ugly, but this was of no importance, to him or to us.

'Plato and I knew Socrates, as no-one else could know him, and now we are all that is left of Socrates. He called Plato the child who is older than the earth and young under the sky, but that is what he was himself.

'Socrates had nothing, yet he had infinitely more than other men: his eyes were open. For him no day was like another day, everything was always new. He said: Possession is the beginning and the end, but the search goes on for ever. He possessed only two things, and these he gave away before he died, but he was always searching, to the very end, and beyond the end. The search goes on for ever.

'It is true that he was ugly, compared with other men, but there was a beauty in his kindliness and in his simplicity and in his wisdom, which was a finer kind of beauty. He was a man at peace with himself. In his heart the real and the ideal were reconciled. He loved life. He wanted everyone to share this love, but he said: Search your own heart, for in your own heart is both the reality and the ideal: you will not find it in another. This was something he couldn't give, except to point the way.

'Socrates was a man who was at peace with himself. Socrates –

'His beard curled, and the lines of his face softened when he slept. He liked coffee, and sometimes he ate pistachio nuts.'

Julius fell silent, and saw that the crowd was motionless, held by the words they could not understand.

'But Plato knew Socrates, too – better, and longer, than I. Plato shall tell you about him, for Socrates said that Plato was older than either of us, in the end he would reach beyond us, towards the sky. The gods have smiled on him.'

He lifted Plato onto a table, and the crowd looked at him with a different kind of interest, because his was a grief they could understand. Plato began his speech:

PLATO

. . . . . .

Plato spoke in Greek, which was better, because they understood him – but I can't write his speech down here, because I don't understand Greek: though Julius, by then, knew some. It was not a very long speech, and probably it wasn't very important, except to Plato himself. A few people in the crowd wept, but none so much as Plato. When it was finished, they went home.

THE INHERITORS

I

Usually they spent the days on one of the hills of the city, wandering through the week from Lofos Strefi to the Ardittos above the Stadium; to the Areopagus, to the Pnyx, to the hill of Philopappos and to the Acropolis. Julius carried the camera, although he was never a very good photographer, and Plato wore the hat which was too big for him. They did not positively go together, but their ways always crossed, and sooner or later Julius knew that the boy would appear silently beside him, swinging his shoeshine box, his black eyes quiet and inquiring under the wide brim of the Panama. Plato seldom spoke, but there was a sort of conversation in his silence that Julius enjoyed. Imperceptibly the summer stretched and lengthened, drawing them gently in its wake.

Socrates lived on. They knew he still lived – round every corner they felt the certainty of his presence, in every place that he had known and loved he seemed to linger. Often Julius thought he saw him, sleeping under an orange tree or climbing straight-backed and marvellously upstanding along some dusty path ahead. Plato saw him too, but Plato never told what he saw, and Julius could only guess. In the Old Town they sometimes spoke of Socrates; in the *tavernas* and on street corners, on the worn steps of the hill, his name was heard, told quietly in the evening, as of a man who was still with them, yet mysteriously removed. In sunlit doorways and in shaded gardens the legend grew, and men who had never known Socrates remembered him.

Julius and Plato walked in the streets, and people saw Socrates passing: they saw a ramshackle camera and an ancient Panama, and the old man was there in the street again. They told of the funeral of Socrates, and some said one of the old gods had come down from the Acropolis and spoken in a strange tongue, and they crossed themselves, more in wonder than in fear.

To Julius the Old Town was a different and secret world; there his eyes saw nothing that was not thousands of years old, and when he looked up, the temples of the Acropolis shone whole and glorious on the hill. It was a feeling that he had for the past, not a desire. He was not tormented by the inexorable centuries, because he did not notice them; for him the past and the present were one, and the future was simply tomorrow before it was today.

II

They stood by the Monument of Philopappos, on the Hill of the Muses. Further down the hill the air was filled with dust and shouting, where a new road crept slowly up in a wide curve. The road was square-cobbled and edged in stone. Chisels rang on marble, shaping seats in quiet corners. The Hill of the Muses had been rescheduled for *tourisme*: vacant possession, the Muses had moved out long ago.
   To the south the sun breathed on the blue depth of the Aegean, and Salamis slept in reflective mystery. In the distance the mountains of Sparta grew hugely out of the summer haze. Below them the wooden trains of the Metro rumbled towards Piraeus. But Julius turned back towards the city. The Parthenon was a second sun, shining from the Acropolis.

III

In Constitution Square the heat was oppressive; it was reflected from the wide dusty expanse of asphalt and from the bleached walls of the buildings and it could not escape. Julius picked up his camera, thinking he would prefer the airy heights of the Acropolis or the clean heat of the Theatre of Dionysus. Among all those thousands of people he thought he was alone, but today he was not.

A figure detached itself from the crowd and grew purposefully and implacably in his path; a face tugged painfully at his memory, and he saw eyes which looked curiously and disbelievingly into his own.

'Julius *darling*, what on *earth* do you think you're doing?'

It was Dulcibella.

Julius recognized her, and at the same time recognized that he no longer knew her.

'I couldn't *think* what had happened! – you weren't at your hotel.'

'At my hotel?' Julius made a desperate effort to adjust his mind to a forgotten past. 'But you wrote – you wrote months ago, from Naples. I got your letter.'

'From Naples?' Dulcibella was suitably vague. 'Of course, that was – Antonio. Darling Antonio, you should have seen him, Julius,' – she warmed to a refurbished passion – 'so strong and terribly handsome. He was delightfully cruel to me, too,' she smiled happily at the memory; 'but he ate unbelievable quantities of garlic. Honestly, I couldn't stand that.'

'No,' said Julius politely. 'I suppose you couldn't.'

'But my poor Julius, what *are* you doing in those simply terrible clothes? – you look like a native. And what's that – thing?' She pointed.

'That is my camera,' said Julius. 'It is the All-Seeing Eye. Or at least,' he added with a sigh, 'it used to be, when it belonged to Socrates – but I'm not very good at it, I'm afraid. It doesn't see very much for me.' He stopped, conscious of some lack of understanding in Dulcibella. He tried to put things right.

'Would you like me to take your photograph,' he asked hopefully – 'it might be interesting?'

'For heaven's sake, Julius, stop playing games. And

you'd better put on some decent clothes. We are going to Istanbul.'

'I haven't got any decent clothes,' said Julius quietly. 'And *we* aren't going to Istanbul.'

It took him a long time to convince Dulcibella, and he wondered if it was worth the effort; in the end she understood.

'You are going to Istanbul,' said Julius, 'or anywhere you like. I am staying in Athens.'

'I *could* stay too – for a week perhaps, if you like; then we could go – ' but there was no conviction in her words, for this was not the Julius she had known. She stopped then, and smiled, and shrugged her shoulders; for even Dulcibella had her philosophy.

'I think it will have to be Berlin, after all. I don't know a soul in Istanbul, and do you remember that simply ravishing young German count, von . . . von Something-or-Other – you were so jealous of him?'

'That might be a good idea,' said Julius gravely. Her way was not his way, but he was anxious to help her, even to her own ends. He had chosen for himself, but he knew his choice was not a judgement on hers. Who could say where the reconciliation of the real and the ideal might or might not be found? In Athens, perhaps, for one; in Berlin for another. There was nothing here for Dulcibella; in Berlin, at least, there was count von Somebody-or-Other.

'Well,' said Dulcibella, 'I suppose I'd better go. Goodbye, darling.'

'Goodbye,' said Julius.

He watched her while she melted back into the crowd, into her world: watched her until she was gone, and he was alone again.

I wonder, thought Dulcibella, if I should have given him some money – poor darling, he looked as if he needed it dreadfully. She almost turned back to look for him, but something stopped her. She had heard of people going native before, but never among her own friends. And Julius, too, of all people! She wondered if Greeks counted as natives – perhaps they didn't – but howsoever, Julius had contrived to look astonishingly Greek. It was too late to go back now. Poor Julius, he really had looked as if he needed some money.

But Julius had already left Constitution Square. When Dulcibella returned to her hotel, smiling with automatic invitation at the handsome lift boy, Julius was already climbing towards the Acropolis.

IV

They sat on the steps of the Parthenon, Julius who had walked from Constitution Square, and Plato who had appeared silently to join him as he passed through the gates of the Acropolis. Plato was chewing pistachio nuts. A party of tourists streamed between broken columns, coming from the temple of the Winged Victory, and spread out to settle in the shade of a crumbling wall. Kostantios waited until they were silent, and then spoke.

'Ladies and gentlemen, the Parthenon ... *Messieurs et Mesdames, le Parthénon* ... the most famous building in the world ... *l'édifice le plus célèbre du monde...*'

'Today,' said Julius, 'I discovered my last possession. It's something I can't give up, except by forgetting it: the chance to go back.'

'It is always there,' agreed Plato.

'It's hard to forget. Much harder than to give. When you give, the thing's done, but when you forget you have to go on doing it all the time, for ever.'

'You will not believe me at first, my friends ... *mes amis, d'abord vous ne me croirez pas...*'

Julius was absorbed in the problem of forgetting.

'There is not a single straight line in the Parthenon ... *pas une seule ligne droite au Parthénon...*'

'We are always going back,' said Plato, 'all the time. But

we can choose where we should go. We,' he said slowly, 'have chosen the Acropolis today, and tomorrow perhaps we will choose another place... It does not matter – time is always waiting.'

'But this choice was different. It was a chance to go back to another world – to none of these.' He gestured at the fallen marble in front of them and the marble that still stood behind them. 'As a matter of fact, it was a chance to go somewhere quite else, and far from here. To Istanbul.'

'I have heard of it,' said Plato.

'Here,' said Kostantios, 'you see man and art and nature, working together to produce perfection ... *ici vous voyez l'homme, l'art et la nature, travaillants ensembles à produire la perfection.*'

Plato smiled.

'We are free,' he said. 'We can go where we will: there is always the choice. I have chosen to stay here.'

'I've chosen too,' said Julius. 'It seems to me I made the choice a long time ago. Each time, it becomes a little easier.'

'Ladies and gentlemen ... *Messieurs et Mesdames* ... the Parthenon was at first a Greek building ... *autrefois le Parthénon était un édifice grec...*'

'It is giving up,' Plato said, 'the unimportant things. All that matters is here – is left to us.' He was thinking of Socrates.

'But it is no longer Greek ... *mais ce n'est plus grec...*'

'We have nothing,' Julius said – 'And the world is ours.'

'It belongs to the whole world ... *il appartient à tout le monde* ... it belongs to me, and it belongs to you.'

Plato cracked a nut with his teeth.

'Possession is the beginning and the end,' he said, 'but the search goes on for ever.'

Julius stood up, unhurried, and stretched in the sun. A few yards from him an elderly American Millionaire stumbled in bewilderment against a rock.

'We'll go, then,' said Julius, and 'search.'

He leaped to hold the foundering American's arm.

THE BEGINNING AND THE END

Zeus, on Mount Olympus, had passed an exhausting day, harrassed by tourists. They pursued him with careless fervour, from the black pine forests of the foothills to the edge of those impenetrable snows on the peak, which he hated because it was cold up there and he was not as active as he had once been. But the tourists ... they crawled over the lower slopes of the mountain, like flies on a midden.

When evening came the tourists went home, and Zeus could rest. He had chosen one of his favourite places, high on the mountain but below the snow, a rocky ledge sheltered from the cold winds, where he could catch the last of the evening sun. He sat there, while dusk crept over the valleys and over the quiet sea, watching and waiting. His face was inscrutable, his thoughts were his own, but in any event there was nobody there to see his face or share his thoughts.

Presently a small piece of paper came floating lightly out of the darkening sky and settled with the soundless delicacy of a moth's wing on a rock beside him. A breeze whispered up the mountain and stirred it where it lay. Zeus stretched out an enormous arm and held the piece of paper, looking at it.

The paper was skilfully folded to give it wings, and in its journey the caressing sky had held up those wings across many miles of secret and uncharted ways.

It was a five-hundred-drachma note.

Zeus tucked it away carefully in an inner pocket, and there was a distant and unfathomable smile on his ageless face.

It was late. It had taken longer than he had expected.